More Than

Lisa Geraghty

Copyright © 2021 Lisa Geraghty

All rights reserved. No parts of this publication may be reproduced, distributed or transmitted in any form or by any means, including photocopying or recording, or any other electronic methods, without the prior written permission of the publisher, except in the case of brief quotations or embodied in critical reviews and certain other non-commercial uses permitted by copyright law. For permission requests contact the publisher at the email address below. Contact details of the publisher: Lisa Geraghty – lisageraghtymediation@gmail.com.

Disclaimer
The story, all names, characters, and incidents portrayed in this production are fictitious. No identification with actual persons (living or deceased), places, buildings, and products is intended or should be inferred.

Contributors
Editor: Liz Hudson, Dublin, Ireland. thelittleredpen.com
Illustrator: Donnacha Geraghty, Galway, Ireland.

Prologue

Jennifer Burke stared at the two people in front of her. She doubted they had been listening to a word she said. The pretty, red-cheeked nurse glanced across at the tall, skinny man beside her – a doctor, Jennifer presumed, judging by the stethoscope dangling around his neck. *What are they waiting for?* she asked herself. *Can't they see I need help?*

Then the man spoke. 'Tell us again what brought you here, Jennifer.'

'I've already explained this,' she replied. 'I have a headache.' Her eyes were glistening now. 'There's something seriously wrong with me. Why aren't you ordering a CT scan or something?'

The two glanced at each other once more. 'Okay, we will take care of that,' the doctor said, his attention never moving from Jennifer's face. 'Tell us how you got here, Jennifer. Does your husband know where you are?'

'I drove myself,' Jennifer answered. 'Don't tell him I'm here. Don't tell any of them. If they think there's something wrong with me, they will take my kids from me. I know they will. They are waiting for the right opportunity. They keep pushing and pushing so that I will break and then they can take my kids.'

More shared glances.

Jennifer continued. 'They hate me, you see. It's jealousy, of course. They never wanted me here. John has been completely brainwashed by them – my husband's sisters, I mean. They cannot find out that I am sick. Promise me? If I could just get this headache sorted, I would be fine.'

Taking Jennifer's chart from the nurse's hands, the doctor turned to his colleague and said, 'Why don't we find Mrs Burke a bed in one of the wards so she can be more comfortable while she waits for her tests?' The nurse looked instinctively at him and nodded.

Tests sound good, Jennifer thought. She needed to know what was wrong. She worried that she could have a brain tumour, or an aneurism, or meningitis. Whatever it was, she just needed to know. She needed it to stop.

Minutes later, she followed the nurse into a large six-bed ward which already accommodated five female in-patients. The middle cubicle on the left was free. Jennifer sat on the bed and watched as the nurse drew the sterile blue curtain around her. She suddenly felt self-conscious. The reality of where she was unnerved her momentarily, and she felt the need to explain the situation to the nurse, to justify herself and how she had arrived at the emergency room that day.

She really did have *such* a headache, she explained. The nurse smiled sympathetically. Jennifer continued to talk, rattling off the prequel to this impromptu admission to hospital: how she had been under so much stress lately, her struggle to cope, walls closing in on all sides, and this goddamned headache. Minutes passed. Jennifer was still explaining. The nurse was still nodding. Eventually, seeing the distress on Jennifer's face, the nurse reached over, took Jennifer's hand and promised her that everything would be all right.

In that moment, Jennifer believed her, but as she rose to pull back the cover on her bed, she heard a murmuring from the other side of the curtain. She stopped moving and listened. No, she wasn't mistaken. She could hear a woman's voice saying the words 'Burke' and 'solicitor' and 'must know her'? Her blood boiling, Jennifer pulled back the curtain to witness a middle-aged woman in her nightgown, hand covering her mouth and phone, divulging the information she had collected in the past few minutes.

'Do you have everything you need there?' Jennifer barked in a temper. Aggressively, she took a step towards the nervous woman in the bed beside her. 'I mean, can I help you with any personal information that you might have missed? Why don't you invite your friend in and I can arrange an interview? What do you think of that plan, you nosy bitch!'

At that point, the nurse pulled Jennifer by the arm and sat her back on the bed, while at the same time paging the doctor for assistance. Jennifer was fuming and still ranting about the breach of privacy.

'Well, seeing that you know I'm a solicitor you should also know to be careful what you say about me,' Jennifer shouted in the direction of the curtain.

The doctor's return was not before time. 'Jennifer, how about you lie down and rest? I am going to give you something to make you feel calmer and less stressed.'

'Will it take away my headache?' Jennifer asked.

'Yes, it will take away your headache,' the doctor replied.

Jennifer complied, and in what seemed like one second, the nurse secured an intravenous line through which the doctor injected a cold, clear liquid. Jennifer felt warmer now. The bed felt softer. The nurse's voice sounded further away. And as her eyes closed and her thoughts slowed down, Jennifer wondered what on earth she was doing there.

Part I

Chapter 1

Three months earlier, Jennifer emerged from her night's sleep with a thumping headache and a racing heart. She hadn't heard the alarm. Or had she set it at all? She sat upright, fighting back the nausea.

John was standing in the door of their bedroom. 'Hi,' he said. 'I've taken the girls to the school bus.'

He seems okay about it, Jennifer thought. It was her job on weekday mornings to get their fifteen-year-old twin daughters Ava and Alannah up for school and deposit them at the bus stop on her way to the office. Thankfully, this morning John was at home. He generally took early clients at his physiotherapy practice in the town. Jennifer had never understood the appeal of getting down to your underwear at dawn on a cold February morning, even if it was for a rub-down.

Sheepishly, she thanked John and recalled the interaction she had with him the night before. She felt embarrassed and guilty. She knew it had been her fault, and she hated herself for it. He was such a good husband and father. She knew this. He was so good to her, and she relied on him. He was steady and grown-up and predictable – all the things she wasn't. Not always exciting or original, but she looked up to him in so many ways, and she loved him.

He deserved better than what he was getting from her these days. She wanted to do better for him. In her heart she knew that she was gradually transforming from an intelligent classy woman into an unpredictable mess. Last night had been just another example of her unacceptable behaviour. Within minutes Jennifer felt a by-now too-familiar wave of anxiety gush from her chest into her pounding head. She felt nauseous and light-headed as the panic gripped her body. She lay still and took deep breaths, believing it would pass. It always did.

She thought it best not to mention last night to John at this early hour. In fact, if he didn't bring it up, she might not either. Once he left the room, she palmed around the bed for her phone. This was the ritual any morning post alcohol consumption. Typically, in the final hour or so before losing consciousness, she was inclined to get opinionated on social media or, worse, text people she felt a sudden urge to share her current thoughts and emotions with. She held her breath while she scrambled through her Twitter, Facebook, LinkedIn and WhatsApp accounts. All clear, thank God. She lay back on her pillow and took a breath of relief.

She knew she had overdone it with the wine again last night, and by the time John arrived home at 9.30 p.m., she had worked herself up into a state of agitation and had rehearsed some fightin' words. It was the same old conflict over and over in their marriage. The same cliché. Too often these days Jennifer turned to her husband for support and was cast aside, swatted away like a bug.

After more than seventeen years of marriage, she was exhausted, almost broken, by two of John's older sisters who had instigated a campaign of bullying against her since the day she arrived – more accurately, since the day she decided to go back to work and open her own legal practice in the town. While Liz, the eldest of the Burke siblings, was the main instigator of the abuse, facilitated by her proximity to Jennifer and John's home, it was extremely well choreographed from a distance by the real ringleader behind the scenes: John's youngest sister, Geraldine.

The whole saga had become a dysfunctional cycle for Jennifer and John. Liz, prompted by Geraldine, would prod Jennifer with a passive-aggressive stick or blatantly insult her, but never in front of a witness. Jennifer would dump her disgust and hurt onto John with the eternal expectation that he would do or say anything supportive. John would tell Jennifer that she was misreading the situation, and what exactly did she expect him to do about it anyway? After all, Liz had her own troubles. Jennifer would then withdraw from the conflict, deflated and having achieved nothing except more disappointment in her husband and a feeling of perfect isolation in this place.

Yesterday evening, Jennifer was clearing up after the dinner, her two daughters were upstairs working on a school project, when she heard the front door open and close, followed by the stabbing sound of Liz's footsteps walking down the hallway of her home. *Why can't she knock, just once?*, Jennifer thought. Her pulse accelerated and the weight of her heart fell like a ball of lead down low in her chest. She closed her eyes, dropped her head between her shoulders and took a deep breath.

Since Liz had moved home to Castlebar after her divorce three years before, she had made a habit of arriving in to Jennifer's kitchen in the evenings. Not every evening, but often enough for it to trigger anxiety in Jennifer, something she had never experienced until recently. Jennifer believed Liz to be a miserably unhappy woman, and had Jennifer not been a regular target of Liz's misery, she would have felt sorry for her. In fact, of late, Jennifer's empathy for this woman was running on fumes and gradually turning into unadulterated contempt, not because the abuse was becoming more blatant, which it was, but because of the wedge it was driving between Jennifer and John.

This evening, like all the others, as Liz walked through her kitchen door, Jennifer clenched her body and greeted her sister-in-law with rehearsed exaggerated enthusiasm. This was always the time when Jennifer performed her best amateur drama. *A tragedy*, she thought to herself. For some reason beyond her control Jennifer was unable to tell Liz how she felt. About the house calls in the evenings. About not knocking on her front door. About the passive aggression. About the overt rudeness. About the intrusion and the disrespect and the insults.

Despite the fact that she was able to take to the stage in the courtroom and cleverly, with poise and dignity, put manners on the cockiest of characters, Jennifer's native Kerry confidence, of which she was so proud, always let her down in this particular case. She couldn't even imagine the repercussions for her if she stood up to John's sisters – not because he was protective of them but because he saw this conflict as an inconvenience, something that he was forced to endure because his sensitive wife couldn't get over herself.

Even if Jennifer found it in her to confront Liz, she knew that no matter how she approached the problem, worded it and explained it, Liz would summon her inner Burke drama queen and a spectacle would ensue. Jennifer had seen that stage production too many times before – from Geraldine, Liz and her husband.

So, for this evening, like all the other evenings, Jennifer went into autopilot, making conversation with Liz as best she could while at the same time trying not to share too much personal information for Liz to use as ammunition against her in the future. It was always a fine line, and Jennifer had learned the hard way that Liz would cling to her words in search of a stick. So many times, Jennifer had asked her husband to explain what she had done to offend his sisters so much, and so many times her queries were disregarded. Eventually, Jennifer took solace in the fact that while Liz was finding fault with her, then she must, at least temporarily, be feeling better about herself, and there was some logic in the whole thing. *Yes, I get it, Liz*, Jennifer always thought. *That doesn't make it okay.*

'Is John working late again?' Liz asked, looking around as though he might suddenly emerge from behind a door on hearing his sister's voice.

'Yes, he sometimes takes late clients. Remember, I mentioned that before,' Jennifer answered. She already knew where this was going.

'It's not right that he has to work such long hours, you know. You need to encourage him to be at home with you and the girls. That's how marriages end, Jennifer. But, of course, if you want a house like this,' she said, looking at the walls around her in exaggerated fake admiration, 'I suppose he hasn't much choice.'

Jennifer could already feel her heart start to beat through her chest. 'I work too, Liz, and John doesn't have to work in the evenings. He chooses to. He likes the work he does with professional athletic types, and they want evening appointments.' *Why am I even answering her?* Jennifer asked herself in annoyance.

'He should be at home with his wife and children. Where are they, by the way?' Liz asked.

'They are upstairs working on homework,' Jennifer answered, feeling more annoyed with every second. This woman was so obnoxious.

'They should be down here with you. Do you not help them with their homework? My mother, God rest her, was always there for us. She didn't work, of course. She never needed the luxuries that women have now. I always said that I would give up my job as soon as I had kids, but it wasn't to be.'

'I guess people should be allowed to make up their minds about how they live,' Jennifer said. She wondered if she was going to be able for a full-on session with Liz tonight. What she should have done, of course, was ask Liz why her own marriage didn't work out, if she was such an expert on the matter. But Jennifer knew that Liz's ex-husband was a compulsive liar and serial cheat, and thought better of shoving Liz's face in it.

Liz had given up her job as a nurse in Dublin several years ago and was now living off the proceeds of her divorce from a wealthy property developer. She didn't have children of her own, and, in fairness, Jennifer acknowledged, she adored the twins, showering them with gifts and money at every turn. She did have some human qualities, Jennifer conceded.

'Is that another new dress?' Liz continued. 'I don't remember seeing that one before?' The look on her face was not one of admiration; the words were not intended to compliment.

'Thank you. I like it too,' Jennifer said. She wondered if Liz's motivation was jealousy, but in truth she knew there was more to it. It was a sort of wariness, or mistrust of Jennifer that fuelled the swipes she had been enduring for years. She was never able to identify the source of this. The woman seemed overtly offended by the notion that Jennifer was living the good life on the back of her brother's hard work, but at the same time knew, and resented, the fact that Jennifer was actually earning more than her husband.

In truth, Jennifer believed that this fed the fire. She had never acted in a way that called for such treatment, at least to her knowledge, and yet, it was relentless, exhausting. Jennifer knew it was time to change focus before this conversation deteriorated.

'So, Liz, how is Helen?' Jennifer asked. This was a calculated move and would shift the focus from herself. Helen was the black sheep, the middle sister, the oddball. Jennifer often wondered if Helen had been Liz and Geraldine's first victim. Helen was a different woman entirely. She had trained as a teacher in Galway and at the age of twenty-four bolted to New Zealand, barely setting foot in Ireland since.

Jennifer had met her a few times over the years at family gatherings and could hardly believe that she was related to the other two. Helen was witty and self-confident and generally unperturbed. Jennifer would have traded a body part to have that sister at home as an ally now. She knew, however, that Helen was unlikely to ever live in Mayo again.

'Oh, looking after herself, don't worry about her,' Liz answered. 'She doesn't appear to have any plans to come home this year, and any time you pick up the phone to talk to her she hardly has time to talk to you,' she said, eyes rolled to the sky.

I don't blame her, Jennifer thought to herself.

'No, she's way too good for the likes of us now,' Liz continued.

Helen was a full-time teacher and mother of three who had married the owner of one of the biggest sheep farms in New

Zealand. The woman was genuinely busy, but Jennifer knew better than to bother opening it up for discussion.

More and more now Jennifer could see that these encounters with Liz had nothing positive to offer. They were no more than an endurance test for her, a source of anxiety to bear in silence, or a source of conflict in her home.

From what Jennifer could see, since the death of their mother almost thirty years before, John's sisters had pampered him and raised him to believe that he was quite exceptional, even special, and that he could do no wrong. Jennifer used to joke about it with John in the early days of their relationship. Now she could see that John had grown up to have very little respect for his sisters while also believing that he was, in fact, never wrong. The whole thing was dysfunctional.

Jennifer poured a second cup of tea and sighed internally.

*

Post purge, and refuelled for another evening, Liz left. Jennifer sat in the kitchen, seething. It would be a couple of hours before John was home. He rarely joined the family for dinner during the week. If he wasn't seeing clients at the practice he was working on his master's, a taught postgraduate programme in exercise physiology through distance learning with the University of Liverpool. It appeared to Jennifer to be an intense course of work, and John often struggled with the assignments.

She didn't resent him the opportunity to upskill, nor did she mind the extra work. Tonight, she really needed him, not as much for company – she was used to her own – but for support and maybe even a bit of comfort. She wasn't sure how much more of this abuse she would be able to take. If he wasn't prepared to stand up for his wife in the face of unashamed bullying by his sisters, Jennifer feared that it would very soon boil down to a 'them or me' showdown.

Reaching for a bottle of Malbec from the wine rack, she noticed the shake in her hands. No one had the right to make her feel this bad in her own house, she thought. As she sipped the first glass and folded her legs up onto the couch, she painfully goaded herself through the too-familiar ritual of self-doubt about the type of mother she had been to her kids. She knew that she worked a lot, and she had the occasional bottle of wine. In fact, she knew she preferred to work than be a homemaker. She felt that she had achieved a lot in becoming a solicitor and achieving a master's in EU law while looking after her young daughters, not to mention a handful of Law Society certificates.

She worried that she may have neglected her duties as a mother along the way, but she reminded herself that her teenaged daughters were happy and – importantly – independent. She knew that they were okay, but in the face of brazen intimidation her self-confidence abandoned her. This only ever happened when she thought of her duties as a mother, never otherwise. She took another sip. She would never have thought herself capable of hating anyone, but she hated that woman.

By the time she heard John's Mazda pull around the back of the house, she was well into the second bottle of wine. He looked disapprovingly at the remains of the cold dinner on top of the cooker. This had not always been their routine. When their daughters were young, and Jennifer was at home, John would rush back after work to join his family for the evening. But something had changed in the past few years.

'Drinking on your own is becoming a bit of a habit, Jen,' he said.

That was the only incentive Jennifer needed to drag both of them into a dialogue that should have waited for another time. In what must have been somewhat slurred speech, she relayed, possibly through gritted teeth, the events of the evening. He didn't even wait for her to finish or ask again for his support in managing his sister's behaviour. His voice predictably ascended into a loud bark, and, throwing his arms in the air while pacing around the kitchen, he yelled, 'What the fuck do you want from me? What the fuck do you expect me to do? She just doesn't like you, Jennifer. Can you not just fucking get over it? I am not putting my sister out of my house for you! I swear you do this for attention! Can I not just come home and have an hour's peace in my own house?'

Jennifer, as usual, defended her position more eloquently and with more self-control than her husband, even under the influence of the alcohol, but there was no point continuing. There was no point trying to explain that she had the right to privacy in her own home. There was no point reiterating that she thought Liz's treatment of her was abusive. And, most of all, there was no point asking him to defend and help her.

The more Jennifer tried to plead her case and ask John to change his view on the subject, the louder and more aggressive he became. The row ended when he slammed the door behind him, leaving Jennifer deflated and injured for a second time that evening. She didn't see much of him for the remainder of the night. He left her to her wine and went to bed.

By the time she got to the bottom of the second bottle, she was the worse for wear. Her thoughts, however, were racing. She felt outside her own body as she climbed the stairs, almost certainly making enough noise to wake the girls. Swinging open the door of their bedroom, she shouted at John, 'Where exactly were you tonight?' No answer. She repeated her question more loudly.

He brushed her off, saying, 'What the hell, Jen? Get into bed for the love of God. You'll wake the girls.'

'No. I want to know what you are up to. I sit here at home dutifully every evening, and I never ask where you are. So now I want to know. You are having an affair, aren't you?'

'Jesus fucking Christ, Jennifer. You are pissed again,' John shouted, less concerned now about his sleeping children. 'You are a fucking alcoholic. *You* are the problem here.'

Jennifer began to sob drunkenly. She didn't know whether she was or was not an alcoholic, but she did know that she was tortured.

Chapter 2

Now, with the house to herself, Jennifer clambered out of the bed and ran a shower. She caught sight of herself in the bathroom mirror and was ashamed. Black eyeliner was smudged under her eyes – she hadn't removed her make-up, again. She struggled to remember how her life had become so difficult and unhappy. It didn't make any sense. She had it all: a husband who adored her and who worked so hard to give his family a comfortable life; two children who, in her eyes, were brilliant and so much fun to be with. And she was an accomplished professional woman herself. She knew she needed to get her act together before she ruined everything.

Despite the perceived exhaustion and regular hangovers, Jennifer looked great for her forty-two years. Dark-brown hair, cropped in a pixie cut, framed an attractive small face, and her deep-set blue eyes were offset by her perfectly formed lips and teeth. Growing up, she never saw herself as beautiful, but the amount of attention heaped on her by men during and since college – her blooming years – had to be significant, she realised. Now she knew she had something. At five foot eight and fifty-eight kilograms, her long legs and square shoulders were striking.

As the hot shower water revitalised her, she reminded herself that she had been looking forward to today. Recently, it had been passing in and out of her mind that she might someday like to expand her practice into corporate law. Tomorrow was the much-anticipated conference in London on the legal aspects of corporate takeovers. She would have to be at Dublin Airport by about five, so that morning it was just going to be a fleeting visit to the office, a rented premises in Castlebar town. Susan, her assistant, would manage without her for a couple of days.

Feeling much better after the shower, she packed an overnight bag and chose her new sky-blue Victoria Beckham dress and nude pointed four-inch heels from her extensive wardrobe. She always felt better when she dressed well.

On arrival at the office in Castle Street, Susan greeted her fondly and reminded her that Charles Roche was due in at ten.

'Shite! I totally forgot,' Jennifer said. 'Susan, babe, pull out his file, will you? He wants to sell a huge portion of his agricultural land and wants me to oversee the sale.'

'And I doubt you'll have any complaints about that, girl?!' Susan replied. She had the thickest West Cork accent Jennifer had ever heard. Despite living in Mayo for the past twenty-three of her fifty-two years, it had never wavered.

Jennifer blushed slightly, answering, 'Not sure what you mean!' Even though she did.

'Stop it, girl! Sure, you practically purr when there's a good-looking man in the vicinity,' Susan said, laughing.

'Stop it!' Jennifer laughed too, although inwardly acknowledging that Susan was right. She did enjoy the energy in a room when she shared it with an attractive, charismatic man. Harmless, she told herself, and not necessarily bad for business.

Just then, Charles strode into the reception area. He was a fantastically handsome man, fifty-five years old and oozing self-assurance. 'Good morning, ladies. You both look astonishingly well this morning,' he announced.

Both women blushed, looked at each other, and Jennifer gestured for Charles to follow her into the boardroom.

*

Jennifer was in the car and on the road eastward at 1.15 p.m., still slightly hungover but high from her meeting with Charles. She was really looking forward to this night away by herself in London. She rarely ventured out of her routine these days. Even her days in court were routine, meeting the same people and doing the same things over and over. The life of a solicitor in rural Ireland became very predictable very quickly, she thought. So, when the opportunity presented to take part in some continued professional development in London, she had grabbed it.

Her mind flashed back and forth to the row she had with John the previous night. She knew him as such a good man. He tried so hard to keep her happy. Sometimes, in the middle of one of their rows, she could see real pain in his face as though he wanted so badly to please her but did not have the raw materials or the instruction book on file.

Jennifer regularly spoke to her friend Sinead about her turmoil over the difficulties in her marriage in the face of what seemed like a perfect life. Apart from John, Sinead O'Malley was Jennifer's dearest friend. She wasn't, however, the ideal choice for a bitching session about John. The three of them had met in their younger days in University College Dublin and had remained close ever since. On graduating from college, all three of them moved west – John and Jennifer to Castlebar and Sinead to her native Ballina where she too worked in a law firm.

Sinead was quite fond of John. They were fellow Mayo natives and very proud of it. Sinead's almost automatic response to Jennifer's complaints of rejection by John in the face of his sister's bullying was that he was 'just a man' and that men were not able to stand up to their sisters. She always told Jennifer not to take it personally.

While she could normally be relied on to row in on Jennifer's team any time the call went out, giving advice that was invariably right, and too often with a helping of tough love, when it came to John, Sinead could see no wrong. What's more, Jennifer knew that

Sinead was, in fact, seldom wrong. Jennifer decided she would call John from the airport and make sure everything was back to normal.

Dublin Airport was surprisingly quiet. Jennifer made her way relatively painlessly through airport security and settled in what looked like a welcoming bar with comfortable leather seats and a modest wine list. She let the tension she had been carrying all day rise upward and off her shoulders and ordered an Australian Chardonnay. With every sip that trickled down her throat she sank into a familiar alternate life, a sort of pretend place that she liked to go when she was on her own sipping vino and taking in the atmosphere.

She loved her life, her husband and kids, her career. She knew how lucky she was in the grand scheme of things, but sometimes in these rare moments of make-believe she imagined that she was sitting on the bank of the Seine waiting for her Latin lover to meet her back at her apartment on boulevard Saint-Michel. She loved to fantasise – one of her diversions that was indeed harmless.

Having slept through most of the flight, Jennifer took a taxi from Heathrow to her hotel in the city centre. It was a gorgeous four-star, and she bathed in the luxury of the interior. She was looking forward to the lounge tonight: the opportunity to wear something spectacular, the unfamiliar atmosphere and the nameless cast of actors on the stage she would create for herself.

She pulled out the black Marc Jacobs dress she had packed that morning. High neck, long sleeves and mid-thigh-length, it complimented her stunning figure. She laughed as she looked at herself in the mirror of her hotel room. Some bold red lipstick and a pointy white guitar and she might be mistaken for one of Robert Palmer's backing dancers in his video 'Addicted to Love.'

Halfway through her fillet steak and selection of green vegetables, she finished a second glass of Montepulciano, feeling insatiable. She never felt this sort of escapism back home in Mayo, but that was okay – she was getting it now. Jennifer was competent in the art of compartmentalisation. She was very happy with her life in Mayo, with John and the kids, as long as she got the odd opportunity to get away on her own and use her imagination to fill the defects in her life.

She ordered a third glass of wine and took a stool at the bar. This was a very bold move, she thought to herself, but then she was feeling a bit bolder. By now, her long legs and striking face had caught the attention of several men in the room. With every sip of wine, her inhibitions dissolved. She felt invincible, like she was playing a part in a movie. The seductress.

It wasn't long before the barman caught her eye. He was at least six foot tall with dark-brown skin and a voluptuous head of black curly hair. She had noticed his glances, his attempts at making conversation. She didn't make conversation. That wasn't her thing. Tonight, she communicated solely through body language and eye contact. At midnight, and with two additional glasses of wine in her, she beckoned the barman one last time. He duly made his way towards her and asked, 'One for the road, miss?'

Jennifer reached into her Gucci purse, looked directly into his black eyes, and handed him her spare room-key card. Slightly shocked for a second and then clearly pleased with himself, he took the key. 'Room 140,' she said.

'Give me twenty minutes to close,' he answered, with no hesitation.

As she moved away from him, as though on a catwalk, he followed her curves with his eyes. Her walk was Marilynesque. She knew this too. Glancing back over her shoulder on her way to the stairs, she felt the anticipation intensify in her.

The knock on the door sent a current of excitement down through her body. He stood there, white shirt open enough to see his broad chest, black chest hair almost pushing through the fabric. His thighs were bulging through his black trousers. She gestured him in and, without speaking a word, pulled him towards her. He needed no instructions. With one hand, he guided her back against the wall and with the other lifted her skirt up to her waist.

Her breath stopped for a moment to allow for the surge of pleasure that shot up between her legs. Her breathing quickened. He kissed her somewhat aggressively. She didn't care. She kissed him back. She wrestled open the buttons of his shirt. She had been fantasising about seeing that chest all evening. She wasn't disappointed. It was glorious.

She quickly took a condom from her purse. She had packed it this morning. Even then she had known how she was about to spend her night away. He wasted no time in obliging, and in a finely polished move he pulled her underwear aside just enough to push himself inside her. Any control she may have retained up to this point escaped her, and she screamed out with pleasure.

There, in a hotel bedroom in London, with a man whose name she didn't know, she felt ecstasy. But more than that, she felt alive and she felt free. The weight and strength of the man drove her back against the wall. With every surge she held tighter to his hair and shoulders. The pleasure was euphoric.

There was no more conversation between them in the aftermath of the passion than there had been beforehand. Jennifer thanked him for his time. He was not offended when he was asked to leave. He understood the contract he had entered into. She fell into the bed in a state of tingling bliss. She was drunk, but not so drunk that she could blame the alcohol for her indiscretion. In that moment she knew what she was doing. She always did. She would sleep now and deal with the hangover in the morning. She would compartmentalise then.

Chapter 3

Jennifer looked out the aeroplane window and saw the lights of Dublin in the distance. The city welcomed her just like it did the first day she stepped onto the campus of University College Dublin as a naive, excited eighteen-year-old girl from West Kerry. Dublin was her second home. Castlebar was not. She was never able to tell John the truth about how she felt in his native county. Mayo had never welcomed her. It had judged her, and it rejected her. In truth, the people of Mayo had not rejected her, but the aggression she so often felt from John's family represented Mayo to her now.

As the plane made its descent, the cabin crew prepared for landing, and Jennifer descended too – into another agonising post-alcohol anxiety attack. A wave of panic was forming a veil over her face and spreading downwards around her body. A recurring distress these days, but Jennifer had experienced this terror enough times now to know that it was the alcohol in her system causing the irrational fear. It was not real. It was not her.

During these waves of anxiety she would freeze, literally and metaphorically. Her face would become cold and stiff. She would feel her heartbeat thumping in her ears. While the physical symptoms of the attack were harrowing, the psychological defilement was worse. In this moment she would descend into a state of dread in anticipation of losing everything in her life that was important to her. She would believe in that moment that she was about to lose her husband and children, her home, her career, her comfort. She would believe that everything she had ever done in her life would come back to haunt her – the recent infidelities, the drinking, the risk-taking – and, worse, she believed that she would deserve it.

Mercifully for Jennifer she had been through this ritual enough times to know that it was, in fact, the alcohol trash-talking her, and as soon as the drug metabolised out of her system these misapprehensions would no longer exist.

When her car merged from the M4 onto the M6 motorway, Jennifer's anxiety began to abate, and she started to look forward to seeing John and the girls. After all, it had been two days. Despite the enduring internal struggle in her relationship with the West of

Ireland and the Burkes, she worshipped the sanctuary of her house in Castlebar and being inside it with her own little family.

Her body and mind gradually relaxed as she moved westward. It was about 9 p.m. now, and dark. She forced a flashback of the night before. She was okay about it. She felt nothing. She asked herself if she should feel guilt, interrogating the cognitive, rational and emotional parts of her brain, but there was nothing. Of course, she knew that it was wrong and that it would devastate her husband to know that she had been unfaithful, but the act itself had such little emotional significance for Jennifer that she somehow felt detached from its conventional meaning. As far as she was concerned, this minor indiscretion was insignificant. It was barely real. It had nothing to do with her true life, the life she had with John. She saw it as a blowing-off of steam, comparable to an intense workout in the gym or getting a massage.

She wasn't even justifying her behaviour to herself. From prior experience, she knew that this was outside of her. However, she knew enough to know that it had to be a secret, a hidden, grotty part of her life that no one could ever know about. She sometimes wondered why she did it – why she did any of it, in fact: the drinking and the fantasising and the seedy encounters. She wondered if this was just her way of getting through the life she had found herself in.

Did she believe that she was entitled to this behaviour to make up for some subconscious deficit in her life? Possibly, but every time her thoughts ambled down this road, she reminded herself of how fortunate she was compared to other women – with her comfortable lifestyle and beautiful, healthy family – and then duly banishing the memory of the night before into the vault in her brain that would remain closed forever to everyone but her. The irony of all of this, Jennifer knew, was that she prided herself on her straightness, her loyalty and honesty with people. That was how she was reared, and that was what she knew was present in every aspect of her life.

Then there was the barman. The realness of his body and her tenure in the encounter. So she acknowledged it, owned it and placed it in the vault.

Making her way down the long, concealed driveway to her home, Jennifer saw the lights on in the house and smiled. She couldn't wait to see them. She hauled her case in through the front door and headed for the kitchen where John was finishing up the dishes from a late dinner.

He turned to her and smiled. 'Well, Jen, how did you get on? Welcome back.'

Jennifer strode directly to him, wrapping her arms around his waist and reaching up to kiss his handsome face. She loved kissing John. He was a great kisser.

'Hold onto something for tonight,' he laughed, and nodded towards the kitchen door where the girls, Ava and Alannah, came springing into sight. They were thrilled to see their mother and immediately started to recant the carry-on of the previous two days. Ava had been selected to play on the school's ladies football GAA starting fifteen. She was an athletic kid and a great strategist on the field, talents she did not get from her mother. Alannah was more academic. She wanted to be a marine biologist when she was older. The science element she took from her father, Jennifer presumed, but she knew deep down that the interest in marine life came from her side. There was West Kerry blood in this child.

Jennifer's father was a fisherman his whole life. He provided well for his family, running a fleet of fishing boats off the West

Kerry coast. When Jennifer was young, she regularly accompanied him on runs out of Dingle Bay that didn't involve long, overnight hauls. Therefore, when Alannah hinted over dinner one day that she had an interest in marine biology, Jennifer barely hid the internal satisfaction that her bloodline was alive in another generation.

Once the ladies were settled upstairs, Jennifer threw herself on the couch beside John. It was late now, and she was wrecked. Her body felt battered. She lay her head on his chest and folded her feet up underneath her. She always got comfort in lying her head on his chest as if it were a pillow created just for her.

They chatted about his master's. He seemed to be working day and night at the moment. He was in the middle of an assignment on the rehabilitation of athletes following knee-joint meniscus injuries. He was enthusiastic about the subject and very knowledgeable, but on paper he grappled with presenting his research in a professional way. Jennifer was always his go-to in this matter. She wasn't a scientist, but she was a skilled writer and always seemed to be able to logically and expertly present his research and his ideas in a way that simply eluded him.

Frequently she had taken his work and rewritten it so that it was presented in a structured way, a way that was simple, eloquent and invited the reader to read on. She never objected to doing this for him. She believed that what was hers was his, and vice versa. She wanted him to thrive in his chosen career. So tonight, when he asked her to take a look at his current draft, she did not hesitate. She would do it in the morning.

*

Jennifer switched off the bathroom light and turned to find John already in bed. He was smirking at her in a way that did not need interpretation. She walked over to his side of the bed and began to take her clothes off item by item. She knew what he wanted.

He was ready for her. Sliding her slim, toned body underneath the bedclothes, she lay on top of him. She kissed his chest, by far his most gorgeous attribute, broad and muscular, and inhaled his skin. *Man smell*, she thought, a combination of cologne and sweat. That was her aphrodisiac, the fuel for her sexual desire. She realised how primitive this was, but she didn't care.

John wrapped his right arm around her waist and in one swoop turned her on her back. Her breathing was deepening now. She wanted him, and he knew it. She accepted his body as though she were starved of it. With every second in her husband's arms, she felt a penetrating love and belonging.

Jennifer loved having sex with her husband. She still fancied him immensely, and he satisfied her sexually – for the most part. She had learned not to expect anything too unconventional or to make any specific demands of him. One night she recalled when she was on the brink of climaxing, she cried out at him to go harder, to force himself into her, to hurt her. It was immediately clear that she had made a mistake. John abruptly withdrew, slighted that she might suggest he was not good enough, and, with innate insecurity, he had sulked. Jennifer knew not to do that again.

Tonight, however, she lapped up the sexual stimulation that her husband was providing for her. It was comfortable and loving and safe. It was exactly what she needed in her life.

The following morning arrived in a slightly less harrowing, less hungover fashion than the previous two. John was gone before she woke, and the girls were already downstairs, Ava scrambling to finish homework that Alannah spitefully refused to share with her, and Alannah organising her diary for the coming week. She would be making a presentation to the school SciFest committee on Friday, and she believed that she had a real shot of getting on the team.

Jennifer was very proud of her girls. Far too often of late she had suffered moments of self-doubt that her deficiencies as a parent – her shameless neglect as Liz and Geraldine had said in one of their assaults – were real, and worried if perhaps it was her own stubborn refusal to accept this that might eventually harm her daughters. Her only wish for them was that they would be happy in the lives they chose. That was all that really mattered to her. She did not care a morsel whether they were academic, or wealthy, she just hoped that she hadn't damaged them beyond repair.

It was at times like this that Jennifer thought of her own childhood. She recalled her mother being home, but not particularly involved in her daughter's life. They were a family of modest means, and, while Jennifer always had enough, she often did without the extras. She believed that despite this her mother had done a great job instilling that well-known, formidable Kerry confidence in her. Once as a young girl, she had gone to her mother in a state of distress for advice, expecting to be instructed how to remedy the problem at hand. Her mother's answer stayed with her every day since then: 'You're an intelligent girl. You can work it out for yourself,' she had said in her musical West Kerry accent.

Not impressed at the time, Jennifer later realised the value of her mother's approach, and it was the same approach she now took with her own girls. 'Live and learn, ladies. You will thank me later for it,' she could regularly be heard saying to them – to their incessant annoyance.

In her office later that morning, Jennifer and Susan sat down to look over Jennifer's caseload for the week. She would be in court all day Thursday; that was a given. Outside of that there would be a lot of prep work and documents to proof. A trespass case, two probate cases, two family-law cases and a quarry-full of conveyancing. This morning, however, she would be spending her time trying to talk sense into Pat Keane, a horrible, spiteful little man, determined to go to his grave fighting rather than settle with his neighbour – 'nothing but a badly bred bastard of a blow-in jobber' – over what amounted to a ditch between their land. Jennifer laughed as she thought about the ridiculousness of the case, but if Pat Keane wanted to pay her to get that ditch for him, the ditch she would get.

Jennifer enjoyed her job, and she loved the courtroom. It offered some high stakes and high tension – not all of the time, but enough to give her a buzz. She loved the rush of the performance, especially when she was forced to think on her feet.

Her true love was the law itself. In college, jurisprudence, or legal theory, was her favourite class. 'What is the law?' her professor would advance to the room full of eager young faces, and they would debate for hours the philosophy of H. L. A. Hart, Lon L. Fuller and Oliver Wendell Holmes. Pat Keane was a far cry from that, she conceded, then sighed, rolled her eyes and laughed.

It was at moments like this that she briefly allowed her mind to wander again, to the 'other' life, the one that might have been. The Paris apartment, the single lifestyle, the gentleman callers, the professorship at the Sorbonne. Jennifer didn't even really want it. She never understood why her mind always went there. The escapism caught her off guard sometimes. Whatever the reason, she knew that her fantasies helped to fulfil her. They were that bit of

Polyfilla that sealed the crevices in her life, and that was okay with her.

With that, she grabbed Pat's Land Registry maps, reapplied her lipstick in the mirror, and walked out into the sharp spring day.

Chapter 4

Three months later, sitting in traffic in her Audi A4 on the Stillorgan dual carriageway, Jennifer was beginning to feel the sweat patches creep out from her armpits. Granted it was a roasting day by Irish standards, but it was the anticipation of the meeting she was heading to that had her autonomic nervous system in overdrive.

As she rolled down the window for air, she listened to the voice on the satnav directing her to St Michael's Hospital, just four more kilometres east of the city centre. This neighbourhood was known to Jennifer, and the familiarity of the place was a comfort to her now. She recognised it well from her days as a law student at University College Dublin, days she always remembered with love, even longing.

Today, however, her journey to the capital was not for old times' sake. She had left Castlebar two and a half hours before. She knew that she had broken a few speed limits, but that wasn't new for her as the six penalty points on her driver's licence attested. *Only about fifteen more minutes*, she thought. She was wrecked. She hadn't slept well, again.

Following clear street signs designed to facilitate visitors from outside of Dublin, she rolled into the car park of St Michael's. Her heartbeat was in her throat now. *Inhale*, she reminded herself. Oxygen would help. And Sinead. Sinead would help now too. She had twenty minutes before her appointment and so dialled her friend.

'Hey lady,' chirped the familiar voice on the other end. 'Did you get there okay?'

'I'm here. Jesus, Sinead, how the hell did I end up here?' Jennifer answered, her voice starting to break.

'You drove yourself to Mayo University Hospital Emergency Department on Sunday morning and demanded a CT scan because you had a headache. That's how you got there.' Sinead paused and then changed her tone. 'Look, babe, everything is going to be okay. You know this. You've got this. You are completely drained with that job, with John, with the girls. This is a sign that you need a break. That's all.'

'Sinead, please be honest: am I mental? Have I lost it?' Jennifer's voice was no longer hiding the tears that were forcing their way out. 'I do feel a bit out of control lately.'

'The only "mental" thing you did was drive yourself to hospital on a whim. I mean, that was a bit of an overreaction I guess you could say. You are stressed. This referral will help you to see that you need to make some changes to your life. You've got this.'

At that moment Jennifer felt as vulnerable as she had done in an exceptionally long time. Whatever the outcome of today's consultation, she knew that things could not stay the way they were. She needed help. She cringed as she thought about the irrational – even crazed – drive to the A&E five days ago. The recollection of that morning was mortifying now. At Jennifer's insistence, the medical team had reluctantly agreed to perform a CT scan. It turned out that she did not in fact have a brain tumour.

'Deep breath, Jen,' Sinead said. 'One foot in front of the other. Call me when you come out.'

'Thank you,' Jennifer exhaled, and then turned her phone to silent.

Jennifer sat alone in a row of seats outside a door that read, 'Dr Ann Cullen, MB, BCh, BAO, MRCPsych, Consultant Psychiatrist.' She picked at the edges of her nails and resisted the urge to pull out her phone and scroll meaninglessly through some social-media app. *Just inhale*, she thought.

'Mrs Burke, Dr Cullen is free now. You can head in,' a very happy-looking young receptionist called in a sing-song voice. Jennifer wasted no time in picking up her bag, her beloved white Prada, from the seat beside her. Folding her jacket – beige linen vintage – over her forearm, she walked straight in. The room was small with a desk and three chairs, two of which had their backs to her as she entered. She was greeted by a smiling lady, aged somewhere in her fifties, who held out her hand and welcomed Jennifer by name, inviting her to take a seat.

Okay so far, Jennifer thought, attempting to ignore the box of tissues on the desk. She guessed that in this line of work there were bound to be some tears shed during a consultation. Par for the course.

Jennifer believed she was there that day for a chat about how to manage her stress levels and maybe get a prescription for some anti-anxiety meds. She accepted that she had been finding things tough lately. In truth, she just needed a holiday, but nonetheless here she was in a psychiatrist's consultation room.

'It says here that you're from Castlebar, Jennifer?' said Dr Cullen, half inquisitively, half already all-knowing. 'You must have been up early this morn—'

'Actually, I'm from Ballyferriter in West Kerry, but I've been living in Castlebar since I left college. So, yes, I guess I'm from Castlebar.'

Dr Cullen began by explaining to Jennifer that the referral had come about because the A&E doctor in Mayo University Hospital had concerns about her mental state when she presented there by herself the previous Sunday. Jennifer felt like saying, 'Yes, I know – I was there!' Instead, she nodded. But before Dr Cullen could continue, she launched into a rapid explanation for the incident, clarifying that she was generally in control and that the stress of juggling work and home had seemed to overpower her lately.

She went on, unprompted, to tell Dr Cullen how she had set up her own law company five years before and now ran it single-handedly. Without taking a breath, she described how she had ambitions to expand the practice in the future.

'You are quite a driven person, Jennifer,' the doctor said, watching her face for a reaction. 'What do you like to do in your downtime? Tell me about some of—'

Once again, Jennifer interrupted the doctor, insisting that she was not really a driven person. She just liked to work. She liked to keep achieving. She found it difficult to slow down or to stop. She was happiest when she was working. That was just her personality. The concept of downtime seemed a bit strange to Jennifer in that moment. She explained this to the doctor. She needed to explain.

'Jennifer, do you realise that since we have been chatting you have interrupted me twice, not given me a chance to finish my sentences and spoken over me when I was still talking? Do you think that you do that a lot? Do you think that you regularly converse with people in this way, not giving them the chance to have their say?' the doctor asked.

Jennifer was silent. She was taken aback by this bluntness, and suddenly embarrassed. She wasn't aware that she did that, but she certainly acknowledged that she was doing it now. 'I'm really sorry, doctor. That was rude of me,' she said.

'No need to apologise, Jennifer,' said Dr Cullen with a smile. 'It's a symptom we call "pressure of speech". Can I start by asking you a few questions about your medical history?'

Jennifer looked at her confused but nodded. *Symptom of what?*

'From your GP records, it says here that you were treated for depression in the past. Can you tell me a little about that?'

Jennifer was pasted to the seat and silent. What on earth was she talking about? She looked at Dr Cullen curiously and said, 'I'm sorry, what do you mean?'

'It says here that shortly after the birth of your babies you were prescribed a selective serotonin reuptake inhibitor used to treat depressive episodes. Do you remember being prescribed and taking a drug for six months?'

Jennifer flushed. At the time, she had discussed with the GP that her mood was a little low after the birth of the babies. He prescribed a drug to get her through a tough patch. As far as she was aware, all post-natal women went on these drugs for a while. It was no big deal. Sitting in front of a consultant psychiatrist, having it referred to as a depressive episode made it sound like a big deal, as though she was ill – mentally ill. The sweat patches under her arms were being tested for the second time that day.

Jennifer confirmed that she had depression in her past.

'And since then, have you ever gone through a similar low where you experienced symptoms of hopelessness, lack of motivation, irritability, anxiety or suicidal thoughts—?'

'Not suicide,' Jennifer butted in again. 'Sorry,' she said again. 'I am way too fond of myself, I assure you.' Both women smiled. 'I think I get bouts of anxiety when my heart pounds and it's hard to breathe and I feel like I might collapse. It happens for no apparent reason, and it's frightening when I'm in it. But I am sure that I have never since felt that soul-destroying feeling of hopelessness and disinterest in my life that I felt back when the girls were babies. It's nearly impossible to describe it.'

Dr Cullen smiled as if to say that Jennifer was in fact excellent with words and a very capable describer. 'Okay, Jennifer. Now tell me what happened at the weekend,' she said.

Jennifer looked into Dr Cullen's face and said that honestly she didn't remember much of it. She had become progressively more agitated during the week preceding the hospital admission. She recalled that she had aggressively turned on a client in her office in Castlebar, in front of her receptionist and anyone in the street who was within earshot of the law office. Also, she had drunk a ridiculous amount of red wine on Friday night and had confronted John in a state of what could only be described as hysteria, ranting about where he had been that evening and what he was up to. And not for the first time.

In hindsight, she could see that her behaviour was paranoid, even occasionally delusional, especially when she drank. All she knew was that her crazy-lady routine on Sunday at A&E had culminated in her being drugged to within an inch of her life in hospital. She could feel the tears gathering behind her eyelids again.

Dr Cullen continued to throw question after question at her, which she answered in all honesty. An unusual serenity started to come over her, a faith in the process and in this doctor. Dr Cullen asked Jennifer about her history with money, any impulsive spending. Jennifer admitted to occasionally getting trigger-happy while shopping online, but generally it wasn't an issue. The doctor also asked about her sexual past, whether there had been any impulsive or risky encounters over the years. Jennifer admitted that there may have been the odd one, praying it would be glanced over by her examiner. It was.

Then, Dr Cullen, scribbling away on her answer sheet, asked, 'What would you say was your best ever achievement in your life to date?'

Jennifer didn't hesitate for one second. 'My children,' she answered, not even needing to think about it. Despite her flaws, she hoped that she had raised them to be very happy and confident girls. With that, Dr Cullen raised her head from her notes and beamed a generous and reassuring smile at her patient. They both knew in that instant that Jennifer was going to be just fine.

Eventually Dr Cullen put her pen down on her desk and, still smiling, said, 'Jennifer, you have a condition called bipolar disorder.' Jennifer didn't interrupt. 'It is one of the more serious psychiatric illnesses that we come across, but with the right treatment and the determination I can see in you, it is a very manageable condition. It is generally characterised by a swinging of mental states, or moods, between depression and various states of mania and hypomania. The immediate problem facing you right now is that you are in a state of hypomania. Have you noticed recently that you often feel full to the brim with energy, super confident, invincible even?'

Jennifer immediately recognised what the doctor was talking about. She regularly felt unstoppable at work and could recall a time recently in court when she went into full Johnnie Cochran mode.

The doctor went on to question whether her states of euphoria had ever gone too far, or whether her drinking had ever led to exaggerated thought patterns or behaviour, like paranoia, for example. Jennifer was about to cry but laughed out loud instead. 'Jesus Christ, this is terrifying,' she gasped, placing her hand over her mouth to camouflage the reality of the words.

'Once you have received the diagnosis, the hardest bit for you is over. Trust me,' Dr Cullen replied.

Jennifer did trust the doctor in front of her, but she knew that, in truth, she had shared only a snippet of her life with her. This was especially true of her life over the past twenty-four months, when she had hardly admitted some of her outrageous behaviour, even to herself. In that moment, she knew that she was bipolar. It made perfect sense.

Dr Cullen informed her that she would be prescribed lifelong lithium treatment and that she would be referred into the care of the mental-health unit at Mayo University Hospital. Jennifer thanked the doctor, shook her hand and turned to walk out of the room. As she did, she realised her life had just shifted in titanic fashion. She was the same person but changed in some way – not because she had a mental illness but because she was now going to get better.

She walked out into the scorching May day feeling a little lighter than before. Even though she had just been diagnosed as bipolar, her immediate sense was one of relief and hope. The inner struggle, the guilt, the lack of reason … it all started to make sense now. For a long time, it had felt like she was in a constant state of conflict with the people in her life, and especially with herself. Maybe now she would begin to understand it, to understand herself. Maybe now she would be happy.

Jennifer was confident by nature and had always believed in her own potential. Since her schooldays, she knew that she could do whatever she set her mind to. This theme followed her through her college years. She had never failed yet, and she was not going to start now.

In the car, she rested for a few minutes before facing into the three-hour journey home. She needed to call John. He had tolerated so much from her over the past couple of years. She winced as she recalled the rows, the paranoid accusations and her drunken performances at the conference banquets with his professional colleagues from the physiotherapy world. He was as invested in this as she was. But it was all going to be okay now. She reached for her phone with excitement.

Without a second's thought, John said, 'What? Are you serious? Jen, you had better go back in there to that doctor and you tell her that are not bipolar! Do you understand what this means? You'll never get a bloody job again.'

Jennifer listened, incredulous. The sense of hope she had felt walking out of the consultant's office ten minutes before was being wiped from her system. All she wanted to feel was respite and healing. But now, sitting on her own in a car park in Dublin, the one person she trusted more than anyone on earth was drop-kicking her out of this brand-new secure reality.

She stopped John in his tracks and tried to explain that this was, in fact, what she wanted and needed. This was going to be the start of a better life for all of them. 'Don't you want your wife back?' she asked.

'Yes, Jen, of course I want you to feel better and to get some help, but you are very wrong if you think this is the way to do it.' He was angry now. It was then that Jennifer copped the source of the outrage, a perpetual source of contention in their relationship. John's West of Ireland 'what will the neighbours think' genes were becoming activated again, and, with a pain in her chest, she resented him for it. Of all the times she needed him to put aside his insecurities and put her first, this was one of them.

She ended the call, telling him they could chat when she got home and reassuring him that things really were going to be better now. She set her satnav for the M50, then sat for a minute looking at herself in the rear-view mirror, running her fingers through her hair. No matter what, she was going to make this work for her. Then she turned the ignition and cried her heart out.

Chapter 5

Jennifer felt more exhausted that evening than she had in her whole life. She couldn't even tell whether the conversation she had with Dr Cullen in Dublin that morning had really happened. For a split second she was not sure. In recent months she increasingly struggled with her imagination, which had a tendency to grow legs. Last Sunday, in the A&E, she had truly believed that John was taking her kids away from her and moving them in with her in-laws. She remembered being hysterical at the prospect and pleading for help. She also recalled the look on the triage nurse's face, a look of scepticism and suspicion, but mostly pity. The nurse had looked at Jennifer as though she was crazy. Jennifer realised that now, and she felt nauseous.

Pottering about the kitchen and generating small talk until the girls went upstairs, Jennifer and John avoided making too much eye contact. Jennifer knew this was not going to be an easy conversation. The more she recalled John's reaction to her diagnosis earlier that day, the more uneasy she became. Surely his was simply a reaction to a gut instinct and did not represent his true feelings about her condition? She knew she would need him now more than ever. He was concerned for her reputation, she accepted this, and she hoped she would be able to convince him that today would be the turning point in their lives.

'You just don't get it, Jen. You are so naive sometimes. People don't accept that kind of thing around here. If you are officially labelled "mental" then your life as you know it is over. Who is going to hire a bipolar solicitor?' John spoke sincerely but in a slightly perverse way that made it more about himself than her. 'I've been researching it online,' he continued. 'I mean, some of the symptoms are completely mad – not you at all. I know you have had a tendency to get anxious, and sometimes you get worked up and excited, but mania, euphoria, promiscuity? Jennifer, really, they got this wrong.'

Jennifer wanted to answer, but her brain let her down. She was shattered. The news she had received in the doctor's office today was bad but listening now to these words from the man she adored and looked up to as a friend was breaking her heart. She knew he did not have all the facts about her behaviour, especially over the past year, and there was no way she was about to set him straight on the matter.

'I don't agree,' she said, defending herself even though she knew very well she should not have to. 'Mental illness does not have the stigma attached to it the way it used to do. John, surely you know that I have not been myself. My behaviour has been "unusual", let's say.' She felt a tremor in her voice. All she wanted for her life right now was to feel calm and happy and normal, and she wanted John to be happy for her because today she had found a way to finally achieve this.

She reassured her husband that, once she began the treatment, he would see that their family would have all the peace and stability they had been missing for so long. She went so far as to accept that the problems they were having in their marriage were her fault. She told him this, in an attempt to win his support.

'Okay, Jen. Look, whatever you want. But my advice is don't tell a soul. This is your business. No one needs to know. Please trust me on this,' he said. He may have conceded to giving the treatment a try in the secrecy of their own house; however, he was most definitely not willing to make it a reality by announcing it to the world.

Suddenly Jennifer felt a bolt of panic. Liz and Geraldine. They would destroy her. Nothing would give them more delight than to know that Jennifer the snob, Jennifer the money-grabber, Jennifer the unfit mother, was 'mental'. She looked at John, and in feigned agreement said, 'Yes, you have a point. At least until I get my head around this, let's not tell a soul. That includes our families, okay? Do you agree? We will keep it between you and me for now.'

As soon as John put his foot on the stairs, Jennifer dialled Sinead. Bypassing pleasantries, she regurgitated the events of her day step by step as they had unfolded. Sinead did not interrupt. She listened to every word her friend told her and, when Jennifer took a breath, replied, 'Babe, you are the most intelligent, capable, clever, caring person that I know. If your brain needs lithium, then give it lithium. It's a metal, for fuck's sake, hardly hard-core narcotics.'

In that moment, Jennifer knew why this amazing person was her oldest friend. They didn't speak regularly. In fact, it could go weeks between meetings, but Sinead was the one who balanced Jennifer out every time. She felt the tension leave her body, and the tears took advantage of the gap in her armour. 'Thank you. I am so disappointed in John. I understand that this is incredibly stressful for him, but sometimes I wish that he was a stronger man. Don't get me wrong, I appreciate everything that he does for me, and in truth he has tolerated a lot from me recently. I just wish he was more confident,' she said.

Sinead listened, and offered advice when it was called for. She comforted Jennifer, telling her that everyone was made the way they were made, and that was life. She had a great way of seeing things. They eventually concluded the hour-long conversation with Sinead reassuring Jennifer, 'This too will pass. You've got this, babe.'

Later in the week, Jennifer presented for an appointment at the weekly mental-health clinic in the day hospital in Castlebar. On arrival, the friendly woman at the desk directed her to a room where she was to await her turn. She was scared and excited – completely out of her comfort zone. She had quite literally never been ill a day in her life.

Stepping into the waiting room, she locked eyes with a man she recognised, a local farmer who had once hired her to purchase land. She froze temporarily, then bolted backwards out the door in the direction of the nearest bathroom. She was hyperventilating now as the reality slowly dawned on her. Was John right? Would she never again work as a solicitor if everyone knew she was mental? There she was, they would say, sitting pretty in the waiting room of a psychiatrist's office with all the other nut-jobs in the town.

But Jennifer did not believe she was mental – whatever mental was. She had a condition that required treatment, like any other condition. So why did she just bolt from a doctor's waiting room and hide in a bathroom? She was not ready for this.

Dr Philip Raz was a middle-aged man, well dressed with an air of control about him. Jennifer was glad of it, because she was about to put her life in his hands. He introduced himself in a tone that seemed to indicate real dedication to his work. It was comforting. It allowed Jennifer the opportunity to gradually open up at her own pace.

'I'm terrified. I won't lie,' Jennifer told the doctor. 'My life has been on a collision course this past year. I've been risking my marriage and my business. I thought the problem was the alcohol. I mean, I know it is. I just didn't realise how unstable my mind had become.'

Dr Raz nodded in a comforting and accepting way, facing her head-on. 'Bipolar disorder is a serious psychiatric condition with many different presentations ranging from melancholic episodes to anxiety attacks and psychotic presentations. It is a disorder with many faces. You presented last weekend with psychosis and paranoia, and you were categorised as hypomanic. It sounds scary, I understand, but believe me: the fact that you are now diagnosed and getting treatment is great news for you. Not everyone with this condition is lucky enough to have the presence of mind to walk in the door of a hospital. Even in your state of psychiatric distress, you had the foresight to ask for help.'

Jennifer took one deep breath after another. She was grateful to the man sitting in front of her. She realised that she did not have surplus people in her life to ask for help. Normally she would turn to John for comfort. Now her chest hurt with every acknowledgement that she did not have him by her side this time. Sinead was her solid ground right now. Selfless Sinead. Jennifer's family in Kerry were terrific too, but she didn't want to involve them in this yet. She had

Susan in the office, but this was far too private to engage the help of her employee.

Then it hit her. She really was a loner. She had never really thought about it before now. She had always loved her own company, spending many happy hours in blissful introspection. She enjoyed socialising as much as anyone, but the notion of having a close group of friends, girlfriends or otherwise, was foreign to her.

Turning to Dr Raz, she inquired about the plan of action. Ready or not, she had already decided that conquering this was going to be her finest achievement. There was nothing she wouldn't do; failure was not on the menu. She desperately wanted the life of calm and comfort with John and the girls that she knew was possible, a happy marriage and a successful career. That's all she wanted. She did not want notoriety or excessive wealth. She just wanted security and harmony, physical and mental.

Scribbling and talking at the same time, Dr Raz explained that Jennifer would be taking lithium at night for the rest of her life. The dose was individual to the patient, and in the initial period of the treatment they would have to monitor her blood lithium levels very carefully in order to maintain therapeutic levels in her system at all times. This meant recording the time at which she took the tablets and then taking a blood sample twelve hours later, when the level of lithium was at its lowest, until the dose was stable. She was confident she could do this.

A bigger challenge for Jennifer was the instruction to curb her drinking habits. It was becoming clear to her that the alcohol would have a negative impact on her attempts to manage the symptoms of the condition. Basically, Dr Raz explained, if she did not stop the binge drinking, this condition would continue to hammer her. With painful acceptance, she nodded at this.

The doctor's final instruction for the day was that Jennifer should link in with the team of clinical psychologists at the health centre. Jennifer was not sure how she felt about this. He explained that they were qualified professionals. At least psychology was a regulated profession. Jennifer worried the myriad of so-called 'qualifications' out there – written on the back of a brown paper bag, people who stuck the word 'psychotherapist' outside the door of their garden shed and off with them. She needed to know who she could trust right now. She would make an appointment – one anyway, she agreed – and thanked her new doctor, shaking his hand.

She knew they were going to be seeing a lot of each other in the future.

She had one last stop before she could curl up inside the cosy refuge of her home that evening. The dilemma was whether she should use her regular pharmacist to dispense the lithium or should she employ subterfuge and slip under cover of darkness to another town. Again, Jennifer checked herself. She was clearly apprehensive about people finding out that she was crazy. She said the word out loud – 'crazy' – and laughed. She reckoned if she took the piss out of herself then surely it would soothe the soreness of it all.

Torn between her own natural confidence and independence, which guided her to be herself and not hide, and the fear of what would become of her if the people of Castlebar got a whiff of her current medical status, she made a decision. She walked into her local pharmacy, where she had been collecting her contraceptive pill since the day she arrived in the town, handed the piece of paper to her pharmacist, Marie O'Loughlin, and braced herself for the reaction.

There it was: Marie's eyes widened to the maximum, and Jennifer knew it was too late to protect herself.

Chapter 6

On the advice of Dr Raz, Jennifer agreed to take some time off work so she could rest and pamper herself. The initial thought of walking out on her law practice and abandoning her clients was a non-runner, but when Sinead suggested that she 'knew a boy' who was available to provide locum cover, Jennifer conceded. Mark Clancy was no boy. He was a very handsome, sociable thirty-year-old solicitor from Galway who had helped Sinead out recently when her workload engulfed her. In truth, he was inexperienced, but Jennifer was in dire need and reluctantly accepted the help.

At first, Jennifer enjoyed the sabbatical, falling into a routine of homemaking that included adventurous dinners and the rearrangement of furniture. Despite the fact that the doctor was satisfied he had stabilised her lithium levels, she still buzzed with an underlying uneasy energy.

'Sit back and let your body heal now,' he told Jennifer.

The irony was that the sitting-back was the singular source of stress in her life now. Jennifer had gone out to work every day of her life. She needed a purpose, and being a wife and mother was simply never going to fulfil her. Over the course of her leave, she habitually turned to her husband for company and distraction, but he seemed more interested in maintaining the status quo: working from dawn till dusk as she saw it.

He reassured her that he was glad she was feeling better, but apart from that he did not engage in conversation about her health. It was a topic he avoided if possible. She sometimes nagged him, as he called it, to speak to the clinic managers about cutting his hours so that he could spend more time at home with his three ladies. But he would brush her off, aggressively at times, with the same excuse: his employers relied on him, and he was obliged to take all the work he could get. Ultimately, she abandoned her appeal for his time, placing it among the rest of her discarded cravings.

As the weeks progressed, Jennifer found it ever harder to motivate herself. She could muster enough energy to get the girls to school, often in her pyjamas, but nothing productive. In her previous life, she would not have been caught dead in anything less than a finely tuned outfit, stilettos, mascara and lipstick. She would spend countless moments deciding on the perfect outfit, balancing classic design with her unique style. Her look was part of her identity. She lived to get 'dressed up', as people called it. For her, there was nothing 'dressed up' about it. It was who she was. She didn't wear fabulous clothes and make-up to get reinforcement from the world: she did it to remind herself, every day, of who she was. 'Your appearance tells your story and portrays what you stand for,' she always said. 'If you look like you don't care about yourself on an outing to the supermarket, then you don't care.'

She taught her girls to have respect for themselves too, to portray themselves to the world as they wanted to be seen. That did not necessarily mean make-up and heels. What it meant, she told them, was when they looked in the mirror, on any given day, they should be confident that they were putting their best foot forward and radiating personality.

When Jennifer caught a glimpse of herself in the hall mirror that particular morning, she looked like a middle-aged woman, beaten into submission by a life filled with failure, a woman who had given up. Four weeks into her lithium treatment, she was suffering the worst hangover of her life. Once the gloss of her heightened mood had worn off, she was left with a rough, seedy reality that she struggled to deal with. Thoughts churned in her mind, and regurgitated memories of events from the past few months filled her days.

Vividly now, she recalled an encounter she had with one of her neighbours in the town centre. An arrogant man at the best of times, he had scolded Jennifer one day for parking too close to his jeep in the street. Her reaction, which she now relived in graphic detail, was nothing less than an eruption. 'Oh, I'm sorry, can you not manage your big jeep in this small space? Maybe you would like me to help move it for you, would you? Or maybe you just like pushing women around? Listen here, little man, you might get away with bullying your wife at home in private, but you will not get away with doing it to me!' she had yelled, the entire street in earshot. The man had driven off in silence.

Jennifer cringed now and retreated into resigned acceptance. The arrogant man in the street was not the only recipient of her uncharacteristic wrath. There were others, and the more she thought about them the stronger the recoil in her body and mind became. She now knew that her coping mechanism during this gargantuan hangover would have to be this: she would accept what she could not undo, and if there was a chance to make an apology to someone then she would. She would do her best with the shit storm she was in, salvage what she could and vacuum-pack what was unfixable into a watertight, impermeable grave. That was going to be her strategy. Draw a line. She had been ill, she conceded. Not herself. Once she resigned herself to this, her recovery advanced.

A couple of weeks later, when Mark called in need of her help on a case, Jennifer was reluctant. She had wilted in recent weeks. But maybe this was her chance to get back to some semblance of normality. When she heard it was a defamation case, notoriously difficult to win, she was annoyed that Mark had taken it on. After all, it was the reputation of her law practice at stake, not just his case.

What was worse, the plaintiff had opted for a jury trial. Juries were standard procedure in criminal law but unheard of in civil cases. Defamation was the only civil-law case that allowed for the option of trial by jury, and Jennifer knew absolutely nothing about jury trials. According to the Defamation Act 2009, a defamatory statement was one that injured a person's reputation in the eyes of reasonable members of society. An actionable defamatory statement had three ingredients. It had to be published; it had to refer to the complainant; and it had to be false.

On the face of it, it looked like Mark's case had all three of these elements. The client, a local vet, was claiming that he had been defamed on Facebook by a well-known animal-rights activist who alleged that he was 'cold as ice', 'an animal hater' and had 'ripped her off'. The vet in question was asserting that his professional reputation had been gravely tarnished and his income had suffered as a consequence. Apprehensively, Jennifer agreed to go into the office to help prepare Mark for the case.

The following morning, Jennifer made an effort. She selected a deep-red sleeveless dress with dark-brown pointed snake-print stilettos. The transformation in her mood was striking. She knew there and then that she needed to get up and get out again. It was time to reclaim her life.

On the way into town, she could feel herself inclining towards anxiety. She dismissed it. As she pulled into the car park in front of her office, she saw that Mark had taken her parking spot. It surprised her when she felt possessive, almost insecure. She dismissed that too. The sun beamed down on her as she strode to her office front door. Susan glowed when she saw her and welcomed her in with such intensity it was as though she had been gone a year. She had in fact taken leave for just six weeks.

With every step Jennifer took towards Susan, she felt a ripple of cold sweat run down her body, then a wavelike surge of blood from the periphery of her extremities to her heart. Simultaneously, her vision grew blacker until she could barely see. *Please God, no, not now*, she cried internally. It was too late to plead with God. She was smack in the middle of a full-on anxiety attack. She felt her trachea constrict, and, like a cat in a car, frantically looked for the exit. 'I just need to run back for something. Be one second,' she spluttered at Susan.

Thankfully, experience had taught her that the outward manifestation of a panic attack never looked as bad as the internal horror. She briskly exited the building to the safety of the footpath outside. Then she sat in her car while her body regained its normal physiological functions. She was devastated. This was her world, and she was losing it. She was losing control. Not like when she was out of control in her hypomanic days. She was not ill now, and she was losing control of everything. If she was not able to get it together and function at the level that she had always done, she had no Plan B.

On the second attempt, Jennifer had a good meeting with Mark. Despite the fact that he was young and cocky, she liked him. Checking herself, she laughed and admitted that what she meant was *because* he was young and cocky she liked him. This glimpse of her mischievous personality every now and then gave her the glimmer of hope she needed to see that things were going to be okay. She would recover from this. The Jennifer she knew and liked very much was in there somewhere.

For the rest of the day, and many days after, whenever Jennifer thought about going back to work, the same panic surged through her chest. It made no sense. She loved to work. It provided the backbone to her existence and was integral to her personality. What if, she wondered, without the 'bipolar' part of her brain she would no longer be able to do what she did? What if she had lost her edge, the risqué fringe to her personality and the element of her skill set that allowed her to negotiate on behalf of her clients and win cases?

What was worse, she admitted to herself that the thought of going into a courtroom again terrified her. She could not believe this was happening to her. Her brain sizzled. She did not even know who she was anymore. Later that week, stopping off at a petrol station on the way home from doing taxi duty with the girls, she bought a bottle of Shiraz. She needed it, and a few glasses of wine were going to do no harm, she bargained with herself.

While her girls spent the night on their grandad's farm, helping out with the newborn calves, Jennifer relaxed for the first time all day. She knew that she had spiralled again. If the past couple of weeks were anything to go by, her transition back to work and life as she knew it was going to be hell. She had been anxious a lot recently, but she knew she needed to make the leap back to a routine.

Her head was pounding by now, so when she saw Sinead's name and gorgeous face light up her phone, she jumped on it. As usual, Sinead had all the right lines. She reassured Jennifer that she was still in the transition phase of her recovery and advised her not to overthink things. Just because she had a panic attack in the office one day did not mean it would happen again. As usual, Jennifer submitted to Sinead's Kung Fu Panda ability to dissipate peace and tranquillity.

'And who knows, Jen, maybe there is another path for you? You are a skilled solicitor, but maybe this illness is a sign that you are destined for greater things.'

'Or maybe it's a sign that I can't stay the course and am going to be a housewife on medication for the rest of my life,' Jennifer added, half joking, half deflated. Whatever the analysis, the two women agreed that they would not unravel the mystery that night and signed off with mutual affection.

Creeping into bed beside her sleeping husband, an exhausted Jennifer wrapped her arms and legs around his warm body. Slightly fuzzy from the wine, she reminded herself that she knew only this for sure: she had to believe in herself, in her resilience, her breeding, her spirit. Losing to this disorder was not an option. She would rather be dead.

Chapter 7

Mark Clancy was a natural. Jennifer sat through Susan's worship sessions on the phone, listening to how the clients adored him and how he really knew his stuff. That was according to Susan's self-professed expertise on the matter, of course. His handsome face and tight trousers had nothing to do with it. Jennifer laughed. *Well, if you've got it use it*, she thought. He was a capable lawyer, and that gave Jennifer ample reprieve from her other worries.

She had built her law practice from the ground up, and knowing that her clients had confidence in Mark was invaluable. Equally, Mark revelled in his new role as commander-in-chief of a law practice. He was bursting with enthusiasm and had even hinted to Jennifer that he would be interested in staying on at the end of her leave had she some use for him.

His recent defamation case had been quite the conquest. His brave move to go to court paid off for his client, and for the Jennifer's law practice she conceded. On the evening of the trial, after an excited blow-by-blow account of events from Mark, Jennifer received a telephone call from Thomas Acton BL, Mark's barrister on the case, to tell her how cleverly Mark had put the argument together, and how professional he was to deal with. Jennifer thanked him and smiled like a proud mother. Such reassurance of Mark's ability had healing powers for her now.

While her law practice was in competent hands, her days had become a cycle of mothering and basic household chores. She was endlessly entertained by the drama associated with being a fifteen-year-old, and in the evenings she looked forward to catching up with news from her husband whenever he got finished at the clinic. She had begun to rely on him more now. He was patient with her, but he had hinted that it was time for her to get back to work for her own sake.

His encouragement to get back to normal caused Jennifer anxiety. She felt safe in her new routine, but as soon as she thought about going back to the office – going anywhere in fact – she regressed. She knew that the current situation could not continue indefinitely and that she would have to face her fear soon. And she would, she promised herself. Any day now.

That night, she dozed off to a podcast about true crimes in Ireland. Sinead had recommended it, and Jennifer was enjoying it so far. It was superb, she thought, really engaging, nauseatingly descriptive with great narrative pace. Criminal law was something she had thought she might have a flair for when she was at university, with its fast pace and endless variation, but instead she had sold her soul for the financial reward of mainstream legal practice. What she liked about this podcast was that she always managed to drift off to sleep to the hypnotic voice of the narrator. Falling asleep had been difficult since her diagnosis, and this was her go-to night-time routine lately.

In her sleep, she was disturbed. In a haze of semi-sedation, she began to feel aroused, her breath quickening to the sensation of something between her legs. She drifted in and out of consciousness, not knowing whether she was dreaming or awake, disorientated and confused yet aroused. Awakening, she felt her husband's hands on her body. He ripped at her clothes wildly – not like him. She turned to face him, but he forced her away, climbing on her back and holding her down.

Jennifer felt her blood rush between her legs. She was more turned on right now than she had been in months. She called out for him, encouraging him to take what he wanted. He did, and his body groaned with satisfaction. Jennifer lay there lounging in the aftershock of the erotic encounter. Heat engulfed her body. She knew then that her libido was one fragment of herself that had not been lost to this bipolar nightmare. There was no illness, no disability, no natural disaster that could take her sex drive from her. She celebrated silently. Jennifer Burke was alive still.

Her husband was already asleep.

Sunday morning brought new energy and possibility. Jennifer arose to find John and the girls chatting and preparing breakfast in the kitchen. It filled her with a warm fuzzy happiness, and she felt an internal calm that she had not felt for a long time. She sat in their south-facing conservatory with her tea and let the sun warm her, enjoying the glow that was around her in that minute. With the sustaining chatter of her family in the background she remembered what it felt like to be filled with life.

There was a time when she oozed vitality – not a false, bipolar-fuelled vivacity but a confident, self-assured contentment.

Today she began to experience a hope that she had recently lost. She looked over at her husband, who winked at her mischievously, acknowledging the encounter of the night before. Jennifer smiled bashfully. She really did love him. She knew there were things about him that she would change if she could. She craved more support in dealing with his spiteful sisters, and she longed for him to show more courage and understanding in the face of her newly diagnosed condition, but marriage and family meant more to her than that, and she was willing to make sacrifices to keep hers.

She allowed a short surge of guilt, even panic, as memories of her infidelities charged into her head, and then she simply said *no*. The line is drawn. That was not her, not the real her. She would do her best by her family from now on.

Early the next morning, Jennifer noticed a voicemail on her mobile phone from Charles Roche. Charles always called her on her private mobile when he needed her. Most of her other clients used the office number, but Charles liked to know he had personal access. She hadn't heard from him since she closed on his land sale last year.

'Jennifer, darling, where have you been? I have something I think you might be interested in. Give me a call,' said the mature, masculine voice on the line. Jennifer's gut reaction was to stall. It had been two months since she had done any legal work with her old clients. She stood there, momentarily, deciding whether to press delete or redial. Without giving herself too much time to deliberate, which would surely have resulted in flight, she dialled and inhaled. 'Charles, lovely to hear from you,' she said sincerely.

'Jennifer, how are you love?' he answered in a sensual tone that made Jennifer melt as usual. 'I'm calling because I recently came across something that made me think of you. Bear with me,' he said, going on to tell her about a position that was about to be advertised in a large start-up pharmaceutical company in the West of Ireland, a company in which he had a substantial shareholding.

According to Charles, the new company was looking to expand its in-house legal team, and he recalled how Jennifer had once told him of her interest in company law and also, more significantly, how she had written her master's dissertation on the intricacies of new drug authorisations with the European Medicines Agency. Charles had immediately thought of Jennifer for this role. In his opinion she was smart, fresh, ballsy, progressive – everything this company was looking for.

Jennifer sat in silence, not knowing how to respond. Eventually she mumbled, 'Thank you, that's very flattering, but my practice—'

'Jennifer, you are destined for better things than spending your days dealing with spoilt-brat children fighting over their auld lad's farm,' Charles protested, his West of Ireland accent leaking through. 'Think about it. I'm going to email the details to you. And Jennifer, this is Castlebar. Opportunities don't ride in on a horse and carriage every day,' he said. Then he was gone.

Jennifer was stunned. The conversation had been so abrupt and out of nowhere. She instinctively disregarded it. How ridiculous it would be to even consider leaving private practice. After all, her business was just in its developmental years. How would her clients manage without her? She repeated this mantra over and over all morning, but there was a spark in her. Something had ignited in her that made her muse over this new opportunity. She knew it was outrageous, yet she could not stop thinking about it. She would mention it to John that night.

By the time John got home, Jennifer had worked herself up into a state of muted excitement. She had begun to imagine what it would be like working with a whole team of people. She thought about the support network that she had sacrificed in recent years by working alone in her small law practice. And she imagined the opportunities she might have with this company. She knew she had so much more potential, academic and personal, than she had been achieving. She even fantasised about the friends she might make. With that thought, a lump grew in her throat. She was a solitary person and had never believed that she needed friends, at least not in abundance. Maybe it was time to reassess.

John was silent at first as he listened to her recount her conversation with Charles. She could not read him. He was definitely not brimming with the same enthusiasm that had begun to shine from her. 'Why would you consider closing your practice now that you have invested so much time and work in building it?' he said. 'This is very impulsive, Jennifer. In fact, it's just typical of you.'

Jennifer's heart dropped in her chest. She did not know why she expected support; she was getting used to going without. She did expect it, nevertheless. 'John, you know I have been struggling with the thought of going back to work in the practice. Maybe this opportunity for a new start has come along just at the right time for me. It is possible that the diagnosis is a sign that I need to make some changes in my life,' she explained.

She went on to suggest that if she were able to secure this new job, she could sell her practice. She would have it valued, but if what she knew about the valuation of a solicitor's practice was correct, she could pay off her debts and have a tidy lump sum left over. It would be the first time in her life that she would have some money for herself.

John looked at her, disillusioned. 'Jesus, Jennifer, you are never satisfied. One minute you want your own solicitor's practice, the next you want to drop it and run off to some new company. Do you actually know what you want? Maybe some day you will just settle into a role and stop running away.' Then he barked, 'Why do you always have to chase drama and look for attention?' With that he left the room, and she was alone.

Despite that fact that she had taken more than one hit from her husband's bottomless black hole of selfishness in recent years,

Jennifer was hurt this time. She was distressed by his reaction. With a spinning head she weighed up the pros and cons of moving to this job in an attempt to fathom where John's reaction had come from. She understood that there would be a lot of work in selling the practice, but if she was able to pull it off, her family would be financially better off. The salary that Charles mentioned today was comparable to her current income, and, vitally, the workload would be more structured. This was not to mention all the other hidden benefits to Jennifer's mental health from working in a team and having professional support and maybe even friends.

Jennifer could not grasp the reason for her husband's reaction. For a split second she considered jealousy. Up to now John had been Jennifer's main source of backing, the scaffold on which she built her life. Perhaps he was insecure about handing that role over to others, an alternative system of support. She dismissed the notion, reassuring herself that it was rubbish. She would wait until he was less tired and approach it from another angle.

Later in the night, when John had gone upstairs, Jennifer searched her inbox for an email from Charles. There it was: BioWestPharma Ltd was seeking an experienced, driven lawyer to join their team of experts in securing authorisations for the development of novel human and veterinary medicines in Europe. The company was in the process of setting up in Westport, less than twenty kilometres from Castlebar. Could this really be for her? As Jennifer read the job spec, she felt herself refuel as if lost energy was returning to her body. She wanted to do this. She believed that she could do it. She knew she had the skill and the drive. At least, the old Jennifer did.

As she read on, there was no anxiety or dread in her – only an eagerness to be part of it. With nervous determination, her unsteady fingers filled out the application form. She wouldn't mention it to John. If she was called to an interview, she would deal with it then. If not, he need not know. She would take it one step at a time. Maybe nothing would come of it, and she would prepare herself for going back to work in a couple of weeks. On the other hand, if she was called to interview, she would do the finest research work of her career, and she would do the best damn interview of her life.

Chapter 8

More than a week later, Jennifer sat in her garden sipping an iced Diet Sprite and looking over the hedge at a herd of suckler cows owned by her neighbour. These ladies had calves at foot, and she laughed as she watched the young vasectomised bull on a mission, tirelessly shadowing the ones he sensed were coming into season. Jennifer did not come from farming stock, but she often spent long summer days on her best friend's farm in West Kerry. The family owned a pedigree herd of Hereford cattle in Dingle, and she used to seize her opportunities to look after the calves once school was out.

She had considered becoming a vet for a while during secondary school, but her love for the law and the art of debate won out in the end. She was glad now. The vets she knew worked harder than the animals in their care and for less financial reward. For now, she enjoyed watching the beautiful animals in the field close by.

Caught reminiscing about her summers in Kerry, Trish the post lady bounced in front of her, handing her an envelope and yapping for at least two minutes without a breath about the unusual heat and the grass burnt from the lack of rain. Trish was a neighbour and although somewhat eccentric Jennifer absorbed her energy and positivity. Refusing the cold drink that Jennifer offered, Trish disappeared in a cloud of dust, leaving Jennifer alone to stare at the envelope in her hand. Her legal post went to her office, but this was addressed to her home. She opened it and immediately saw the headed paper, 'BioWestPharma Ltd.' She drew her breath. This was it. If it was going to be a PFO, then she was going to be okay with that.

She scanned, probably too quickly, and read only every second word. She was cordially invited to interview for the position of Head of New Drug Authorisations at the above company. She beamed then read again to be sure she had read it correctly the first time. The interview was to take place in four weeks. She had so much preparatory work to do, but first she would have to tell John.

'Please try to see this from my perspective, babe,' she said to her husband that evening after dinner. 'It's such a good opportunity for me to use my skills, potentially progress my career in a big pharmaceutical company and make some new friends and colleagues. Even the doctor said that my professional lifestyle is very isolating and possibly does not suit me.'

'This company could be gone in a year, Jen, and then where will you be? You will have given up everything you have been working for,' John retorted. 'Look, I think it's a very rash move, but if you want to do the interview, then I won't try to stop you. You have always done exactly what you want. That's not going to change now, I guess.'

Jennifer could see the rationale in John's concerns, but by now she was already so excited about the prospect of the new start that she had been prepared to overrule him anyway. A new start is exactly what this would be for her, she thought, and possibly the salvation of her too.

'Have you spoken to Mark about whether he is interested in the practice?' John asked, feeling slightly defied. Jennifer hadn't broached the subject with Mark yet in case she failed in her bid to get the job. She didn't want to raise his hopes. Yes, she would wait. Her securing the job was so doubtful anyway that there was no point in discussing it with him now. And what was the worst that would happen? She would get the job and Mark would not want the practice? Someone would take it surely. She would cross that bridge another day.

Jennifer spent the next three weeks researching her ass off. She studied everything she could learn about the company, as much EU law about EMA drug authorisation as she could find, and Irish and EU good manufacturing practices. She knew though that the company would not hire her because of her knowledge of the law. Lots of people knew the law. This company was looking for someone clever, quick, organised, someone who worked easily with all types of people, someone strong and steady in the face of a problem, and someone who would stay. Jennifer knew that she would have to sell her personal as well as her professional skills to these people.

The interview day approached like a train, and Jennifer grew progressively more nervous. The more nervous she was, the more nervous she became. The panic felt like an exponential curve. She knew that she had to find a way to get her anxiety under control. She had been patient, had tolerated that bipolar beast up to now, but this time there was no way she was going to let panic rob her of a chance to move on. She would not allow herself to regress into the state in which she had lived a few months earlier.

On the advice of her medical team she employed the use of meditation and relaxation techniques. Normally an eye-roll-inducing prospect to Jennifer, she was more surprised than anyone to find that this offered her some crucial release. She was converted.

As the days disappeared, she practised some interview answers in the mirror. She even got Sinead to phone randomly, putting her on the spot, and ask questions. She felt confident about the legal questions. She was a little more uneasy about the questions that would test her personality and character. She accepted eventually that she actually liked who she was. She was extremely competent and efficient, and she was confident that she would be a great asset to their team. If they didn't agree, then it would be their loss. She believed that there was something great waiting just around the corner for her.

Amid the turmoil of her life, Jennifer housed an endless amount of fight and self-belief. She was a strong, intelligent lady with great integrity and humility. She just hoped that the interviewers would see this.

The day arrived, and Jennifer stopped to look at herself in the mirror as she walked out the door. She had considered pointedly the perfect outfit. She was aiming for sophisticated, not dull, aka not 'solicitor'. She wanted to express her personality because she was determined to be herself today. At this stage she had done all that was possible, and they could take her or leave her. Jennifer never dressed in the traditional solicitor drab black skirt suit and blouse – grey if they were being exceptionally adventurous. Some days she would walk into a courtroom, and the red exit sign would be the most glamorous thing in the room – until she got there, that is.

Today she settled on a cream pencil skirt, a light-blue fitted blouse and brown Ralph Lauren stilettos. No jacket. This was her look, and she was making a statement. She looked great. The blue in her blouse made her eyes sparkle. *Of course, that could be the lithium*, she couldn't help joking to herself. She picked up her brown vintage purse that she scored at a second-hand market for five euro and inside it a card from the girls that read, 'Kick ass Mom x'. She would do this for them. She knew she had not been a textbook mother, but if her daughters grew up to be strong, fair and honest people she would go to her grave happy.

Sitting in the lobby of BioWestPharma Ltd headquarters, Jennifer practised her relaxation techniques and did not think about the interview. She was happy with her level of nervousness. *Normal,* she thought, *not mental.* Good so far. With that, a young man rounded the corner of the lobby and called her into the biggest boardroom she had ever seen in her life. The table was the size of a spaceship, Jennifer thought, and the skylight was spectacular.

The young man smirked and said, 'It's pretty impressive, isn't it?' Jennifer smiled, a little embarrassed that they had noticed how wowed she was at this early stage. She gathered herself and said hello. She was momentarily flustered, wondering whether she should go and shake their hands or not, given that they were quite literally twelve feet away and she would have to walk around half the circumference of this monstrosity. *Damn it, do it,* she thought, and, dropping her bag on her seat, she rounded the table – a feat that took almost a century – and shook hands with all four interviewers.

Then she walked back to her seat, conscious that they were doubtless staring at her ass the entire time. *Get your act together, Jennifer,* she thought to herself as she eventually turned to face them. The panel consisted of two women and two men, and Jennifer was taller than three of them. She relaxed as the interview settled into a comfortable conversation about her education and professional experience. She had practised this part plenty.

The 'tell me why we should give you this job' part came next. In what Jennifer could only describe as a moment of nervous energy, she ejected 'I've got great style.' It just came out. Both women smiled. The older of the two, a Ms Caroline Montgomery, smirked in a confident 'been there, done that' sort of way, while the young woman, Dr Anna Browne, followed her lead, although clearly giving a shift of discomfort at Jennifer's confident, even cocky, presentation. The young man, Mr Anthony O'Hara, who had led Jennifer into the room, also seemed entertained by her answer. The older man, however, Mr Kenneth Regan, a senior board member at the company, looked at Jennifer in a way that might have suggested he was worried she could be trouble. Jennifer recovered quickly with a more appropriate response to their question and hoped she had done herself no harm. Maybe what they needed right now was just a little bit of Jennifer, she thought, not the full show.

She went on to explain what her management technique would be in the event that she was heading up the drug-authorisation team at their firm. In this section of the interview Jennifer felt that her personality got a chance to come through. She was satisfied with this. It was what was going to set her apart from the other candidates.

All in all, she felt that her interviewers were impressed with her. She had great leadership qualities, excellent legal knowledge, and, let's face it, she was easy on the eye. Yes, they were all impressed – apart from Kenneth Regan. He did not smile once during the entire interview. She bet if she'd worn the damn black suit he would have liked her.

As the interview closed, Jennifer believed that she had done her best. Mr Regan concluded by thanking her, and then, out of nowhere, said, 'You have come highly recommended to us, Mrs Burke, and in truth I think I speak for my colleagues here at BioWestPharma when I say that we are very impressed with you.'

Jennifer was bursting with happiness on the inside but strained to keep a professional outward façade. She thanked them for their time and for making the interview so pleasant for her. She thought of Charles Roche, the rascal. What the hell had he said about her and why? He had always flirted with her, blatantly, but surely he had no plans to progress the platonic relationship with her or ask for a return of the favour? *Jesus, Jennifer, get a grip. Maybe you actually are very good at your job and Charles wants you at the firm because you are a great lawyer – not to sleep with you. You idiot.*

For a second time, Jennifer rounded the semi-circumference of the spaceship and shook four hands. When she took the hand of the Mr Regan, he said, 'You will be hearing from us, Jennifer. We are only considering one other candidate so it will be between you both. We will contact you by post and ask you to arrange a routine medical. We aim to start this position within the month.'

Jennifer's entire volume of bodily fluid drained into her feet. All she heard was 'medical'. What was worse, the man into whose face she was staring when she virtually exsanguinated saw the look on her face. Someone had just stuck a pin in her head and deflated her where she stood. It was over, she thought. She could not believe that the fact that she would be required to do a medical exam for the job had not entered her stupid head before now.

She made her exit quickly from the room and out into the fresh air. This diagnosis was going to cling to her like a murder conviction for the rest of her life. It was a life sentence. She was well. Healthy. She knew this. She was intelligent and competent and a great worker. It didn't matter. She was 'mental' on paper.

She told John that the interview went really well but that there were lots of people in line for the job with more experience than her so she wasn't going to get her hopes up. There was no way she was going to admit to him that he had been right all along, that she would never again get another job as long as she was diagnosed with bipolar disorder. In seeking treatment, she had done what she thought was best at the time. Now, like everything else she had ever done, she would have to accept it and move on.

Later that night, she couldn't sleep. Her disappointment kept her awake. Every ounce of legal training in her body was telling her that an employer could not discriminate against an employee or potential employee on the grounds of mental illness, which was legally categorised as a disability. She knew this. She also knew that with all the intent in the world the equality legislation did not protect people from the realities of these situations. All that should matter to her employers was that she was fit to do the job. In actuality, a sniff of the word 'bipolar' and they would find a dozen reasons for her unsuitability to the position. The doctor who would examine her would have her medical records, but they would not be allowed to disclose the contents of them to the company – at least, in theory that was what was supposed to happen. This would of course depend on the professional independence of the doctor in question. Once again, for the fourth time in this year, Jennifer's life was in the hands of a doctor she had never met.

Almost a fortnight after her visit to the company doctor in Westport, Jennifer stared at the white envelope on the hall table. Trish had shoved it in the door earlier, and Jennifer had placed it there until she was alone and ready to read it. In a silent house, she sat on the second step of the stairs and opened it carefully, not tearing it. She reminded herself that whatever happened it was meant to be. If not this, then something better. She would bounce back like she always did.

'Dear Mrs Jennifer Burke, having considered your application to BioWestPharma Ltd for the position of Head of New Drug Authorisations, we are pleased to offer you the contract. We anticipate that your employment will commence on 1st November. Please contact our Human Resources Department in advance of this date for more details. We look forward to working with you.'

Shedding a rare tear, she folded the letter back in its envelope and picked up her phone to tell her partner in crime.

'Sinead, I did it.'

Part II

Chapter 9

Sunlight beamed through the window of her first-floor office as Jennifer read through the projected timeline for the clinical-trials strategy for their new veterinary chemotherapeutic drug, currently in development. From her newly acquired knowledge of the veterinary pharmaceutical industry Jennifer felt that this drug was a runner. The R&D team on this one had discovered a gap in the pet-care market. Between the spike in uptake of pet health insurance and the explosion of vet reality-TV shows, podcasts and blogs, it appeared that pet-owners were happy and willing to invest in the health of their pets. This new cancer treatment for dogs and cats looked like it might be a success story for BioWestPharma, providing Jennifer pulled off their manufacturer's authorisation, a legal requirement for any company wishing to put a new medicine on the European market.

She was fixated on the data in front of her when Sean Clifford, a recent graduate scientist from the University of Limerick, strode into her office. He had knocked – only he just didn't wait to be admitted. Jennifer threw her eyes up and said, 'Hello again, Sean.' She was now two months into her new job, and Sean, her assistant, was probably the person she interacted with the most, along with Kate the intern. Kate was fresh from Sligo Institute of Technology's Pharmaceutical Science programme and was on a year-long funded internship. Human Resources had decided that Jennifer's office was the spot for her.

So there it was: the entire drug-authorisation department of BioWestPharma Ltd. Jennifer had been assured when she accepted the job that in the coming year or two the company would invest in staff for her, but at the moment this was it. In truth, it was adequate. Jennifer was currently working on only two applications: the novel chemotherapeutic molecule destined for the veterinary market, and a new formula for a human antidepressant. The irony of that was not lost on her.

As team leader, Jennifer had given Sean the task of compiling the clinical-trials data for the upcoming pre-submission meeting with the EMA, and Kate was working away busily on the pharmacovigilance protocol for this new vet drug. This was the part of the application that detailed to the EMA how the manufacturer would oversee ongoing monitoring of the safety of this drug into the future. Of course, Jennifer would be developing this document herself, but she needed to keep Kate busy somehow.

She smiled when she thought about her little team. She was very fond of her teammates. She would never admit to them that she thought of them as kids who needed supervision and guidance, at least not any time soon.

'I think that we have enough data to take this to the pre-submission meeting,' Sean said as he smiled at Jennifer. 'We have reviewed the results, and in terms of efficacy, safety and quality, we really like them. We are still working on the format of the risk–benefit analysis document, but I think we can give them a call and set up a meeting.'

When Jennifer started the job, she knew that the clinical-trials team was well into the testing phase, but she didn't realise how close they were. It was now her turn to go to work for real and earn her keep. If the data were ready for the pre-submission meeting with the EMA, then she was no more than six or seven months away from the submission for market authorisation. This would be her first submission. She was excited and nervous at the same time. Pre-submission consultations were not obligatory as part of the process, but because it was a novel molecule, and this was new territory for Jennifer, she had decided to go through this stage. She knew she would learn a lot from the preliminary meetings with the EMA panel. She would submit the documents and set up a meeting immediately.

Jennifer scanned through Sean's work. The data were professionally presented. She decided to work non-stop, and at the stroke of eleven the following night, she pressed send, requesting pre-authorisation feedback from the EMA on her first-ever market authorisation. Her body may have been wrecked, but her mind was bustling. She was delighted with herself, and very proud of her little team. She knew this was just the first baby step in the process of having their new drug authorised, but she was chuffed with herself nonetheless.

Everyone was in bed when she got home that night. This was not what she had planned for her family life when she accepted the job, but she knew that late nights would be a rarity for her and so relaxed. She poured herself a glass of Malbec in the silent kitchen, took off her pinching Kurt Geigers and, turning off all the lights, tucked her feet underneath her on the conservatory couch. She never sat here in the dark. It was surprisingly peaceful.

Sinking back into the couch surrounded by nothing but moonlight, Jennifer felt alive. It was just after midnight, and even though her body ached, she felt fulfilled and grateful. She had come a long way this past year. She rarely permitted herself to reflect on the 'crazy times' as she called them, but tonight she allowed herself a few moments of self-applause for how she had survived and thrived this past twelve months. She recalled that fateful day in Dublin when Dr Cullen had assured her that, with the right medication and a strong will, she was confident that Jennifer would overcome the condition.

Jennifer hated to admit it, but she knew she had done it on her own. John had taken a 'do whatever you like' approach with her ever since the diagnosis. As long as she wasn't asking him for emotional support or too much time, then he was happy for her to get on with her life in any way that suited her. Neither hindrance nor help. That seemed to be the best he could do. She accepted that he was busy at work and with his master's, and, in truth, men were not equipped to deal with more than one thing at a time, but she always harboured an underlying disappointment in her husband that scratched away at her, never breaking the skin, just causing an itchy flare-up of inflammation every now and then.

Life at BioWestPharma was settling nicely for Jennifer. She reported directly to the board of management and so had no actual boss to speak of. This was just as well, she thought, since she had never really reported to a direct line manager before and wasn't sure how her personality would take to being ordered about. As it stood, she was ruler of her own little patch, and that's how she liked it.

In general, she rarely spent much time away from her desk. She liked to get as much work done as possible during the day in order to make the most of her evenings off with the girls. Even though the BioWestPharma campus was always buzzing with a myriad of different people from various departments, Jennifer never seemed to get round to mingling. She was crap at it. She realised that now.

On her break the following day, and rewarding herself for her mini-milestone the previous evening, Jennifer was content to sit on one of the black leather couches in the very luxurious staff communal area, shoes off, feet tucked up underneath her, reading whatever news came her way on her phone.

'Hi, would you like to join us?'

The words fell upon Jennifer's ears from nowhere. For a moment she didn't even realise the lady in front of her was speaking to her, she was so engaged in her own world. She raised her head and saw a beautiful blonde woman about her own age with huge blue eyes and a beaming smile.

'No, thank you, I'm fine here,' Jennifer answered. For a second, the woman looked at her, evidently not expecting that answer. Jennifer knew she was doing it again. She was a loner by nature, and it did not occur to her to seek out the company of others. She always believed she could go through life alone and genuinely enjoyed her own company. She didn't need friends. Except she did. The doctors had told her to make an effort and seek out and enjoy human company.

'Actually, yes, I would love to, thanks,' she said and hurried to put back on her shoes and gather her sandwich wrappers.

The friendly blonde lady held out her hand. 'Ruth O'Neill, Marketing,' she said.

Jennifer reciprocated: 'Jennifer Burke, Authorisations.'

For the first time since she had joined the firm, Jennifer spent her lunchtime in the company of a group of other employees. These women seemed familiar with each other. They worked together, scattered throughout the various departments in the firm. Some were toxicologists; some were data analysts; one was a zoologist. Ruth O'Neill was responsible for the marketing strategy for a new drug once the authorisation was secured. She was effectively the face of company.

In Jennifer's opinion, these women were all very comfortable with each other. The conversation seemed to her to be on a very personal level. They discussed each other's lives as though they lived in them. They also discussed the lives of other employees who were not present – a habit Jennifer found unacceptable. She sat there in silence knowing that the conversation would eventually come to her, but not inviting it.

'Nice to finally meet you, Jennifer,' said a thirty-something-year-old woman with a formidable Midlands accent. 'You have been hiding away in your office since you got here. Are you afraid of us?' she said.

A bit familiar, Jennifer thought. *So this is what the doctors were recommending?* 'It's nice to meet you too,' she replied. 'I'm afraid I've been busy finding my feet.' She eye-rolled on the inside of her head. *Come on, Jennifer. Give them a chance. You need them more than they need you.*

'Your shoes are amazing, Jennifer.' Ruth quickly changed the subject – to great relief from Jennifer who acknowledged the bail-out. It was obvious that Ruth O'Neill had an impeccable sense of style herself. Cream culottes with a baby-pink silk blouse over brown leather Louis Vuitton boots. Her hair and make-up were perfect. She even smelled of style. It wasn't just her appearance that caught Jennifer's attention, however, it was her ability to read that Jennifer was uncomfortable in this group, and to know when it was time to hold out a friendly hand.

Mercifully, the conversation turned to shoes, and Jennifer caught her breath. She settled eventually into a relaxed chat about her drug-authorisation department, the work that they did, and their imminent meeting with the EMA. She didn't bother mentioning the fact that she would more than likely be going on an all-expenses-paid trip to the headquarters of the EMA in Amsterdam in the coming month, to discuss feedback on the authorisation procedure for the veterinary chemotherapeutic drug in the pipeline. She decided they had enough gossip for today.

On the dot of two, several of the girls in the group scattered to their respective workstations, and Jennifer began to make her way to her office. She wasn't sure how she felt about her lunchtime experience. She was programmed to not make friends easily. She had been so traumatised by Liz and Geraldine Burke's vile gossiping about their neighbours over the years and the way they would ambush her for information when she was on her own, that she believed she had lost the ability to trust people and make friends.

She had always been a loner, but because of her experience with the Burkes she was now simply mistrusting and suspicious of people, especially people who poked into her private life. It was easier to be on her own. Her psychologist had told her that she should not let her experience with the Burkes ruin her chances of moving on in life and meeting new people. In this regard, Jennifer was happy that today was a good first step.

Later in the day, Jennifer thought about Ruth O'Neill. Jennifer didn't get an opportunity to learn anything about her today.

The other women were too busy asking questions and talking about people who were not there. Jennifer liked Ruth for some reason. She recalled noticing her rolling her eyes a couple of times when the ridiculous commentary called for such – at the same moments that Jennifer would have been rolling her eyes had she not had an unfamiliar audience. This had to mean something. *A kindred spirit*, she thought, and smiled. Okay, Jennifer would give Ruth a chance. She would go find her tomorrow and be sociable. She would be friendly.

Chapter 10

Later in the month, Jennifer and Ruth shared a black leather couch on one of their extended tea breaks. Neither of them worked on the clock, unlike many of the other employees at BioWestPharma, and so they enjoyed regular dates in the comfortable staff recreational area. The campus oozed an American tech-company vibe which meant that cosy couches and a well-stocked canteen were permanent fixtures.

Despite the recent office news that a third novel drug had entered the R&D phase with the company, ominously increasing the workload for everyone, the employees of BioWestPharma seemed happy and grateful to be working there. Jennifer and Ruth were no different. Both women had moved from jobs that had offered much less support and opportunity and where the options for managing stress were limited. At BioWestPharma everyone worked hard, but the pay-off was worth it in so many ways.

In spite of herself and her self-professed loner status, Jennifer really enjoyed Ruth's company. They had exchanged mobile numbers weeks ago, and now they spoke or texted every day. Ruth was a Co. Sligo native but had spent most of her working life in Dublin on the prestigious marketing team at Brown Thomas. She had literally travelled the world with what seemed to Jennifer to be a dream job before resigning and moving west about a year ago to be closer to home.

In truth, Ruth had dropped her life overnight to get away from her long-term boyfriend whose alcoholism and cocaine use had resulted in breaking point for their relationship. Jennifer revelled at the bravery of it. She could not imagine being able to walk away from a relationship that she had spent years building. Jennifer did not have the details, but she knew that Ruth still loved this man by the way she spoke about him. She imagined the relationship must have been especially abusive to force this seemingly strong, confident lady to leave behind everything she had worked for and start from scratch in a new place. Looking at Ruth now, and listening to her retell stories of her life, Jennifer admired her very much. She believed that she was truly lucky to have found her. Jennifer realised that this was the type of therapy the doctors had been talking about. Human contact. Emotional connections with people. *The doctors might have been onto something*, Jennifer thought.

'Another cuppa, Jen?' Ruth asked with a grin, knowing that they really should be going back to their offices.

'Yes. Bring lids. We can take them back with us.' Both women laughed at the absurdity of the suggestion. On her return from the canteen, Ruth quizzed Jennifer about the upcoming Burke family gathering that was looming at the weekend. She had been filled in on Jennifer's difficult relationship with the Burke women by now and wanted to ensure that Jennifer had a plan of action for surviving the impending encounter.

Jennifer's approach to any meeting with her sisters-in-law was to grin and bear it. Even now, the thought of being in a room with them filled her with anxiety. The worst part was the aftermath when she invariably threw her frustration at her husband, resulting in another row and eternal deflation.

Ruth's proposed methodology was more aggressive. 'Give it back to them,' she said. Jennifer knew that the chances of her answering back their rude taunts were just as likely as both women spontaneously combusting in front of her. It was more probable that she would turn into a stupid, useless child in front of them so as not to cause a scene and upset their father and her very insecure husband. These family affairs always turned out to be lose-lose scenarios for Jennifer. The anxiety they caused, however, was very real and accumulated after every encounter.

'Okay, if you are not yet ready to stand up to them, let's just set a few ground rules,' Ruth said. 'Firstly, do not get caught on your own with them. Be strategic. Make sure that no matter what you are doing you never end up in a room on your own, or with one of them. That way at least, whatever they say will be witnessed, and they can't serve up the Burke speciality, "that never happened, you have a great imagination," blah blah, okay?'

'Got it,' Jennifer answered.

'Secondly, if one of them makes a dig, whether it is supposedly in jest or not, pretend you do not hear it. Do not react. Do not make eye contact. Turn to the nearest person to you and start a completely unrelated conversation. Just act like it never happened,' Ruth said. 'That will put manners on the bitches.'

This made sense to Jennifer, and, importantly for her, it was not confrontational or aggressive. She would be able to pull this off. Ruth reminded her that although this was a great first step, she would still have to deal with the issue of Liz walking into her home uninvited, and she would still have to deal with the issue of John repeatedly letting her down in this conflict, but that was for another day. For now, Jennifer was happy to take one step at a time together with her new friend.

That's how it felt to Jennifer now. She was in it with someone. She had support.

Sinead had always been a great support to Jennifer, but Sinead was far more philosophical in her approach to the sister-in-law torment. Ruth was practical. Sinead was a fantastic friend, but she was miles away. Ruth was here.

Jennifer strolled back to her office feeling lighter and more positive about the upcoming Burke dinner. More importantly, if this plan of Ruth's worked, Jennifer would feel empowered, not frustrated, and hopefully this time she would not need her husband to provide redress. There would be no row and no stress and no let-down and no disappointment. If Jennifer could learn to handle this abuse on her own terms, then the lingering bulging abscess always hanging over them in their marriage waiting to pop at any moment might resorb of its own accord.

A few times over the years, Jennifer had thought she could handle it. She thought she could convince herself that Liz and Geraldine's treatment of her wasn't worth worrying about, but she always failed. Instead, as the years of unresolved hurt went on, it got progressively worse. Now, with Ruth's help, Jennifer thought she might at last be able to do it. She felt stronger than she had in years, mentally and physically. She would go into battle ready this time – not already defeated.

Later that afternoon, Jennifer anticipated her first encounter with the EMA. She was confident about her application and wanted to make a first impression that would have an impact. A Skype call was scheduled for 4 p.m. She would have preferred a personal meeting but knew that was not possible today. In actual fact, Jennifer hated video calls. She dreaded standing in photographs too – anything that involved a recording of her physically. She was incredibly good-looking, and she knew it, but for some reason she felt more confident in person. She would often get up and walk to someone's office rather than phone them. Back when she practised law, she would arrange a face-to-face meeting rather than make a long phone call. She could never explain it. She put it down to growing up in Ireland comparing herself to all those pushy American kids but knew that was rubbish. It was just another Jenniferism she used to say.

Once she settled into the call, Jennifer found her feet. She was disappointed to discover that it was not with one of the rapporteurs in person but a young assistant simply on a mission to get the meetings organised. The initial consultation would take place on site at the BioWestPharma campus as soon as the preliminary documentation was reviewed. It transpired, to Jennifer's horror and excitement, that this was going down in about four to six weeks. *Jesus*, thought Jennifer, this was really happening.

The young lady with perfect English and blinding white teeth informed Jennifer that the committee with responsibility for authorising veterinary medicines, the 'Committee for Medicinal Products for Veterinary Use', had appointed a rapporteur from France to conduct the scientific assessment. Jennifer knew that the lead assessor in this process would be from the Member State that had the greatest concerns about the authorisation procedure itself, or possibly the mutual recognition procedure between Member States. Typical. France, she thought. At least it wasn't one of the Scandinavian countries. That thought released some tension slightly. There was some give in the French, she thought, some bit of manoeuvre to be had, especially if she could establish a good relationship with the representative.

Once Jennifer had clarified the procedure for the visit to Westport with the young lady, the call ended. *Very efficient*, Jennifer thought. If efficiency was their style, then they were coming to the right marketing authorisation department. She smiled then took a long deep breath.

As the day turned into evening, Jennifer felt a familiar and disgusting rise of anxiety in her chest and throat. The minute she noticed it she shook her body as though to rattle it out of herself. There was no way she was going to let herself down with this task. A bit of nervousness would be grand, she accepted – even useful in a situation where her performance would have real implications for the company – but not anxiety. For the remainder of the workday she was filled with nervous energy.

Maybe she should share it with someone? She wasn't supposed to be on her own with her thoughts and anxieties, the professionals had said. She thought of Sinead. She hadn't seen her for months, and she realised that she hadn't spoken to her for a few weeks. Sinead would most likely be with a client now, or possibly in court, but Jennifer decided that she would call her on the way home.

Jennifer loved her morning and evening commutes in the car from Castlebar to Westport and back. They lasted no more than twenty minutes, but this was Jennifer's time alone. Usually she drove in silence, assembling her thoughts and practising her mindfulness – a valuable habit she had picked up from her psychologist. But this evening she would give her time to Sinead. She laughed out loud. What she meant was she hoped Sinead would give her time to her.

Arriving home that evening, Jennifer was met inside the door by the sound of teenage girl screams. This bolted her out of the lovely haze of happiness and positivity that she had enjoyed since her chat with Sinead. 'Seriously! What the hell is going on here?' she asked. She promptly worked out that the argument involved the subterfuge acquisition of a white Tommy H T-shirt by one sibling from another and the subsequent accidental inclusion of a pair of red knickers in the washing machine. Ava had taken the T-shirt that Alannah had saved up to buy and had ruined it. *Reality check*, Jennifer thought light-heartedly. *Welcome home.*

She was accustomed to dealing with parenting issues on her own. While she kept John informed of all the teenage carry-on in the house so that he would not miss out on the experience, he was rarely there to deal with it at first hand. Jennifer knew the reality of the situation was that even had he been on site for these ruckuses he did not possess the skills to manage them anyway. In the face of any conflict, not necessarily including himself, he would invariably pace around the kitchen, his face getting redder, his voice rising in volume and pitch. The man had absolutely no skills in the art of conflict resolution. Jennifer resigned herself at this stage of their family life that it was easier to manage all teenage conflict situations on her own.

'Ava, you did not have permission to take the T-shirt. In the eyes of the law that constitutes stealing. In case you are not aware, theft is a criminal offence. You are lucky that Alannah did not report it to the Guards. In this case we will deal with it ourselves. You will give Alannah the 75 euro that you owe her over the next three weeks. Your weekly 25-euro pocket money will go to her. You had better start learning how to cook lunches and pack sandwiches for school or you are going to be very hungry!'

Alannah beamed at her mother and clapped her hands, clearly delighted that justice had been served. Ava stood in a state of disgust with her mouth in a grimace. 'You have got to be joking,' she yelled and practically spat, 'It was a bloody accident.'

'The taking of her T-shirt from her wardrobe without permission was an accident?' her mother inquired.

'I fucking borrowed it,' retorted Ava. 'You are not a judge, you know!'

Jennifer's eyes darted to her daughter. 'Never again use that language with me or in my house. Do you understand? Or it will be more than a 75-euro fine next time, lady.'

Ava pounded up the stairs while Alannah trotted contentedly back to her homework. Jennifer was fuming with her daughter's outburst, but was she really surprised? Her father spoke to Jennifer like that all the time. Any time there was conflict, if she were honest:

raising his voice, slamming things, swearing, deflecting the issue at hand, turning the conversation around on Jennifer and even denying that her concerns existed. Not to forget the obligatory storming out and slamming of the door.

In fairness to John, it worked for him. The conversation would be well and truly over, and he would have succeeded in not having to deal with it. She knew that the girls witnessed a lot of it. In truth, Jennifer realised how fortunate it was that they had grown up to be as respectful and balanced as they had. They were great kids and would both be amazing young women.

Jennifer took a deep breath and poured a generous glass of Shiraz. With the first long swallow, she felt her muscles relax again. She soon forgot the domestic conflict of this evening, and her thoughts drifted back to the upcoming French guests. She was grateful for the way her life was unfolding after the year she had endured. This was going to be her time. She believed now for the first time in ages that she was exactly where she wanted to be.

Chapter 11

Saturday evening arrived, and the four Burkes piled into the Mazda. Jennifer took a nice calm breath as they drove the five kilometres from her home to her father-in-law's house. She always encouraged the girls to walk into their grandfather's house first in the meagre hope that they would suck the attention from the room and distract everyone inside from her own presence.

John would also absorb a lot of interest for the first few minutes of any visit. This usually gave Jennifer adequate time to scan the room for potential risk of ambush and allow her to strategically choose her spot for setting up camp. Sometimes, depending on how many people were present, Jennifer would busy herself at the sink or take on the waiting duties. Not today. The house was full: John's father – also John Burke; two Burke sisters, Liz and Geraldine; Geraldine's husband, Derek, and their nineteen-year-old son Darragh were all busying themselves about the catering duties that Liz had set for them.

The occasion today was John's father's seventy-fifth birthday. He was a quiet self-effacing man who, as far as Jennifer could see, stayed out on the farm as much as possible and never got too involved in his daughters' blathering. This was of course Jennifer's own assessment which she conceded to herself may have involved some poetic licence. Liz had decided to cater a small gathering for the group at the family home today.

Jennifer got on great with Derek and Darragh. She often thought about asking Derek how he found it in himself to spend his life with Geraldine. To Jennifer, Derek was so lovely, so normal, and he seemed to have a God-given power that enabled him to see the best in Geraldine. Sometimes, his commitment to their marriage made Jennifer question her contempt for the woman. Sometimes. Rarely.

Geraldine worked as a doctor's receptionist in Galway, and Jennifer's blood would run cold when she thought about the unfortunate clients whose medical records Geraldine had access to. She could just imagine the data breaches and assaults on people's privacy that were going on unbeknownst to them. She thanked the Lord every day that this malicious gossip was nowhere near her medical records. Bile rose in her stomach at the thought of what Geraldine would do to her if she found out.

Nevertheless, when Geraldine addressed her in a friendly tone and offered a glass of wine, Jennifer accepted both. She put the wine to her lips and let it get to work. Despite the underlying tension in her, she enjoyed the meal and the light-hearted chat from Derek and Darragh and, of course, her own two girls. Geraldine was noticeably quiet and maybe even a little sour. Something was bugging her. She wasn't her usual nauseatingly vocal self.

While the adults were having coffee and allowing the delicious roast-beef meal to settle, the twins and Darragh went outside to the shed to play with some brand-new sheepdog pups. Spring was well under way on the Burke farm, and the new lambs and calves were an annual attraction for the grandkids.

Hardly kids anymore, Jennifer thought.

In the dining room, the conversation eventually turned to Jennifer, which was inevitable, she accepted. Liz congratulated her on her new job and offered a toast. John winked at her. This was not so bad, she thought. She had just begun to explain some of the details of her role in the company when Geraldine piped up, 'Yes, a big swanky multinational. John told us.'

Jennifer realised that Geraldine had been putting away the Shiraz all evening.

Geraldine then turned to John and claimed, 'You will soon be able to stay at home, John, and be a kept man. You can let your wife be the breadwinner, wear the trousers. She must be earning twice as much as you at this stage?'

There was silence in the room, but not in Jennifer's ears as the arteries pulsated in them. Was this bitch really talking about what she and her husband were earning? Was she mocking John or having a dig at her? Every promise Jennifer had made to Ruth earlier in the week evaporated, and she answered, 'With respect, Geraldine …'

Everyone knew that a sentence that started with the phrase 'with respect' never really intended respect.

'With respect, Geraldine, what John and I earn in our jobs is not really an appropriate conversation for around this table. I would appreciate it if we didn't discuss it.'

'It's grand,' John said, the colour changing in his face.

Jennifer's hands were trembling with rage at this stage. She had taken enough from these women. Enough was enough. She was going to tell John tonight at home that she was finished with Geraldine and Liz, and he would have to find a way to deal with it.

With that, Geraldine flung her cutlery on her plate, and in what seemed to be a resonating shriek, let fly: 'Who the fuck do you think you are? You think you are so much better than the rest of us. You are not! You never set foot in our home unless you are summoned. When was the last time you graced us with your presence? Visited my father? You are a fucking snob.'

Jennifer stared at John, who dropped his fork and got up from the table. His face had already made it to explosion zone – the usual reaction. Jennifer continued to maintain her silence, her gaze never leaving her husband's face despite the fact that Geraldine was still screaming directly at her.

When Geraldine eventually shut her mouth, Jennifer looked at her. 'Geraldine, I was making it clear that my earnings and those of my husband are out of bounds for your dinner-time conversation. I believe that was a fair comment.' Jennifer amazed herself at her poise and control. She did not raise her voice. She did not defend any of the other accusations that Geraldine was screeching at her. She stuck to the original argument and did not engage with the assault. Instead, she watched her husband and followed his face with her eyes.

'Stop it, Geraldine. Stop it, for fuck's sake,' John reluctantly grunted. His pacing was getting more erratic, and sweat was accumulating on his forehead. Geraldine's father and husband also made attempts to mollify the out-of-control sibling, but she was oblivious to them.

'I mean, you swan in here like you are better than us. You are too good to talk about your fancy new job. Who the fuck do you think you are? After everything my family has done for you since you got here, you ungrateful bitch. You have no respect for any of us.' Still screaming, Geraldine looked frantic.

It was at that moment that Jennifer witnessed what crazy really looked like. Jennifer was unusually calm at this point and realised how well she actually was herself – how mentally well she was. She was looking in the face of 'mental', and she savoured the fact that it was not her. This realisation had an immense calming effect.

'Come on, we are leaving,' barked John.

Jennifer looked around and thanked God when she remembered that the twins had finished eating and had run off down the farm. By some act of charity, they hadn't witnessed this. 'No, John, you don't have to leave your father's house because of this one and her bad behaviour. Sit down and finish your drink,' Jennifer said calmly. Then, looking directly at Geraldine, she said, 'If Geraldine needs to take some time to calm down, she can leave the table and go out and get some air.'

Geraldine did exactly that, but the state of John suggested to his wife that it was time to leave. While he searched for the girls in a nearby outhouse, Jennifer walked out of the Burke family home without getting so much as an apology or an explanation. She knew right then that today was going to be her last day in that place.

The silence in the car on the way home was striking. The girls must have sensed that the sudden departure represented turbulence. Once inside the door, and while looking at the ground, John said, 'She was out of line.'

Jennifer shot her eyes towards him. This was the first concession by him that a member of his family had mistreated her.

She wanted to accept his recognition yet not gloat at him about being right. She wanted to take this comment as a breed of apology for not believing her all along. She decided to simply accept his acknowledgement and let it lie.

She had not felt the need to cry up to now. In a way, she was not surprised by Geraldine's abuse. After all, she had born witness to similar contempt for years out of sight and sound of her husband. But now, in the dark hallway of her home with him she felt some recognition for the first time. She looked at John's face and saw a glimmer of anguish. He did not have the wherewithal to deal with this truth. She knew it. What he didn't realise was that she didn't need him to deal with it, she just needed him to believe it.

It was late now, and the twins had gone up to bed. Jennifer took up her familiar sanctuary on the conservatory couch and sipped at a glass of Shiraz. In this spot, her anxieties would seep out of her into the couch beneath. While attempting to slow her breathing and detach from the trauma of the evening, she caught a glimpse of John outside under the moonlight. He was on a phone call and pacing around the patio slabs in his socks.

Her first thought was how unusual it was. It was so late, and they had perfect mobile-phone network coverage in the house. *He must be frazzled from the evening's affairs*, she guessed. It was a given that he would not be able to discuss the incident with her; after all, she was too heavily invested in it emotionally. He must be turning to one of his friends for advice and to offload. He was entitled to that, she thought. He was as inept as a child to deal with conflict and confrontation. She was glad he was enlisting the help of one of his friends. In fact, she recalled during this past year when she herself had started counselling with the psychologists at the health centre in town, she had wondered if John might benefit from some psychotherapy, some stress-management skills. She could never find the right time to suggest it. At least this time he was confiding in someone. She would not ask any questions. Likewise, she would not force upon him a discussion about the evening's assault. She would let it lie now. They had all been through a lot tonight, and for some strange reason Jennifer believed that, despite her intentions, Geraldine may have actually brought them closer together.

Sliding open the conservatory doors, John spoke to Jennifer on the couch. 'Babe, that was the out-of-hours office line. I know it's late, but one of our athletes just had an accident. He is coming straight in, and, apparently, I'm on call. I'll be as quick as I can.'

Jennifer didn't remember John ever being called in to work on a Saturday night, but she accepted the emergency and didn't complain. She was perfectly content on her own, tonight of all nights. She was happy to just breathe and clear her head.

Chapter 12

The early summer sun shining through her bedroom window forced Jennifer to wake from an unexpectedly peaceful night. The French contingent from the EMA was landing in Dublin Airport about now and would be making their way west. Monsieur Jacques Martin and his party of three from the Scientific Committee for Veterinary Medicines would be received by BioWestPharma at about 10 a.m.

Her crew was ready. The data looked great, as did the laboratories. The board of management of this company was experienced and resourceful and had assembled a team of Ireland's finest scientists and analysts to push these drugs over the line. Once EMA approval was achieved, the pay-off would be one-hundredfold.

Jennifer turned to look at her sleeping husband. She thought him distant since the uproar with his sister. Shortly after the assault on Jennifer at the party, he had informed her – with a certain amount of resentment, Jennifer thought – that he had instructed his sister to apologise to her before she was allowed to set foot in his house again. Jennifer had no way of knowing if this was true. She had caught John embellishing stories many times in the past, but she always let it go. All she knew was that no one had apologised and so the stand-off endured.

Jennifer noticed, however, that John continued to visit his old home, meeting both sisters regularly, trading stories and eating dinner together. It was Jennifer alone who had been excluded. This was despite John's aggressive claims that he had 'put his sister out of his house' for his wife. In all honesty, Jennifer didn't care about John's digs anymore. That fact that neither Liz nor Geraldine were visiting her home any longer was worth all the hostility John could throw at her. This was a win as far as she was concerned.

The campus was buzzing with excitement when Jennifer arrived at 9 a.m. She looked fantastic in a cream fitted dress with a high collar and long sleeves. Her brown platform stilettos gave her height and presence. Elegant and authoritative was the look she was going for today. Beauty and brains her mother would always say, and don't be afraid to show off both.

Jennifer was up for it today. The BioWestPharma team had outdone itself in getting the drug as far as here. The purpose of today's meeting was to allow the EMA to guide the manufacturers through the impending authorisation process as seamlessly as possible. They were here to offer help, and Jennifer and the BioWestPharma team were pleased to accept it.

The delegation met in the foyer of the laboratory complex. It was decided that they would start the day with a tour of the facilities. As Jennifer made her way across the site from her office, she was taken by a wave of gratitude and pride in what she had achieved over the past year. It was not until today that she realised exactly what she had survived.

Her doctors and psychologists were delighted with her progress and reassured her that as long as she took the lithium and avoided excessive consumption of alcohol the behavioural changes and extreme moods were unlikely to recur. That was as good as a cure to Jennifer. She knew that the stigma of having a mental illness would always have a hold over her. She realised that the threat of the information getting into the wrong hands still existed, but she hoped that in time this would be a diminishing concern for her. Perhaps when she was more established in her new career or a bit more mature in herself this threat would disappear.

As she rounded the corner into the laboratory complex, Jennifer spotted that Geoffrey Oakes, Head of Clinical Trials, had already introduced his colleagues to the EMA team. The sound of her heels on the tiled floor prompted the entire delegation to turn around and face her. Geoffrey frowned at her as he had done several times in the past when she had waltzed into one of his labs in heels and without a white coat.

While mouthing an apology to him, she locked her eyes on the most beautiful man she had seen in her life. Okay, she accepted this might be an exaggeration, but he was definitely the most handsome creature she had seen in Co. Mayo in recent memory. She stared at him for what must have seemed like a ludicrous amount of time. He looked like he had come straight from the man mould – that perfect body and face that God had intended all men to have except genetics got in the way.

He was at least six foot two inches tall, big, broad, strong. Shirt open and sleeves rolled up like a working man. It was his face that drew Jennifer's gaze: jet-black hair and dark skin. Perhaps some Arab blood, she thought. He had the type of stubble that, no matter how sharp the razor it just can't be shaved clean. Eyes big and brown like only French men have and a huge Roman nose.

Jennifer realised that this particular feature was not attractive to everyone, but she had always loved it. Everyone had their fetishes. Hers was men with big noses. *Sinead would crease herself laughing right now if she were here*, Jennifer thought. During their college days she had taken the piss so many times out of Jennifer over this peculiarity in her taste. Jennifer herself couldn't explain it. She used to laugh whenever Sinead claimed that subliminally Jennifer believed it was code for the size of something else. 'Yet to be tested,' Sinead would giggle.

'Jacques Martin,' said the glorious specimen, holding out his hand and introducing his two colleagues.

His hand was huge and warm. Jennifer pleaded with all the angels in Heaven that she was not blushing right now. 'Jennifer Burke, Head of Authorisations,' she responded.

'Ah, yes, I recognise your name from the documentation. BioWestPharma is doing excellent work here, Ms. Burke,' he said.

'Call me Jennifer, please,' she purred.

'I will,' he answered, still staring directly into her face. Jennifer wondered if she could feel a spark of mutual attraction in the air. It was a lifetime since she had felt attractive to a man, and she did not know how to deal with the attention. All she knew was that it was giving her a glow that she had missed, even craved, in recent times.

The tour of the laboratories continued throughout the morning. The plan was to meet in the boardroom after lunch to allow the EMA team the opportunity to offer feedback on the preliminary documents that had been submitted from Jennifer's office. The atmosphere among the French assembly seemed relaxed and comfortable, and Jennifer was enjoying the process.

On more than one occasion during the tour she thought she caught the gaze of Monsieur Martin. She wondered if she was mistaking his forthright French mannerisms for the unspoken messages she suspected were being transmitted, but she was not imagining it. During her presentation to the delegation later that afternoon, she was conscious of his watching her, his attention never wavering. By the end of the visit, Jennifer was in no doubt that there was a sexual tension in the air when they were both in a room together.

She was surprised to find that it did not phase her. In fact, it gave her energy and confidence. It provided the stimulus that she needed to perform and impress him. This was the real Jennifer in action, bold and confident and capable. In her office that evening, she felt drained and exhilarated at the same time. The visit had gone well, and, as a bonus, she had been invited to the EMA headquarters in Amsterdam later in the month for training. For today she could not have done more.

She rifled through her purse and took out a tiny hand-held mirror with a Friesian cow's head on the lid – a gift from the girls' last trip to Kerry. As she touched up her make-up with it, she heard a knock on her door.

'Bonsoir, madame.' It was him. She felt herself get nervous. This was stupid, she thought. *Catch yourself on, woman. Be cool.* 'As we are not flying until morning, we have decided to spend the night in Westport. A few of us are having a meal and some drinks later. I would very much like it if you would join us,' he said in his provocative French accent. Perhaps provocation was not the intent, but in this room, at this moment, it was.

As he spoke, he walked towards her until he was standing at her desk, towering over her. She stood up. She wasn't going to be towered over; she was feeling vulnerable enough. As she rose, she smelled what she recognised as Dior Homme. This man was strikingly beautiful. He oozed sex appeal from every pore, and he knew it. For a split second she fantasised about what he might do to her if she gave him permission. Then she gathered her thoughts and responded, 'Thanks for your offer, but I have commitments tonight with my husband and daughters.'

Jennifer banished all notions of desire and sexual indulgence from her mind. Having lived through the past year, there was no way she was going to jeopardise her future with John and the girls now. She knew that she had lived a life of risk and madness in the past, but she had survived. Her marriage had survived. She had gotten away with so much unacceptable behaviour. Were John ever to find out about any of it, her marriage would be over.

The day she made it into remission, she vowed that she would never again put herself in that position. John was all she wanted now: John and her family and her home. Her mental-health crisis was behind her, and John had come through for her in her fight to deal with her bullies. No more men and no more craziness. She was grateful for what she had.

Jacques graciously accepted her response and bid her farewell, congratulating her again on her very professional work. His departure symbolised a sort of acceptance in Jennifer of her transitioning from a past life and entering into a new, safer, more secure but possibly less exciting one. This was what she wanted. She would find a new type of excitement with her husband.

John was home with the girls when Jennifer arrived that evening. She was overjoyed to see him. She dropped her bag, kicked off her shoes and hurried towards him, wrapping her arms around his neck and planting her lips on his. He responded in kind although a little surprised by her amour.

'Get a room,' Ava blurted, and they all laughed.

For a moment, Jennifer felt overwhelmed with emotion. She was so happy right now. Her life was falling into place. She watched John and her little ladies from her perch on the couch and wished there could be more evenings like this. In these moments when they were all together having fun, with no talk of external stressors, her life was perfect. She sat back and enjoyed a *vin rouge* – in Jacques' honour and smiled to herself.

She had secretly revelled in his attention today. It reassured her that she still had it. That's all she needed to know. She didn't need to act on it. She decided that she would start building bridges with her husband from today. She would make amends for the years of … she didn't even have a name for it … whoring? Jesus, no, she could not say it. The woman who did that was not Jennifer. The Jennifer that she was now, the true Jennifer, was going to look after her husband and rebuild their marriage. This would be her next project.

Just then her phone beeped. Ruth O'Neill. 'Well, chick, tell me everything. I heard he was a ride.' With a cheeky grin on her face, Jennifer texted back: 'Ride. Fill you in tomorrow, x.'

Chapter 13

Jennifer checked her phone again on her way to the office. For a third day in a row she had attempted to get hold of Sinead with no success. It was not Sinead's form to let missed calls go unattended. She was not usually this busy. Perhaps she was 'busy' in an 'otherwise engaged' or a 'do not disturb' kind of way, thought Jennifer. She smiled and hoped this was the case.

Way back in their UCD days, it was always Jennifer who ended up engaging in dodgy encounters of the carnal variety while Sinead was happy to facilitate and encourage, always from the sidelines, living vicariously through her more adventurous friend. Jennifer remembered when Bonnie Tyler would come on the radio she would turn the volume right up and sing mockingly at her, 'I'm holding out for a hero till the end of the night.'

Jennifer wished that Sinead would meet someone and share her life. She was an amazing, kind-hearted person, and Jennifer longed for her to find her white knight upon a fiery steed, but Sinead was still holding out. Jennifer would call her again at lunchtime.

On her office desk, Jennifer found details of her flight to Amsterdam the following week, compliments of Kate the intern. The stay was planned for just the one night. Thankfully, Kate had booked the first flight on Monday morning, which would give Jennifer at least a few hours to discover the city. On Tuesday she would participate in a training course at the EMA, and she would be back at work by Wednesday morning. *Hardly even a disruption*, she thought.

She was gagging for the chance to get away on her own. She loved being with John and the girls, but she needed some overdue solitude. It had been almost two years since she had last escaped alone. As she recalled that weekend in London, she barely remembered the details. It was a haze now, more like a movie she had watched or a book she had read. Her anticipation for this trip was fuelled by a need to be alone and at peace for a while. No escapism required. She looked forward to inhaling every minute of the experience.

John had seemed very encouraging when he heard about Jennifer's trip to Amsterdam. He usually didn't pay too much attention to her movements, but this time he seemed happy that she was getting the chance to travel and upskill. While he was still somewhat distant at home, his annoyance at the encounter with his sister seemed to have abated. She hoped that this was a sign they could move on from 'Geraldinegate' and build a better, closer relationship. She wanted to rediscover the intimacy they once shared.

She decided that on her return from The Netherlands she would arrange a getaway for both of them. It had been years since they took a holiday without their daughters. *Bruges*, Jennifer thought to herself. John loved the history of the little Flemish city that had been lost in time. That would be the perfect place for them to reignite their love. She wouldn't ask for permission. She would surprise him.

Her thoughts were interrupted by Sinead's face lighting up her phone. 'Hey, girl, where have you been hiding?' Jennifer inquired. 'Tell me you were off the grid in some country manor with an inter-county full back?' She giggled, half wishing she could trade places with her friend had it been true.

'Hi. Afraid not. Ah, I've been a bit off form. I took a few days off and relaxed at home,' Sinead answered – her voice a bit lifeless if Jennifer were honest.

'Really? Jesus, Sinead, why didn't you call me? Did you call your parents? What's the matter?' Jennifer asked with genuine concern.

'Ah, I'm grand. You know yourself. I just needed a bit of time off. Work is manic. Jesus, sorry Jen, don't mean to use that word lightly.' Jennifer threw her eyes to the sky. 'The workload is mounting. I find it harder and harder to face into it. I feel wrecked tired all the time. I'll be grand when I get a bit of a break,' Sinead explained.

Jennifer knew enough from her own experience with mental health that Sinead might need more than a rest. 'Have you seen a doctor, Sinead? And maybe it's time to ask for help with the caseload at work. You work day and night, and you are not paid enough to do that.' Sinead had always taken on too much, even in college when she was often called on to chair committees and fundraise for various clubs. She was never able to say no.

Sinead reluctantly agreed to take her friend's advice about seeing a doctor but was happy to change the subject back to her. Jennifer continued the call as long as possible, filling Sinead in on the news from the girls and John, Geraldinegate and, of course, her exciting progress at BioWestPharma, but Sinead was missing her spark. It pained Jennifer to hear her friend feeling so low. They signed off with a promise from Sinead to make an appointment to see her GP as soon as possible. Jennifer would give her a few days, not put any pressure on her to talk, and call her again.

Sunday night arrived, and Jennifer had carefully packed a wardrobe to impress. If she were going to see the city of Amsterdam, it would not be on foot. In fact, she hadn't worn flat shoes since those harrowing months following her diagnosis over a year and a half ago. To her, flat shoes now symbolised depression and darkness and giving up. She knew that made no sense, but once she made an association in her mind it stuck for life.

John never got 'the association thing', as he called it. He could not understand how a smell, or the shape of a footpath, could evoke such emotions and memories in Jennifer. In fact, Jennifer believed that it irritated him. He often referred to these 'associations' as drama on the part of his wife. She, of course, would respond by telling him he was missing out on one of life's loveliest experiences. They always concluded that debate with a reluctant acceptance of each other's peculiarities.

Tonight, John was home and settled in front of the television. It was a rare treat to have the evening to themselves. She poured them both a glass of Malbec and shuffled in beside him on the couch. She had been watching him all day in his tight jeans and a white shirt buttoned down at the neck. John had a typically Irish appearance, not particularly beautiful but perfectly structured and in proportion. His daily workouts at the gym in Castlebar did not go unappreciated by his wife. He always turned her on, even after all these years.

She nudged her way under his right arm and lay her head on his chest. Despite everything that had happened between them, this was still one of her favourite spots. She loved his smell and the heat that always radiated from him. His chest, with its coating of dark-blonde hairs, some turning grey, still drew her touch. She was already aroused. She had been in that state for days. She slid her hand from his thigh up towards his chest and began to undo his shirt buttons from the top down.

The sensation of his chest hair in her fingers was like an 'on' button for her body. As she unfastened him and placed her hand inside his shirt, she moved her lips up to his neck and towards his face. She imagined how erotic it would be if he lay her down right there on the couch. That was not his response. He removed her hand from his chest and shuffled free of her.

'Jesus, Jennifer, not now,' he said, rather exasperated. 'I'm not in the mood. Just a bit tired.' He didn't make eye contact with her but picked up his glass and continued to stare at the TV. Jennifer didn't speak. She couldn't predict what would come out of her mouth had she begun. John had never rejected an offer of sex before, not in all the years. In fact, they had what Jennifer considered a vigorous sex life for a married couple. She was stunned and a bit dazed. And she was insulted. Rejected.

She sat there momentarily with her thoughts, trying to stem the disappointment and summon some reasonability. Yes, she would be reasonable. This was not the slight that she had perceived. The man was entitled to accept or reject an offer of sex. If it had been the other way round and Jennifer had been the one to refuse, then he would be expected to assent and get over it. So why did she feel so hurt? Perhaps it was the hard-line tone he took with her? It was borderline aggressive. He was borderline aggressive a lot lately, but this rebuff hurt her.

Without making a fuss, she took her glass from the table and made her way upstairs. She would not make a big deal of it. Maybe she would play hard to get for a while. Teach him a lesson. No, this was not Jennifer's style. She was straight to a fault. The saying 'what you see is what you get' was invented for her. She would forget about it. Bury it. Her psychologist would love that, she smiled. It would pass for sure.

She was in bed before ten. Her anticipated trip to Amsterdam in the morning was definitely not something she wanted to miss. She read through Kate's itinerary one more time to ensure that she was on track. She felt excited, imagining sunshine, sitting in a breezy outdoor café watching strangers go about their lives. She was also looking forward to making the acquaintance of some of her European counterparts at the training event at the EMA headquarters. She secretly congratulated herself for finally discovering some decent social skills. She was less intimidated lately by a full room or a public event.

Her beeping phone snapped her from her musings. A text message from Ruth: 'You all set? Lucky bitch. I'm dripping jealousy here. I think I must be due some "training" too at this stage! So will the French man with the big penis, sorry I mean nose, the big nose, will he be there? No harm looking right?'

Jennifer couldn't help laughing. Ruth always made her laugh. She was as bold as brass. In ways, she reminded Jennifer of herself, at least the way she used to be before she learned to behave herself a little bit. She answered, 'Doubt it, but thanks for your concern regarding my entertainment for the next couple of days! See you Wednesday x.' Ruth was a beam of light in Jennifer's life right now. It was as if God knew what Jennifer needed and had sent Ruth straight to her.

By now, Jennifer was relaxed and happy to let the issue with John dissipate. She turned off the lights and sank into her pillow. She had recently progressed to falling asleep in silence, which she discovered was giving her more peaceful nights and superior-quality sleep. She inhaled, held her breath and exhaled, allowing each muscle in her body to relax from head to toe. She would empty her mind with each exhalation … No, she wouldn't. He was still there: huge and strong and French. She imagined his muscular arms holding her hands above her head while his body pinned her in position, preventing her escape. Jennifer knew it would be some time before she drifted off to sleep that night.

Chapter 14

Jennifer's day in Amsterdam was filled with lazy coffees and lounging by the waterside. An emersion in the world of Anne Frank and Van Gogh would wait for another day. Today was for idling and people-watching. She would have a couple of hours before she had to make her way back to the hotel and then on to the EMA convention centre where the international visitors would be hosted to a welcome dinner.

Jennifer had a fondness for the Dutch ever since her fling with Jacob in her final year at UCD. Jacob was a newly graduated scholar from the Utrecht Law College and was interning at the Law Department at UCD at the time. He had been assigned the task of providing tutorials in European Law to Jennifer's cohort. He was young and nervous, practically the same age as the students, and lacked the air of authority that normally exuded from their lecturers. Jennifer remembered how she fell for his brave face and manufactured confidence. She always bought into the mantra of 'fake it till you make it.' More than that, she liked his funny accent and his long fair hair tied at the back of his neck in a ponytail.

Following an exchange of what now seemed like embarrassingly obvious glances between them in the lecture hall, Jacob had posted a letter to her in the internal mail asking her out. They managed simply fine without mobile phones back then, she thought. It was her first experience with a 'European'. No courtship, and his confident expectation of intercourse was a given. Not like Irish lads her age, she reminisced, who would tiptoe around you, ply you with vodka and poke at you until you submitted.

She smiled now, recalling her memories of that time with affection. Jacob was an adorable man and very kind to her. It was her only experience of Dutch men, and the association stood the test of time. To her, all Dutch men were Jacob. Sitting on a canal bank in Amsterdam, she wondered what had become of him. She hoped he had found a happy and prosperous path.

Dinner was at eight. In her hotel room, slightly under pressure for time, she stepped into a stunning laurel-green dress, sleeveless with a straight neck and cut to the knee. Green was a bit predictable, she thought. Too late now – it was the one she had packed. Wriggling her toes into her nude Ralph Lauren heels, she stood up straight and tall in the mirror. Head up. Shoulders up, back and relaxed. Just like her mother had taught her. She must have been ten years old when her mother showed her how to do that, but she never forgot. She made one final turn in front of the mirror and decided that she scrubbed up well. Right: dinner, one or two drinks and early to bed.

The conference centre was small but beautifully decorated. Jennifer hurried in the door of the room, worried that the delegates may already be at their tables. She was right. Every seated head in the room turned to look at her. 'Every bloody time, Jennifer,' she scolded herself. She had not been conscious of being alone in the crowd until this minute. Any possibility of blending into invisibility was lost, thanks to the damn green dress.

A kind man ushered her to a table of random people who welcomed her politely. They were Dutch for the most part and two German ladies, who Jennifer suspected might be a couple until she reminded herself to stop judging people. Everyone at the table spoke English, to her surprise and gratitude. A glass of unidentifiable red wine later, and she was comfortable in her skin and bringing an unmistakable Irish wit and humour to the table.

The group casually made its way to the bar for a nightcap. It was quiet. She remembered it was Monday night and her group were the only ones in the building. She took a seat at the bar, not planning to be there for long. She would have one glass of something better than what had been on the table, and she would retire at a very decent hour.

Her day had been delightful. With some new-found colleagues and potential friends, she was looking forward to the next one. While attempting to get the barman's attention, she heard a voice from behind her, so close she could feel his breath on the back of her neck.

'Madame Burke, welcome to Amsterdam. May I buy you a drink?'

She didn't need to turn and face him. Dior Homme, with a hint of French testosterone. Summoning every ounce of bodily integrity in her, she coolly and confidently turned on her chair. 'An Argentinian Malbec would be ideal, but I'll settle for French.' She had it said before she realised the cheeky smile and alternate interpretation on her companion's face.

What in the honour of Jesus is Jacques Martin doing here?, she gasped to herself. How had she not known he would be? Oh God, no, please don't let him be running the training course tomorrow. She wouldn't hear a word of it with the distraction. She had imagined this man naked so many times over the past few weeks it didn't bear thinking about, and the things he had done to her in her mind's eye were making her blush now in front of him. She cringed at the thought of it all.

And now he was buying her a drink, and she was going to drink it with him. 'Thank you,' she smiled, but in a fake, controlled way. 'I didn't realise you were going to be here. When did you arrive?'

'Jennifer,' he said, but in a French accent. This was the first time in her life that she thought her name was sexy. 'I had business with the Agency today. I fly out in the morning. I was sitting behind you at dinner when you made your dramatic entrance. Did you not see me?'

Cringing followed cringing when she realised that he had possibly been looking at her throughout the entire dinner. She put her French Malbec to her mouth and gulped it when he wasn't looking. This was going to be fine, she thought. She would have a pleasant drink with a very handsome man and enjoy it. She was in control.

He took a seat beside her at the bar and faced her. His eyes were hazel brown in the centre with a darker brown circumference. Hypnotic. She soon realised that she couldn't stare too long at his face without remembering her secret fantasy scenarios and becoming aroused. *Shake it off lady*, she told herself. *You are a professional, and a damn good one.* She would use this opportunity to milk her companion for some valuable information regarding the drug-authorisation procedure and his opinion of BioWestPharma's application. No flirting and no messing.

Jennifer's attempt at focusing the conversation on all things veterinary medicines failed miserably as Jacques asked about her family, her origins in Kerry and her aspirations for the future. *So much for the professional conversation*, she thought. He made it so easy for her to ramble on. His attentive and inquisitive nature consumed her. He was charismatic and entertaining and glued to her words.

As he handed her a third glass of Malbec, she could feel her cheeks start to glow and realised that she was tipsy. This would have to be her last drink if she were to get out of this situation unscathed. She couldn't attest to her self-restraint after a fourth, she hated to admit.

With every minute that passed now the man was becoming more amorous, gazing at her and complimenting her shamelessly. 'You are an incredibly beautiful woman, Jennifer. I hope that your husband appreciates what he has,' he said, inches from her face. She lapped up the words. She had been starved of affection of late.

'Where are you staying tonight?' he asked.

She didn't answer. It would have been so easy for her to invite him back to her room. No one would ever know. But she knew it wasn't what she wanted. She thought of John at home with her girls and suddenly felt a wave of loneliness for them. Between the wine and the guilt, she needed to leave right then and there. She apologised to Jacques and picked up her bag. She knew that if she left right away and didn't make eye contact with him again that she would be okay, but if he came any closer to her she might lose her resolve.

'Thank you for a lovely evening, but I think I had better go now. I hope to see you again soon,' she said and made directly for the door.

'Wait, I will walk you to a taxi. You can't go out there alone,' he said as he jumped from his stool and followed her. She desperately did not want him to follow her. She needed to dive in a taxi and get away from him. He persisted and walked close by her side out to the street where they waited to hail a car. They didn't speak. She didn't raise her head to look at him. If she had, there would have been no turning.

She spotted a car and called it. Thank God, she would escape and do no harm. As she reached for the door, Jacques grabbed her arm, and with what seemed like minimal effort on his part, he tugged her entire body back towards him. She swung around in one swift motion. There, in the streetlight of an Amsterdam avenue, he kissed her. She didn't resist – partly in shock and partly in lust. She felt her body fall back against the car and the weight of him press against her. He was devouring her. Every scrape of his black stubble on her face caused another wave of contraction in her groin. He was spectacular. She grabbed the front of his shirt and held on.

'Take me to your room,' he whispered.

Jennifer pulled away and drew a breath. She was not going to do this. Those manic days were long gone, and she was now completely responsible for her every action and decision. She would not risk her marriage and her life with John again. Not for a night with Jacques Martin, that was for sure. 'I'm sorry' was the only explanation he got, and she was gone.

As she travelled the short distance back to her hotel, the longing for the French man faded. It would have been a brief moment of pleasure, she admitted, but not worth the guilt and shame in the aftermath. She thought of John at home with the girls. She knew things had been difficult in recent months and their relationship was not nearly as strong as it could be, but she was going to remedy that. Their love was still there. She didn't doubt it.

It was turning midnight at home in Ireland when she climbed into her hotel bed. She was tired now and thinking about her long day ahead tomorrow. Her head hurt from the wine and the events of the night. She wondered if John might still be awake. The sound of his voice now would soothe and reassure her.

She dialled his mobile, but it rang out. She wasn't surprised. He likely had an early start tomorrow. She decided to leave a text message. He would get it in the morning. 'Hi. Long day. Miss you. See you and the ladies tomorrow night. Love you all xxx.'

Her eyes closed as soon as she hit the sheets. *Goodnight Amsterdam*, she thought as she drifted off, placing the night in her vault of memories with so many others.

Chapter 15

It was almost midnight when Jennifer's Audi turned in the gates of her Castlebar home. She was drained from her journey but looking forward to seeing her troops. The girls would surely be in bed, but she hoped that John would have waited up for her. She needed the grounding effect of seeing his face and touching his skin.

On stepping in through the front door, she wasn't disappointed. She could hear one of the songs from the nineties compilation CD the girls had made for John for his birthday: 'Girls who want boys who like boys to be girls.' She smiled. She would still take Blur over Oasis any day of the week.

She found John working on his laptop at the kitchen table. They locked eyes and smiled at each other. She was delighted to see him. Dropping her bag, she walked up behind him, put her arms around his shoulders and kissed the back of his neck. She inhaled him. He was one of her favourite smells. He received her amorously in contrast with their last intimate interaction. She was relieved. It was good to be home.

He closed the laptop and turned to see her. 'I missed you,' she said, the emotion inside her seeping out in the moment. 'How did you all get on?'

'Sure, we missed you too, Mom. The girls are probably still awake if you want to pop up to them. I'll put the kettle on,' John replied.

She accepted the offer and, grabbing her bag, made her way upstairs to the girls. They were dozing off, but she stole a sneaky kiss from both. She would drop her bag in her room and go straight back down to spend some rare alone time with John. She was weary but would happily find the energy to partake in some well overdue lovemaking with her husband if he wanted it.

Turning on her bedroom light, she dropped her bag in the corner of the room. She would unpack it in the morning. Then something hit her like a slap across the face. She stood there in the corner of her bedroom, slightly dazed, evaluating and re-evaluating. Her observations were clear. The information was sound. The bed had not been slept in. The pillows and bed cover were exactly where she had put them yesterday morning when she left for the airport. Nothing had been touched.

John had not slept here last night.

Jennifer's chest tightened, and a dull painful ache emerged where her heart was supposed to be. He didn't come home. He stayed somewhere else. *With someone else, maybe?* Oh God, her thoughts were a lap ahead of her now.

She didn't remember the climb down the stairs, but standing just inside the kitchen door she looked at her husband and asked, 'Where did you sleep last night?'

He glanced up immediately at her. His face told the truth: it drained of blood, and his eyes closed in slow motion as his brain slowly chugged into action. 'I had a few drinks in town and stayed with one of the lads,' he answered, his eyes anywhere but on hers.

'Which lad?' she asked.

'Donal. What difference does it make?' His body was already in defence mode.

'And you left the girls here, by themselves?' Jennifer asked, her thoughts barely still collected.

'Jesus Christ, Jennifer, they are sixteen, and you have no problem fucking off and leaving them,' John said, his volume rising now.

'I left them with their father, and I went on a one-night training course. I haven't left the house in over a year and a half, John.' And just like that she was doing it again. She was defending herself. He was an expert at putting her in this position. She had started the conversation by asking him to explain his behaviour, and within a few seconds she was defending hers. This was textbook behaviour by her husband, and she was exhausted by it.

The first four stages were always the same: deny, defend, deflect, attack. And her money was on this confrontation going into fifth gear any minute: aggressively attack until she shut up. If she refused to back down, he would invariably storm out, slamming as many doors as possible on his way. Jennifer attempted a calmer approach. 'John, this conversation isn't about me. I asked you where you stayed last night. I saw the look on your face when I asked you. You looked like you were going to throw up. Now I'm asking you again. Please tell me the truth.'

'I fucking told you where I was.' The volume went up another couple of notches. 'What's your problem anyway? Oh, you saw the look on my face? Will you cop your fucking self on? I suppose you are going to tell me you have a "gut feeling" next,' he said mockingly. 'There was no look on my face except what's in your imagination.'

This wasn't the first time John had told his wife that she was imagining things. Liz had also thrown that particular 'imagination' concern at her too over the years.

'Okay, so if I call Donal and ask him where you stayed last night, he will be able to tell me?' Jennifer asked, reaching for her phone.

'Yes, Jennifer, phone a man after midnight with your mental queries and wake up his whole family. Jesus, you are a piece of work,' John replied condescendingly. And there it was again, the 'mental' tag. He knew the buttons to press. 'Look, I stayed with Donal after a few drinks. You can choose to believe me or not. If you don't, that's your problem,' he said. And that was it.

Jennifer could have predicted how that conversation was going to go, and yet she walked straight into it. Again. In eighteen years, she had not found a way to effectively communicate with her husband when his back was against the wall or he was in a position of defence. And now she would be carrying the weight of wondering if her husband had met another woman with no way of knowing if it was true or just 'in her imagination'. Standing in her kitchen, fatigued and terrified, she was left alone with her grievance to take it or leave it, like every other conflict she had faced in her marriage. Another hole to plug on her own.

'Please sleep in the spare room tonight,' she said to her husband, looking him directly in his eyes before he stormed outside. 'We can deal with this tomorrow.'

She wouldn't bother phoning Donal. He would cover for John anyway, and, to be honest, she had more integrity than to lower herself to it.

Sleep came to Jennifer for only a few hours that night. By morning, body and mind were crying out for rest. John sulked through breakfast and left without acknowledging her. This was standard procedure – his way of making sure that Jennifer was rightly deterred from approaching the uncomfortable subject with him again. At this stage of the marriage, she knew not to bother. It would only result in a more aggravated response than the first time.

Aeons of attempted negotiations about his sisters had eventually taught her this, but not until they had gone through years of discord. In matters of conflict resolution with her husband, it seemed to Jennifer that she suffered from some form of arrested development. She was a skilled communicator and always sided towards mediation over conflict in every other aspect of her life, but when it came to communicating with this man, she was anything but accomplished.

She had always assumed that this was because of the emotional entanglement she had with him or the fact that she expected higher standards and more consideration from him. Whatever the reason, she was in the middle of yet another soul-destroying conflict in their relationship. She knew enough not to expect her feelings and worries to be addressed in a calm, compassionate way. One option was to let it go. She did not know what the other was.

The clock crawled towards lunchtime. An earlier text to Ruth had booked a seat on the black couch and a friendly non-judgemental ear. Pleasantries were dispensed with as Jennifer vomited the events of the night before to her friend in the knowledge that advice would be forthcoming.

'Ruth, I don't know what to think. If what he is saying is the truth, and he stayed with Donal, then why did he defend himself so viciously?' Jennifer said, looking to her friend for comfort. 'And I know what I saw. His face drained of blood like he was looking at a truck driving at him.'

Ruth took her friend's hand and looked at her lovingly. 'Jen, all I can say to you is this: you need to start trusting yourself, your gut, your instincts. You are an extremely intelligent woman. You are the straightest person I have ever met. You are the strongest person I have ever met. And most of all you are absolutely not mental.'

Ruth's words were reassuring. Jennifer knew all of this, but when it came to her relationship with John, this logic betrayed her. In her gut she knew that John was hiding something. She also knew that this was by no means the first time in her marriage that John had forced her to accept stories under duress. Stories that he needed to sell. She knew he was a liar, but she never had concrete evidence to put to him, and his aggressive reaction always forced her to drop her accusations. That, and the fact that it was simply easier to give in to him.

'What you need to concentrate on now is how you will handle it. You are a lawyer, so think this through like I know you can. What are your options? You can accept what he told you and believe that he was with Donal. You can reject what he told you and believe that he was with a woman. If you do the latter, you are left with three options. You can stay and turn a blind eye. Lots of women do this. You can stay and start an investigation into his movements and communications and build your book of evidence. Or, Jennifer, you can leave him today.' Ruth had a very scientific way of putting things.

Jennifer was silent for a moment as she absorbed what had just been said. The reality of it was striking to her.

Ruth continued. 'The real question is what do you want to achieve? It's your marriage to manage any way you like.'

More silence. Then, 'I love him. I want my future to be with him. He has his faults, but so do I. If I am as intelligent as you say, then I should be able to find a way to make it work. I should be able to manage the conflict-resolution vacuum in his brain and make it work. Right?' Jennifer reasoned. 'Most of the time we get on great. We have fun together. At least we used to. Obstacles got in the way over the years. My illness. His sisters. But most of the time it was good. I would love it if we could find a way to be happy again.'

'Okay, then,' said Ruth. 'Which option are you choosing?'

Jennifer took a sip of her tea and answered her friend in a way that was partially intended to convince herself that she was right. 'I am going to accept his explanation and put it behind me. He has always reacted suspiciously when I put him on the spot, and I know that he has unresolved insecurities from his childhood, so it is understandable that he is very defensive. Ruth, I know you don't know him very well, but John is a really good man, and he does his best for his family. I want to keep my marriage together. I believe that I can make this work.'

Ruth smiled at her friend and said, 'Then I am here for you to help you in any way I can. If you're in, I'm in.'

Jennifer reached across and hugged her friend.

Later that evening, Jennifer took a few minutes to regroup. John had been the only person in her life for so long that she had forgotten how it felt to have someone like Ruth beside her every day, someone so completely in her camp, on her side. Ruth was an incredible person and entirely faithful to Jennifer. It was an overwhelming feeling to admit what she had been missing out on for so long by limiting her world to John and her daughters. Letting Ruth O'Neill into her life was the best thing to have happened to Jennifer in a long time.

Chapter 16

Calm descended over the Burke house that evening. Once John realised that Jennifer would not pursue her investigation into his night away from home, normal service resumed. The chatter of her daughters in the kitchen brought a certain peace to the evening, and the two adults were happy to communicate through them for now.

Looking across the table at her husband, Jennifer longed for him to envelope her in his arms and reassure her that their relationship was solid. She knew, however, that he didn't have the emotional resources. He didn't have the template DNA to find the resources. This was who he was.

He was her husband. She had only ever imagined a future with him. They would grow old together in this house. When they were building it, they had joked that in their old age they would have to move their bedroom downstairs into the small office because they would be too crippled to manage the stairs. They had been through so much together. It was now time to put her cognitive behaviour therapy to good use, she decided, and change the way she was thinking about the relationship. She knew what the man was capable of and not capable of. It was time to stop expecting the impossible and start making things work. After all, she was the more intelligent and imaginative of the two, she boldly smiled to herself. She would find a way.

Morning beckoned a busy day for Jennifer. Today she would brief the board of directors on the progress of the applications for three new drug authorisations. She would discuss the pending approval of the cancer treatment drug, which was almost complete, a novel human antidepressant which was nearly at the end of the clinical-trial phase and a new beta blocker for the treatment of feline cardiomyopathy. Jennifer's newly acquired knowledge of dog and cat ailments impressed even her. There was no such thing as learning too much, her mother would say.

It was critical for her to impress the board today. She had been at the company for under a year, and millions of euro were riding on these authorisations. She was confident in the work that had been done, as were the managers of the R&D and clinical-trials departments, but she understood that the investors needed to hear this from her. Pulling herself out of bed and into the shower, she knew that her mind would have to be on the job today.

The girls were buzzing this morning. They were leaving on a six-day school trip to Poland, and the teenage excitement in the house was at maximum. As John corralled them into his car to take them to the station, Jennifer inhaled an overdue breath of relaxation and solitude. She took her time palming through her wardrobe. She always preferred her winter look to the summer one. It was her penchant for high necks and long sleeves that made it work. The cold of the morning prompted a cream woollen polo with a grey pencil skirt paired with dark-brown leather heels. Simple and elegant. Her hair looked amazing too, cropped into a tight pixie cut that accentuated her beautiful jawline and broad shoulders. This would do nicely, she thought.

As the boardroom filled, Jennifer pleaded with her body not to let her down. Recent experiences with presenting in public had gone well for her, and she reminded herself of this as she battled the anxiety that was creeping in on her. She had done this a hundred times, she told herself, and she was more than capable. 'This is going to be great' was the mantra she had learned to repeat over and over. All she had to do was believe it.

Jennifer had developed her own style for these presentations. She hated using PowerPoint when she spoke to a group. She preferred to speak to the room without the prop. It was a throwback to her days as a lawyer when she would address the court with nothing more than a few notes on her desk. The performance was always more impactful that way, she thought. So today she used the slides to present the data only. She was going to ad-lib the rest. She would instil confidence in these people and demonstrate that she was in command of her patch.

She settled into it as soon as she got started, and eventually she began to enjoy the experience. She was a natural communicator and kept the attention and interest of the board throughout the presentation. She explained scientific terminology and broke the process down in such a way that everyone in the room could understand and no one was bored. Competently fielding questions regarding timelines and potential marketing dates, Jennifer did herself proud and wrapped it up in an hour. She had made an impression.

While she was career-focused, Jennifer was not overly ambitious. She loved to work, but not to the extent that she needed to climb the career ladder at any cost. What she needed was to know that she was doing her best and achieving her goals. She was not a perfectionist, but she liked to know that she was doing things right.

She was thrilled with the feedback and knew that she would benefit from her presentation in the long run. It would potentially mean an extended contract or a better paid position some day. She excelled at excelling. Still bustling with energy, she phoned Sinead on her way home. It had been almost a week since they spoke, and Jennifer hoped that she was feeling better.

'Hi, Jen, how are you?'

Jennifer heard the voice of her friend and was relieved. 'Hey there, lady. How are you keeping? You sound better anyway, thank God,' Jennifer answered.

Sinead went on to explain that she had visited her GP after last speaking to Jennifer, and they had decided that, among other measures, Sinead should start a course of antidepressants with a view to monitoring the progress over the next couple of months.

'Sinead, that's excellent news. One step at a time. And you know how I feel about all things narcotic: take them!' The friends laughed. 'Seriously, girl, those drugs are designed to make you feel better. Just take them.'

Sinead agreed and promised that she would. She had also made an appointment to see a clinical psychologist in the coming weeks. This was progress as far as Jennifer was concerned. It pained her to watch her old friend in this state. She knew at first hand of the horror of clinical depression, and the thought of anyone suffering in this way broke her heart.

Jennifer didn't burden her friend with her tales of woe about John. Nor did she indulge in the success of her day. Instead, she offered to visit at the weekend. However, Sinead had already made plans to see her parents. At least she wouldn't be on her own, Jennifer thought. 'Take care of yourself babe,' she said, signing off, and said a short prayer for Sinead's quick recovery.

It must have been close to seven when Jennifer pulled in the gates of her home. She was delighted to see John's car in the drive. The girls were away, and she was excited at the prospect of having the house alone with her man. Now was as good a time as any to start building bridges with a good old reliable roll in the hay, she thought to herself, smiling. *Start with the easy stuff,* she thought, *and work your way up to the trickier issues.*

In the kitchen, John sat in silence at the table. The house was unusually quiet, Jennifer thought, and he looked unsettled. As he stood to greet her, Jennifer walked towards him, arms outstretched, throwing them around his neck affectionately.

The affection was not received. Unwrapping her arms from around him, John pulled away from his wife. 'I can't do this any more, Jennifer. I'm really sorry. It's just not working,' John said, avoiding eye contact with her.

'Excuse me? What the hell are you talking about?' Jennifer asked, slightly annoyed at yet another rejection.

'Our marriage isn't working any more. I'm leaving you,' he said without emotion.

Jennifer stood in front of him, staring at him, not speaking and not really understanding what he was saying. The words seemed plain enough, but they were not landing on her at all. 'I'm sorry, you are going to have to explain that to me again. What the hell is going on?' she said, still not entirely in the grasp of the conversation.

'Oh, for fuck's sake, Jennifer, I'm leaving you. The marriage is over. We have come to the end of the road. What don't you understand?' he said harshly.

She felt dizzy and very nauseous. She sat down. Surely she was picking this up wrong. Did John just say that he was leaving her? 'You are leaving me? Why? What about the girls? You can't do this to them. They adore you. This is ridiculous, John. I mean, are you having some sort of midlife crisis or something?' she said.

'I'm not leaving the girls, Jennifer. I am leaving you. I will see them as much as I always do. I just don't think I can live with you any more. Our lives have gone in different directions, and we have grown apart. I think we will be happier this way in the long run. Look, I have taken an apartment in the town, temporarily at least. When the girls get back, we can tell them I am helping Grandad on the farm for a few weeks. We will talk to them together. In the meantime, you and the girls can stay here. We will sort out the financial stuff in due course.'

And there it was. All worked out. An apartment taken in the town. John had been planning this move for a while – Jennifer had no way of knowing how long. She stopped for a minute to try to work out how she felt, but she felt paralysed. Her husband had just told her he was leaving her. His bags were in the car. He was walking away.

She stood and called to him. She needed to ask one question. 'Is there someone else? You might as well tell the truth about that. Men don't leave their wives, John, unless it's for someone else. They don't just walk out of their home and into a dingy flat because they have fucking "grown apart" from their wives.'

'There is no other woman, one hundred per cent guaranteed. You have my word on that,' he said.

'Swear on the lives of your two daughters, John,' Jennifer demanded. She needed to hear him say this to be sure.

'Yes, I swear,' he reassured her. 'I'm leaving now. I think it's for the best. You will realise in time, Jennifer, that we are in a destructive, even toxic relationship and it's not going to get any better.' He said this in a way that was designed to pacify her.

Then he was gone.

Jennifer was numb. She was angry. She was distraught. She was terrified. Standing in the middle of their kitchen, her heart raced and her head thumped. She put her hands over her face, but she could not stem the deluge of tears and heaving sighs that erupted from her. This was not happening. She could not do this. She couldn't live without him. She just could not. She would not survive this. She would literally die without him.

Her head reeled trying to deal with what she had just seen and heard. She dropped to her knees on the floor and cried until she felt sick. Her chest hurt. The pain of heartbreak was an actual pain, she discovered. The man she loved was gone. He didn't love her anymore. It was too late. Her life was over.

Chapter 17

She woke in the darkness some time the following morning, the taste of red wine still in her mouth. The memories of the evening before resurfaced gradually like turning up a dimmer switch in a dark room. The muscles of her already dehydrated heart contracted when she remembered that John was gone. In a tidal wave of grief, she pressed her face into her pillow and wept. She wanted her husband.

Jennifer had never experienced real grief before today. She had known stress and anxiety and fear, but never grief. Lying there on her own in the dark she wondered if she had the strength for this. The thought of facing the rest of her life without John was beyond the threshold of her ability.

She turned on her side and placed her feet on the oak floor, one foot at a time as though it required mechanical intervention. One foot at a time was exactly how she was going to do this, the way she was taught after her bipolar diagnosis. She stood and opened the window, bearing the cold air. Then she prayed. She asked God – no, she begged him – to help her. She begged him to send something that would take away the pain. Anything. Closing her eyes, she pleaded with him to help her to understand why this was happening, to send her the means to survive this.

Fighting the wave of nausea and the bigger upsurge of panic, she walked to the bathroom. *How could the skin around her eyes be dehydrated and puffy at the same time?*, she wondered. She was a mess. If she was going to survive this with her mental health intact, she knew that she had to keep moving, to keep functioning. She knew that if she lay down, she would wither.

She showered, dressed, put on her make-up and heels, and got in the car. It was a blur, but she was functioning. She would go to work and focus on what was in front of her. First, she needed to detour to the pharmacy to fill her prescription. Now was definitely not the time to risk running out of her medication. More judgemental looks from Marie the pharmacist, she thought. *Fuck her*, she said to herself, fighting tears and a headache.

'Hi Marie, my usual prescription please,' Jennifer said, checking her phone in case John had made contact. He hadn't. Jennifer could never explain why collecting her medication made her so uncomfortable, but it did, ever since the first day she handed her prescription over the counter. She had felt judged, put into a box, and she hated that.

What was worse, Jennifer learned early in the process that the pharmacy was only allowed to dispense medication that treated psychiatric illnesses one month at a time – in case the patient overdosed, she knew. She rarely if ever thought about her condition anymore, but she was thinking about it this morning.

When Marie returned with the lithium parcelled up as usual in a small white paper bag, she beckoned Jennifer to the corner of the pharmacy, for what seemed more privacy. 'How are you, Jennifer?' Marie asked. Jennifer was disconcerted, but Marie seemed sincere.

'Okay, thanks,' Jennifer answered, not inclined to divulge a morsel of private information to a woman who was, for all intents and purposes, a stranger. Jennifer was uncomfortable with all forms of prying into her life in recent years, and today of all days she wasn't in form for a heart-to-heart with a nosy neighbour.

'I've been meaning to ask,' Marie continued. 'Please know that we are here to support you in your recovery. You look great. I just wanted to say fair play to you, and if you need anything please let us know.'

Jennifer was taken aback. She realised then that she had completely misjudged this woman. She had done to Marie what she was so afraid was being done to her. She felt humbled. And grateful. She felt so grateful. This woman was reaching out a human hand of support. Jennifer felt that she might cry. 'I'm really grateful, Marie. Thanks a million,' she said and with that took her medication and left, overwhelmed with the humanity and the realisation that this time she really had gotten it very wrong. Today, however, the kind act of a stranger was exactly what Jennifer needed.

Walking in the door of BioWestPharma, she opened a video message from the girls, updating her on their fun and mischief. The pain of having to tell them would surely break her. The pain of watching their pain. She kept walking. She kept breathing. She would get to her office, and she would work. This was her plan. She knew that if she could just keep the rest of her life in order, she would be able to handle this crisis with John.

Sitting at her desk, she wondered if she was supposed to tell someone about the break-up. Like when there was a death in a family, wasn't it common practice to inform as many people as possible so they could pay their respects or something? She supposed that she should tell her parents. But how could she tell them before the girls knew? She put her face in her hands and sighed out loud.

'You okay?' Sean asked, sticking his head in the door. She had forgotten that she had invited him in this morning to discuss the feedback from some of the scientists on the draft EMA application. She clearly wasn't okay, but she wondered to what extent that was visible on the outside.

'Yes, grand, thanks. The kids are giving me a bit of a headache, but that's what happens when you are responsible for two sixteen-year-old madams,' she lied.

Satisfied with the explanation, Sean pulled himself up a chair and started into his work. Jennifer threw her eyes to the sky and was amused. There was no way she would have pulled that off with Kate – or any woman for that matter. She surprised herself at how she coped with Sean and the job in front of her.

She switched her brain into EMA mode and did what she had to do. She worried that she was not functioning at one hundred per cent, but she was functioning, and that was good enough; Sean was perfectly content with her contribution. As the morning wore on, she thought about John. She had to speak to him. The more she relived the heartache of last night, the more she questioned John's behaviour. It just did not make sense. 'Why?,' she asked herself, over and over, and she tortured herself by speculating whether it was too late to remedy what had happened. Whatever was going through his head, whatever he believed he couldn't live with, she wondered if she would be able to repair it. Surely they could work this out if she could just get through to him.

    She decided to text him: 'Hi. How are you today? I have been better :(Can we meet and have a chat? Neutral ground if you like? O'Flaherty's Hotel after work?' She hoped that if she approached him calmly, aka 'not mental', and offered to discuss the issues with an open mind, then maybe there would be a possibility that he would change his mind. There was no way she was going to give up her husband without a fight. They were not a match made in Heaven – that was obvious – but surely he had not stopped loving her. She simply did not believe it.

She checked her phone at least twenty times that morning, but there was no reply from him. She messaged Ruth – she needed her friend right now. She was not entirely certain that she would be able to talk to Ruth in public without sobbing, but she was going to try. She needed to share the burden of this with someone who would be on her side and offer truthful counsel.

'What. The. Fuck.' was the only response that Ruth could assemble. Jennifer simply nodded, tears already welling. Ruth stared at her with her mouth open. It almost made Jennifer laugh such was the gaping expression. She had always heard the phrase 'her jaw dropped' to denote surprise, but witnessing it for real was comical. 'Jesus, Jennifer. Are you okay? Why in God's name didn't you call me last night? What exactly did he say? The fucking clown.'

Ruth had never hidden her opinion that John was punching above his weight with Jennifer. While she never disrespected him to Jennifer, she made it clear that she believed that Jennifer was the prize.

'He thinks we have come to the end of the road in the marriage. He doesn't see a future for us. He thinks that in the long run we will be happier apart,' Jennifer repeated without emotion, almost as if she had been a mere onlooker the previous evening.

'Why *now*?' said Ruth. 'I mean, from what you have told me, your marriage was tumultuous from the beginning. "Passionate" was the term you used, as I recall.' She continued, 'I know things had been going downhill since that thundering bitch of a sister had her meltdown, but this is completely out of the blue, isn't it?'

'How did I not see this coming, Ruth?' Jennifer asked. 'I am a bloody idiot. All I see is what is placed in front of my nose. I obviously go around with blinkers on. I literally only see what I want to see, and all I saw was a future for us together.'

Ruth looked at her friend. 'The night he spent away, Jennifer. Think about it. He has a woman somewhere.'

'No, I doubt it,' Jennifer replied. 'I thought of that too straight away, but when I asked him to swear on the lives of his daughters he didn't hesitate. I believe him. He said that this was about me, about us. He simply can't live with me anymore.' Her eyes were becoming progressively redder.

'No fucking way, Jen. He is a fucking liar. We are going to follow him. It's the only way to find out for sure. You need to be certain about this before you can move on,' Ruth said with conviction.

But Jennifer was having none of it. Creeping around spying on her husband was not something that she could bring herself to do. She wondered if, subconsciously, she was happier with those blinkers on. Either way, she would not agree to follow him.

'Okay so,' Ruth reluctantly accepted. 'Let's make a plan, a short-term plan for now, one day at a time. Fuck it, Jen, one minute at a time if that's what it takes. Let's think about where you are. You got through last night. Fair play to you. You got up and dressed this morning and came to work. You are doing brilliantly. What else?' she asked in her enduring best-foot-forward mode.

'I texted him to ask to meet. He hasn't answered yet. I need a better explanation than the one I got last night, and I need to know if there is any hope of him changing his mind,' Jennifer said, her voice lifting slightly at the thought of a possible reunion. Ruth did not object to the meeting but adamantly instructed her friend to 'play it cool' and, above all, 'do not beg.'

Her whole life, the notion of begging anyone for anything was a foreign concept for Jennifer. She would never resort to it.

What she would do was explain that she was open to making whatever changes were necessary to bring them back together. She still had a couple of days before the twins returned from Poland. If she played this well, she might be able to spare them completely.

'No matter what happens, Jen, always remember who you are. You are a strong Kerry woman,' Ruth said. She knew that introducing Jennifer's Kerry blood into the conversation would lift her spirits. 'You will survive. You have up to now, and you will into the future. Failure is not in your portfolio, girl.' She continued, 'And never forget that I am here for you, day or night. I will have my phone on twenty-four hours for you.'

Jennifer welled up at this. She was overwhelmed with the selflessness of her friend. She thought back to her early years in Castlebar when the only people in her life were John, his family and her two young daughters. She recalled the loneliness and coldness that she lived with for so many years without realising what she was missing out on.

Standing up to return to their desks, Ruth reached out for her friend and embraced her tightly. Jennifer did not resist. She accepted every second of it. Walking back to her office, she felt braver, supported. She would take one step at a time. For now, she was choosing to believe that John could be convinced that their marriage was worth another try, that she was worth another try. She would not look back, and she would not look forward. She would stay in the now. That's what she learned to do when she was sick, and it saved her life then. It would be the process she would employ now.

Rising from her desk at the end of the day, she felt her phone vibrate. It was John. She could feel her pulse quicken, but she reined it in with deep controlled breaths.

'Okay, 7 p.m.,' was the entirety of the text.

She was thrilled but knew she must practise restraint now. The purpose of the meeting was not to beg him to come back. It was to encourage him to understand that were he open to salvaging the marriage, she was certainly willing to modify her behaviour or her lifestyle in order to make it work.

She detoured to the ladies' room and stood before the mirror. *Jesus, Jennifer, you've had better days*, she thought. There was no way she would let John see her like this, distraught and struggling. No bloody way. She dabbed some concealer beneath her wretched eyes and swept blush across her cheeks. As she blotted her Mac

Ruby Woo lipstick into her lips, she reminded herself not to get her hopes up. She needed some answers. She would make an offer. And she would retain her dignity at all costs.

Chapter 18

True to form, Jennifer arrived at the hotel on time. She tapped her nails along the outside of her teacup as she sat in a private booth in the hotel lounge. She was nervous, which she thought was ridiculous. She knew this man better than anyone in the world. What she needed was to be calm and casual. She wondered if she should order him some coffee or a drink. Maybe not. There was no way of knowing how late he would be. She distracted herself by watching a cricket match showing on Sky Sports. It was far from the GAA on which she was reared, but her father had once taught her the rules of this noble game and she found it mesmerising to watch.

Suddenly John was by her side. He was still in his work gear, and his runners hadn't made a sound on the timber floor. He was smiling and looked fresh. He had slept, she thought. He certainly hadn't guzzled a bottle and a half of wine to numb the pain. She smiled back and offered him a seat. *Best foot forward now*, she reminded herself.

He ordered a beer and offered her a drink. She was driving but would have refused anyway. She needed to be compos mentis. She did not have a clue how to begin, so she reached for the one sure thing she knew would break the ice. 'Hey, how are you?' she asked, already knowing the answer. 'Did you get the video from the girls? They are hilarious, aren't they?'

She thought that starting the conversation by reminding him of the one thing they actually got right together would be a good idea. The lawyer in her was at work under the surface. He laughed and agreed. 'Look, John, the reason I asked you here this evening was because I didn't get a chance to say what I should have said last night. I got such a shock. I need you to explain it to me again, please. Tell me what's going on,' Jennifer said calmly.

John started to look uncomfortable – the same shift in his demeanour that he displayed every time Jennifer asked him to explain himself. He had zero interest in another showdown tonight. The proposed separation was intended to put an end to the conflict in his life, not to invite more on himself.

'I don't know if there is any more to say, Jen. You have to admit that we haven't been getting on for quite a while. We used to have a spark. There was a time when the conflict and the blowouts were tolerable and manageable. The marriage is just not enjoyable anymore.' He half glanced at her and continued. 'We bounce from one argument to the next, and the peaceful times in between are getting shorter and less frequent. I believe that we will eventually make each other miserable, and I don't want that to happen to either of us. Too much of our lives are ahead of us yet.'

Jennifer watched his face. She struggled to see her husband. This felt so rehearsed.

'You are so functional and happy in every other aspect of your life,' he said, 'but with me you are miserable. Can't you see that?' He seemed so sincere suddenly.

Her stomach hurt as she considered the possibility that he was right. 'Okay,' she said. 'I can see your point. Things have been difficult for us over the years, but that's who we are. We fight, and we make up. John, we have built a life together over twenty years. A home for our kids and ourselves as we grow old. Surely you want to try to save that? This is going to devastate the girls,' she added, hoping that he would soften his stance.

'Living in a house where there is ongoing turmoil is more detrimental to their well-being,' he responded. 'This way they will have two homes each with a parent who is happy.' It rolled off his tongue without a pinch of regret or concern. He had been thinking about this longer than she realised. 'Jennifer, you will be fine. You are self-sufficient. I will help to look after the girls, and I will be fair financially,' he added, getting right down to business.

'Do you not love me anymore, John?' Jennifer asked, her cheek muscles tensing in an attempt not to cry.

'Of course I love you, Jennifer,' he answered. 'I just can't live with you anymore. I can't live in a constant state of conflict. You will never be happy in this marriage. Nothing I do will ever be good enough for you. I'm doing this for you as well as me, Jen. Can you not see that?'

Jennifer was unnerved now by his consistent attempts to make her believe that the separation was for her benefit, like he was doing her a favour. 'John, trust me when I say that this is not what I want, and I am sorry that I gave you the impression that it was. If I were to tell you that I would be willing to try hard to make changes to keep us together, what would you say? Would you be willing to talk about it, maybe go to marriage counselling and try again?' she said, clinging for dear life to his expression and next words.

'I think it's too late, to be honest,' he said. 'I don't think that we can change who we are.'

'John, there is no reason why we can't draw a line under the past and start again. We could get to know each other again. Slowly. We could go out on dates again. We might enjoy it, and, who knows, we might find whatever we lost over the years,' Jennifer said, almost in pain, tensing her face in position so as not to cry. 'All I can do is promise that I will try to change. I will do anything you need me to do to make it work.'

His expression softened. Jennifer thought for a second that she might be getting through to him.

'Look, Jen, I'm actually really flattered by this, but I'm not sure. Maybe there is a way, but I don't want you to hold out too much hope. If you haven't been able to change up to now, I don't think you will at this stage.' There was a sort of cockiness about him.

His words hit her hard and didn't sit well. 'If I haven't been able to change up to now? Surely this is about both of us compromising, no?' she replied.

'See, there you go,' he said. 'Right back with the argument and the accusations.'

Jennifer held her breath. The very last thing she wanted right now was another row, and if she accused him of anything, anything at all, it would start. She began, 'Okay, sorry, but you would be willing to consider a trial period where we could work on the relationship? You could stay in the flat if you want and we could take it slowly.'

'Look, I'm not saying no. Let me think about it,' he said. With that, he rose, kissed her on the cheek and said, 'I'll call you.'

Jennifer didn't leave the hotel straight away. She sat and analysed what had just happened. Her primary feeling was one of relief, then hope. This might work out after all. She had convinced John to consider a reunion. It wasn't a perfect outcome. He hadn't committed, but she would take it. It was a far cry from the wretched despair that she had felt the night before.

As she walked to the car, she felt the fist around her heart loosen. In her rear-view mirror she saw the face of a woman clinging to her future by a thread. If it broke, there was nothing but a void in its place. She wondered if she was also looking at a woman who had held onto her dignity. No, what had just happened in there was nothing short of begging – and she knew it.

Facing the thought of a long evening in an empty house, she turned her car back towards Ballina. Sinead had not answered her previous two calls. She wouldn't be able to ignore a knock on the door as easily.

Jennifer worried how the news of the separation would affect Sinead. She loved both Jennifer and John, and although the women kept in contact more, Sinead was loyal to both. She was still on leave from work, and, from what Jennifer could see, she was hibernating for the most part. Jennifer scolded herself for not making more time for her friend, for not calling to her and encouraging her to get out and exercise. She resolved there and then to try to meet Sinead more often and help her keep active and fit.

She remembered from her own experience that exercise was key to mental health. She reminded herself every day: balanced diet, plenty of exercise, lay off the vino and keep an eye on the stress levels. She broke out in a sweat when she considered what might happen to her under this weight of this stress. Her underlying fear of regressing back into either of the crippling mental states associated with her bipolar disorder was at the forefront of her mind now more than ever.

Sinead responded with delight to seeing her friend at the door. What Jennifer recalled about depression was that the thought of going out and interacting with people was substantially worse than actually doing it. Jennifer refused a glass of wine on account of having the car but noticed that Sinead was now drinking a lot more than she used to. She knew this was a red flag in the fight against mental illness, but one step at a time, she thought – and not for the first time today.

The conversation quickly turned to Jennifer as Sinead inquired about John and the ladies. She promised that as soon as she was feeling better she was going to cook a gourmet dinner for the lot of them and put them up for the night so they could all enjoy a drink. She laughed and asked if the girls were drinking in front of their mother yet. Jennifer's pained face soon quietened her, and Sinead asked her friend what was wrong.

Jennifer tried so hard to fight the tears, but with the first word came a loud sob and then she blurted out the rest. She re-enacted every scene, every word. She reassured Sinead that this was not what she wanted for her family and relived her undignified promises to change for her husband if he would only reconsider. The heartbroken woman could now add humiliation to her catalogue. And desperation. She thought she had hit rock bottom in the aftermath of her diagnosis. At least up to today she believed that she had. Now she was boring her way through the bedrock.

Sinead listened and did not interrupt. When Jennifer finished speaking, Sinead walked to her friend and threw her arms around her. 'You are going to be okay, pet. No matter what happens you have friends and family who love you very much. Never forget that. You will never be on your own.' Sinead always knew what to say. 'Take it as it comes. If he wants to give it another try, then great – but remember, Jen, there must be compromise on both sides. I'm sure there are things you can do better, but please don't forget that his behaviour leaves a lot to be desired. Unless he makes some changes to the way he manages conflict and communicates with you, then nothing will change.'

She was right, of course, but in this moment Jennifer could not see it. She was a terrified woman who would do anything to hold the stability of her life together. Sinead was aware of this and did not push her.

'Would you call him, Sinead?' Jennifer requested. 'You are one of his oldest friends. He would listen to you.' Sinead nodded. Jennifer trusted that she would do whatever she could.

Chapter 19

Two more nights and one full day passed. Jennifer was counting. She had survived three nights without John, struggling not to think of him in his new flat enjoying his new life without her. The girls were expected back this evening, and she had not spoken to John about the plan for managing his absence. Every cell in her body wanted to avoid telling them at least until she was certain that the marriage was over. Her interpretation of John's parting words at their hotel meeting offered a chance that he would change his mind about the separation and she could put this nightmare behind her. Until further notice, this was her brief.

Jennifer had booked a couple of hours off work that morning. It was her appointment at the day hospital for a blood test to check her circulating lithium levels. She wondered if there was any possibility that Dr Raz would see her, just for a few minutes. She felt well. Actually no, she felt wretched, but from a bipolar stability perspective she was well. However, she was rapidly developing a sick feeling in the pit of her stomach that her current stress levels might be more than her constitution could handle.

Sticking a waterproof plaster to her inner elbow, Michelle, the clinic nurse, smiled at Jennifer and told her that she had collared Dr Raz on his way between patients and arranged a quick chat. Michelle was one of the kindest people Jennifer had ever met. In fact, since her first visit to the clinic over a year and a half ago, Jennifer had developed a comfortable relationship with Michelle and also with her clinical psychologist, Diane. More importantly she trusted this team who had been appointed the task of looking after her.

'Good morning, Jennifer. How are you?' Dr Raz said with a soothing voice and encouraging smile. Jennifer smiled back. 'Tell me what I can do for you today.'

'I'm well, thanks,' Jennifer replied. 'I mean, I'm okay. My husband has just told me that he's leaving me. He has moved out. It was sudden. Well, it was sudden for me.' She fought the tears. She really hadn't come here to cry.

Dr Raz looked at Jennifer with real sympathy. 'I see. I'm so sorry, Jennifer.'

'You see,' she continued, 'as you know, my condition is pretty much under control. I am seeing Diane regularly, and she thinks that I am doing brilliantly. My worry is that this stress will push me over the edge again. I remember the state I was in when all of this started. I am literally terrified that I will go back there. It was stress-induced then. That's what I was told. So, it can happen again, right?'

'I understand why you have concerns, Jennifer. Tell me, are you taking the lithium as prescribed?' Dr Raz asked.

'Yes,' Jennifer answered.

'And are you having the lithium levels measured, as instructed?' Dr Raz asked.

'Yes,' Jennifer answered.

'Are you checking in with your clinical psychologist?' Dr Raz asked. 'Engaging in some of the self-care techniques that she has outlined?'

'Yes,' Jennifer answered.

'And have you cut down on your alcohol consumption, as I explained?' he asked.

Jennifer smiled, catching on to where he was going with the conversation. 'For the most part,' she said.

'Jennifer, I do not doubt that this is going to be a tough time for you and your children. But please remember that you have put the work in when it comes to this condition. You are in control of it, not the other way round. So, my advice to you is this: keep doing what you are doing. Check in with Michelle or Diane the minute you feel overwhelmed or worried about your stability. And remember, just because you might suffer symptoms associated with stress in your life does not mean that you are suffering bipolar symptoms. I don't have to tell you that these are completely different things.'

Jennifer nodded at the man. She knew this. She just really needed to hear it from him today. Shaking his hand, she left the clinic, giving Michelle a wave and a smile on her way out. *What fabulous professional people*, she thought to herself. *Some people have such kindness inside them.*

A text from John at lunchtime put a smile on her face. Finally, some contact. 'I'll get the girls from the station at eight if you like and drop them home,' it read. She was thrilled. She would get to see him. This was a good sign – he wasn't avoiding her.

'That would be great,' she replied. 'What do you think we should tell them?' She was determined to exude rationality from now on and not put pressure on him.

John replied immediately suggesting that they run with a story of how he was staying at his father's house for a few weeks to help him with the farm work because he had hurt his back. It was as good a story as any, and it would give them a chance to come up with a strategy for breaking the horrific news to their daughters. Horrific in Jennifer's eyes that was. She felt nauseated at the hurt and destruction this would cause in the lives of two sixteen-year-old girls and was momentarily disgusted with her husband's selfishness. But she agreed to the lie. It would postpone the pain and also give her a chance to work on John, and possibly reverse his decision. In the meantime, she had until eight to prepare for his arrival.

Shortly after eight, the girls came bounding in the door and ran to their mother for a hug and kiss. Jennifer beamed at the sight of them. It was the first moment of genuine happiness she had felt in days. They were starving and more than pleased with the Italian chicken casserole that she had waiting for them. Jennifer smiled at John and invited him to stay for dinner.

'Ah sure, go on. That smells too good to turn down,' he said, smiling back. 'Any chance of a glass of that nice Malbec you have stashed away?' he added, to Jennifer's delight. She poured two large glasses, and the four tucked in. It was hard for her not to be cognisant of the scene: the four of them sharing the dinner table together at the end of the day. It almost killed her to banish the despair and the tears that were emerging just behind her eyes, but now was not the time for despair. Now was a time for positivity and hope.

'Did Dad mention that he will be up at Grandad's for a couple of weeks to give him a hand?' Jennifer got right to the point. She wanted to get it over with. She watched carefully for the reaction on her daughters' faces. They nodded, mouths full.

'Yeah, Dad told us in the car,' Ava affirmed. *Okay*, thought Jennifer. John was obviously taking the lead in this with the kids. She would have to make sure that any future communication about the situation came from both parents together. But for now everything was under control.

For the next hour or so the four laughed and joked as the girls conveyed stories from their trip. The adults listened with incredulity to a story about their history teacher's indulgence in cheap red wine and an accidental tumble down the stairs of the hotel. Jennifer teasingly explained the saying 'What happens in Vegas stays in Vegas' to the two, who concluded that this couldn't possibly apply to teachers.

As Jennifer emptied the last of the wine into her and John's glasses, the twins decided that they were fit for nothing but the bed. They hugged and kissed their dad goodnight, and, like that, the kitchen was quiet.

'Leave the dishes,' Jennifer said. 'Let's finish our wine over in the conservatory.' It was dark out, but this was the most comfortable place in the house.

'You look really well,' John commented, half surprised. 'Were you at work?'

Jennifer *was* at work, but she had made an effort to change into something that she knew John would like this evening. It was a black fitted skirt and black silk blouse with her favourite Gucci heels. She knew that John loved her in black. She had no intention of trying to seduce him, but in the circumstances she thought a subtle undercurrent of physical attraction would do her no harm.

'Yes,' she replied. 'We are almost ready to submit the final manufacturing authorisation for the drug I was telling you about. It should be ready to go within the week. It's a huge deal for the company.' Business as usual was how she was going to play this. No more begging. Her strategy was to show him what he was missing and hope that he would see sense.

They chatted a while about their jobs and friends. Jennifer found it hard to fight the fear that her life with this man was about to end, but for now she did. She smiled and flirted a little. He seemed to respond. He was in great form now, she thought. She hoped that she was getting through to him. *Why couldn't the time they shared always be like this?*, she wondered, with a pang of sadness now settling in her.

'I got a voicemail on my phone today from Sinead. She wants to talk to me. You wouldn't know anything about that, would you?' John asked, smiling.

Jennifer smiled back, avoiding direct eye contact, and said, 'No idea. But I know that she has been feeling down recently. She's been off work. Be sure to return the call,' she added, half wondering if she had in fact been selfish asking her friend to intervene when she should be concentrating on her recovery.

'Okay, Jen, I'd better get moving,' John said, standing up and moving towards the door. Jennifer's chest contracted with sadness, but she would not show him. She followed him to the front door and checked that he was okay to drive. He reassured her that he was. As she opened the door to let him go, they spontaneously moved closer together, their bodies almost touching.

Jennifer looked up at her husband. He moved his face towards hers … their lips touched. They kissed gently at first, as if to test the water, then harder and with more intent. She moved her body towards him and pressed herself against his solid frame. He was aroused. She could feel him against her thigh. Her breathing deepened as her body awakened to his provocation.

'Will we go upstairs?' he asked in a whisper. Jennifer would have run up the stairs with him in a heartbeat, but she collected herself and her thoughts. Her intention was to win him back by making him see what he was losing. If she made herself available to him now, there would be less incentive for him to work on the relationship. He would be able to happily have it both ways.

'Maybe next time. Let's see how this goes for us first,' she said. He accepted that and pulled away from her. 'Will you call back soon to see the girls? We should probably arrange something more concrete,' Jennifer added. He agreed and said goodnight.

Jennifer retreated to the kitchen and faced into the washing-up. She was delighted with how the evening had gone. She refused to relive the trauma of the break-up now. She would solely focus on the potential reunion. *One step at a time*, she reminded herself. The more she reflected on John's sudden decision to leave, the more she believed that she must have played a significant role in the break-up of the marriage. She had not realised how difficult she must have been to live with. John must have been under considerable pressure to feel forced to walk out on his home and kids. If she could convince him that she was still the same girl he had married all those years ago then surely he would come back. It was that thought that would keep her going now, one day at a time.

The following day dragged painfully. With the best of intentions Jennifer dipped at moments – sometimes in anger, sometimes in fear for her future, intermittently in absolute heartache. Through all of it she kept her head up and her lipstick in perfect place. In the moments when she found it difficult to concentrate and focus, she would say to herself, 'Just do it!'

She had read a book a couple of years earlier called *The 5 Second Rule* by an American lady called Mel Robbins. Her story was one of true survival through sheer grit and determination. The advice in the book was simple. You don't have to feel like doing something: you just have to do it. Stop procrastinating. When you are faced with a task that you don't feel like doing, be it getting out of bed or writing a report, simply count backwards from five and on one, *move*. Don't think about it, just do it. Jennifer had used the advice very successfully when she was recovering from her depression. It was so simple. No heavy psychology. She relied on Mel today and was grateful for her.

A phone call from Sinead late in the afternoon was welcomed. She had surely been speaking to John by now and would have news. One way or another Jennifer knew she wouldn't last long in this limbo. Whatever Sinead had to say, it would move the situation along one way or another.

'Hey lady, how are you?' Jennifer asked, conscious that Sinead's mood had not been great of late, although the fact that she had voluntarily made a phone call was a good sign.

'Hi, Jen. I'm good, thanks,' Sinead replied. 'So, I was chatting to John. I thought you might be anxious to know how it went.'

'No shit, Sinead,' Jennifer replied, in an attempt to move the conversation on.

'Well, he pretty much repeated everything he had said to you, as if it was rehearsed, to be honest, so I pushed him a bit more. He is categorically denying the presence of another woman. He swore that there was no way he would do that. So, I guess it's up to you whether you trust his word on that. I asked if there was any chance of a reconciliation. He didn't say no. He said that he believes that you both still love each other and that you would stay together if you could, but it is an impossible relationship. He didn't blame you specifically, but he did say that your issues with his family had taken a toll on your relationship and that there was no point being in marriage if you were going to be arguing most days.'

'Jesus Christ, Sinead. He is impossible to get through to and so aggressive when his back is against the wall.' Jennifer's frustration was seeping through now. 'The man is never wrong. Never. And if you challenge him or you have any grievance whatsoever that could implicate him as being at fault, he just denies everything and turns the whole thing on you. I literally have never met a person like that in my life. I don't know how to handle it. I don't even know how to explain it. It is frustrating and so unfair. Yet he can't or won't see it. He will not accept that there is any flaw in him.' Jennifer was weary at this point. 'Did he rule out couples therapy or some sort of intervention?' she asked, calming down and trying to find solutions.

'He didn't rule it out,' Sinead said. 'My advice to you is to take things slowly, Jen. Don't jump back into bed with him – actually or metaphorically. You are in love and will do anything to save your marriage, I can see that. Give him a few weeks to commit to trying again, but then – and this is important, Jennifer – if he won't commit to a real roadmap for getting back together, don't let him string you along. Either you are married, or you are separated. If you are separated, then you need to put boundaries around him, with your home and your time and attention. If you are not getting back together, then you need to move on.'

Sinead's words were harsh, but Jennifer knew enough about survival at this stage of her life to know that she was getting good advice. She thanked her friend sincerely for her mediation. She knew it could not have been easy for her. 'Love you babe,' she said.

'You've got this, Jen,' and Sinead signed off.

Chapter 20

The following few days in Jennifer's life consisted of an endless loop of relaxation exercises, counting backwards from five, some tears and the occasional panic. She felt as though her mind was doing laps of an imaginary car park searching for somewhere to settle. One minute she was efficient and in control. Five minutes later she was sobbing. The more she felt control slip from her grasp, the more it slipped.

During all of this, John had been in regular contact by text, checking in on her and the girls every day. She encouraged the communication, but it stung hard every time he signed off. She knew that she would have to be patient if she wanted this separation to end. She reminded herself to take one minute at a time, as Ruth had insisted. Jennifer knew that she was anything but patient at the best of times. Waiting around for her husband to change his mind about leaving her was near impossible for her. She became exasperated with every day that passed like the proverbial child in the back seat of a car on a long journey.

Friday brought with it valuable distraction. It was the EMA submission date for the market authorisation. The laboratory technicians had organised a meal and drinks as a sort of celebration after work. In typical Irish fashion they were celebrating before they had ever been awarded the authorisation, Jennifer smirked as she accepted the invitation. She really had no choice. In the middle of a busy, jovial restaurant with friends and colleagues was the last place Jennifer wanted to be these days, but she submitted nonetheless. After all, she was integral to the success of this application, and she knew it would be good for her soul to surround herself with joy and gratitude for a little while.

Ruth parked herself beside Jennifer at the dinner table and ensured that the conversation flowed. She could see that Jennifer was struggling to participate at times. Over the past week, Ruth had made a deliberate effort to rescue her friend from her melancholy. She regularly changed the subject if Jennifer descended into a state of dejection. 'Don't feed it,' she would say. 'Take it one step at a time. Don't wallow and don't anticipate.' Tonight, she was keeping a close eye on Jennifer to make sure that she was engaged in some distraction, possibly even having fun.

Sean and Kate had starting drinking early in the evening, and they were doing a very poor job of hiding their secret affair, which Jennifer had in fact uncovered ages ago. Their body language in the office had been too obvious to miss; Jennifer smiled as she recalled. Of course, she never mentioned it to anyone, especially to Ruth, who would not have been able to resist teasing them.

Jennifer was glad that she had agreed to spend the evening with the team at BioWestPharma. Despite her internal agony, she was delighted to see them relax and bask in their achievement. She was now very fond of her colleagues. She didn't care how much of a cliché it was. To Jennifer, these people felt like the family she never had here in Mayo. Her thoughts drifted to her own little family, and her heart hurt. As she felt her mood ebb, she turned to Ruth and explained that her bed was calling. She knew that she had done well to last as long as she had. By now it was 10 p.m. Jennifer thanked her friend for making the night so enjoyable.

Ruth didn't object when Jennifer hugged her goodnight. 'Call me over the weekend – any time, okay, babe?' Ruth said as she walked her friend to the door 'You are a Trojan of a woman, Jen, you know that?'

'See you Monday,' Jennifer said.

A cool breeze met her face when she stepped outside the restaurant door. She took her Audrey Hepburn scarf, as Alannah jokingly called it and, in a needlessly exaggerated swoop, wrapped it around her head and face. As she did, she felt the back of her right hand brush against something – a person. *Oh no*, she thought, as she realised that she had accidentally given someone a swipe across the face. She immediately swung around to offer a heartfelt apology when she saw the fabulous grin of Charles Roche before her.

'Assaulted before I even get inside the door,' he laughed.

'Charles!' she said and launched to hug and kiss him. His face brought great memories. She hadn't seen him since she took the job at BioWestPharma. She had wanted to send a thank-you note or leave a message on his phone thanking him for the part he played in her appointment, but the lawyer in her told her not to leave any evidence that might incriminate him in favouritism. She realised now how stupid that was. 'It's so great to see you,' she said.

'Likewise,' he replied. 'How have you been? I hear that you are playing a blinder in your new role, young Jennifer, just as I suspected you would. And here we all are, celebrating the achievements.'

Jennifer brushed off the compliment, feeling slightly mortified when she remembered that she had once believed he might someday want to collect on that favour.

'Are you leaving?' Charles said.

Jennifer nodded, tucking herself back into her scarf, more elegantly this time. There was no way that Jennifer could delve into the reason why she was leaving. It wasn't the time or place. 'Prior commitments with the mini-mes,' she said instinctively. Children seemed to be a default excuse for getting out of any situation.

'Such a pity,' he said. 'Are you sure you don't have time for a quick drink?'

Jennifer shook her head. 'Not tonight, thank you all the same,' she said. Charles reached for her and kissed her a second time, and then, as quickly as he appeared, he vanished in the door of the restaurant – *No doubt to flirt with the very next sparkly thing*, Jennifer thought with a smile and made her way towards her car.

On her journey back to Castlebar she was filled with pride in her colleagues at BioWestPharma, and herself, and temporarily cheered up by the lovely, unexpected reunion with Charles, but the heartache that she could not share it with John was overwhelming. She wished that she was going home to him tonight into his warm arms. She would apologise for all the times she started rows and vow not to do it again. If she got one more chance, she would make sure there was not a minute's turmoil between them again.

Tears flowed as she drove, the thought of losing him never far from her mind, until she realised that she was literally minutes from his flat. Perhaps she could call. She could say that she was excited to tell him about the EMA submission and she was passing the door. Maybe he would invite her in. A quick hello and a chance of another enjoyable encounter would be good for the cause, she thought. She dreaded the image of seeing him in his new 'home'. It nauseated her, but a brief cost–benefit analysis suggested that the potential gains to be made in calling to see him would outweigh the momentary pain.

Pulling her car to a stop a short walk from his apartment building, she touched up her make-up in the rear-view mirror and dabbed her Chanel behind her ears. She was nervous about how he would receive her, but she was willing to take the chance. John's Mazda was there; he was inside. As she reached for her purse and turned off the car lights, a black Honda pulled in close to the door of the building. She would wait until the occupants went inside. She wasn't overly conscious of being seen by the locals, but at this moment she just wanted her privacy.

Two figures emerged from the car and embraced as they walked towards the door. A young blonde girl in her twenties and a man. Jennifer watched their body language momentarily, admittedly envious as they stopped to kiss. She looked again. Then she looked some more. The man was John.

Her eyes never left them as they disappeared inside the building. A wave of dizziness overtook her senses for a couple of seconds, and then it cleared. In what must have seemed to a random onlooker a grotesque act of insanity, Jennifer started laughing. Out loud. Followed by a scream of 'You idiot! You stupid fucking naive idiot!' She did not cry now. She was too angry – but not with him. With herself.

Could it have been any more obvious?, she thought. She recalled the lies he had told, the lies she had bought. Eighteen years of lies, she realised now. She thought of the pair of them in the flat, laughing at her, stupid naive Jennifer, poor mental Jennifer. She recalled how he had allowed her to believe there was a chance they would get back together, all the while sleeping with some – Jennifer paused – *child*, who was probably also being lied to.

Despite her fury, Jennifer knew that there was nothing to be gained from confronting him tonight. She believed now for the first time in her life that her husband was a compulsive liar. She would never believe a word out of his mouth again. And she wouldn't give this bitch the satisfaction of thinking she was worth the energy. Instead, she decided to do something that she had never done in her life.

'Hello, Castlebar Garda Station. What can I do for you?'

'Hi. My name is Jennifer Burke. I'm here at Eldergrove Terrace. I'm really sorry to bother you, but I've accidentally tipped my car off a parked car. I have been waiting ages for the owner, but no one has returned to it. Is there any way you could contact them? Or maybe give me their name and I will phone them myself? I'm really upset. I'm so sorry. My kids are at home on their own.' She explained it all to the guard with theatrical precision.

'Do you have a reg for me there?' he asked.

'Thanks a million. It's a black Honda Accord,' Jennifer responded, and read out the registration.

'That's grand, Ms. Burke,' the guard replied. 'The car is registered to a Sandy Gallagher, Malahide, Co. Dublin. I'll give you the mobile number that's registered for her. If you can't reach her, let me know. She'll be on to us anyway when she thinks it was a hit and run, don't worry.'

Jennifer thanked him sincerely and hung up. She could not believe that she had just gotten away with that, and momentarily questioned the data-protection policy of the Gardaí. Then she grinned to herself. *Right, Sandy Gallagher, there's no way someone your age has resisted the lure of social media.* Her entire body was trembling as she typed the girl's name into her smartphone. It took her a matter of minutes to find her Facebook page: Sandy Gallagher, final-year student at University College Dublin, studying a degree in physiotherapy, currently on work placement.

Jennifer stopped in her tracks as it dawned on her. She was his intern. For a second, she thought she would throw up. Her husband was having an affair with some young one who was on work placement with him. It was unethical beyond words. Worse, it was *her* husband who was having the midlife crisis of the century, she thought, her head reeling.

She wanted to call Ruth. But she would be drunk. Sinead would be in bed. She was on her own with this until morning. *Okay*, she thought, *breathe in and breathe out. No one is dead. The kids are safe.* There was nothing that could be done tonight that would fix or change anything. She would go home and remain calm.

As she drove the short distance to her house, the reality of the situation trickled through the protective shell of anger she had created around her, and her heart grew more inflamed. It felt swollen and painful like it might rip through its pericardial sac and bleed all over her lungs. The pain grew more intense as she fumbled the keys and rushed inside. She wanted to cry now. The girls were in bed, but she knew that if she let the first tear flow what would follow would not be a few quiet sobs. She would bawl, and she could not let the girls witness it.

She climbed the stairs and locked the bathroom door, hardly able to suppress her anguish. Turning on both taps fully, she filled the bath and quickly climbed in. And there she bawled, muffled by the flowing water. She cried in wails. Her body had never before experienced such agony. It did not even compare to the ache she suffered the night he left her. This was unnatural pain. She cried out for her lost love. He was *her* husband, and he was gone. She cried until she could hardly breathe through her swollen face. In the end, she didn't know if she was sitting in bath water or her own tears. Then the inside of her body was empty, and there were no more tears. She was worn out.

Sleep happened by default. There was nothing left in her to keep her awake. As she drifted off, she knew that she would have to confront him. Just once. She didn't know how. All she knew for sure was that she would not listen to one more lie. She wondered if there was even any point in confronting him. She was painfully aware of how every confrontation with this man had ended for her in the past. But yes: she would confront him one last time. She would not entertain his excuses, his accusations, his aggression. She would say her piece, and she would leave. But where? There was no way that she was going back to the Playboy Mansion again, that was for sure.

As she closed her eyes, she resigned to call him tomorrow and ask for an evening meeting on neutral ground and in public. That would deter his temper, and she would only have to contend with his lies. She would give him no warning that she knew. No warning. She could play him at his own game if she tried, and from now on she would.

Chapter 21

At a café in Castlebar the following morning, Ruth's head was close to combustion as Jennifer revealed the events of the night before. In fact, Ruth would have gone for John's throat had he been in front of her right now.

'I'll fucking kill him,' she barked, her passion genuine, continuing, 'I'm glad you know, Jen. Can you imagine how much more he would have strung you along? What a fucking coward. Any half decent man would have admitted to being with someone else once he made the decision to leave the marriage.' Her disgust with John Burke was oozing from her.

'I wouldn't be surprised if he was stringing both of us along,' Jennifer replied, her face pale and lifeless. 'You can be sure he hasn't admitted to her ladyship that I'm oblivious to her existence, or that I am sitting at home waiting for him to change his mind about the separation. He is playing both of us, Ruth, feeding his swollen ego the whole time.'

'So, what will you do now? How are you going to play this?' Ruth said, willing and able to participate.

'I've arranged to meet him after work in O'Flaherty's,' Jennifer replied. 'We had a drink there last week, and it was nice. We got on well. He won't suspect an ambush. I'll put the facts to him and back it up with evidence. I won't tolerate the drama that he will throw at me as a decoy. I'll handle it the same way I have done in court my entire adult life. Granted, my track record at managing him in similar situations at home over the years has been a spectacular failure, but the stakes have changed, and we are playing by his rules now.'

Jennifer was surprised at how calm and unruffled she felt as the day wore on. She prayed that her resolve would endure until evening. She wandered around the shops, working her way through a shopping list that the girls had given. Some brand of training shoes for Ava and a pair of high-waist Adidas leggings for Alannah. Jennifer had initially protested at being asked to do this. She claimed that sports shops were an alien planet to her, and she always felt like the young lycra-clad shop attendants body-scanned her from her heels upward as though she had wandered in the wrong door.

The girls were having none of it this morning as they made fun of her, describing how small she looked like in trainers and joking that she had a 'funny run'. She had laughed and just gave in. After all, the princesses, as she often called them, were far too busy for town today: they were at an all-weekend birthday party. So, in her four-inch L. K. Bennetts, Jennifer faced into the sports shop. It was a distraction if nothing else and temporarily took her mind off the purgative task ahead.

As the 6 p.m. appointment with John approached, Jennifer began to feel nervous, but she remained focused. She arrived at the hotel a few minutes early. She would have a glass of wine, just a few sips to settle the nerves. She rehearsed her words in her head – at least the initial lines. There was no way of predicting how John would react to it. The only thing she knew for certain was that it would not be 'Yes, I was having an affair. I did lie to you, and I am very sorry.' Predicting that in itself was helpful, she accepted.

She watched him walk in the door. He looked great. It was no wonder the young one fell for him, she thought. That and the glowing report that would go back to her placement supervisor of course. Jennifer's cynicism was alive and well, she was glad to see.

John smiled at her, saw that she had a drink and went to get one too.

'Hi, how are you?' he asked when he sat down. 'How are the girls getting on at the party? Are they still okay to come with me after school on Monday?'

Jennifer smiled and nodded. She pushed away her glass and waited for John to put away his damn phone. Then she spoke. 'Thanks for coming. There is something I want to ask you,' she said. He looked at her and nodded, confident in the knowledge that whatever it was he could field it. After all, he was an expert at managing her by now.

'Are you seeing another woman? Is there another woman in your life?' Jennifer asked and waited, not diverting her stare from his face.

'Jesus, Jennifer, how many times do I have to answer the same questions? And you even sent Sinead on a mission. I've already told you that I left you because I can't live with you any longer,' he blurted, maintaining eye contact.

'I'm not asking you how you feel about me, John, or about why you walked out. I'm asking you if you are seeing another woman,' Jennifer said firmly. There would be no deflections today.

'No, Jennifer, for the tenth time. I am not seeing another woman,' he answered, a hint of condescension in his tone. He really needed to wrap up this conversation. It was making him uncomfortable.

'Sandy Gallagher?' Jennifer continued. 'Ring any bells?'

John stiffened and his eyes narrowed. He was visibly uncomfortable now. 'What about her?' he grunted, his body clenching. 'She's on placement with us from UCD.' He had no idea how much Jennifer knew or how much was speculation. Either way, he would stick to his story. It had always worked with her in the past.

Jennifer continued calmly. 'You are having an affair with her. You have been having an affair with her for quite a while. Long before you left our home. Maybe for the first time in your life you could tell the truth and stop wasting my time.'

John could feel his anxiety rising. He had no option but to fight now. He would shut her up and put an end to this. 'What the fuck are you on about now, woman? More bullshit to torment me with. The marriage is over. I don't see what your problem is,' he retorted.

'Let me make this clearer for you, John,' Jennifer responded. 'I am not asking you whether the marriage is over. I am asking you whether or not you are sleeping with this woman.'

'And I said no. Now, are we done? I'm busy,' he said, getting ready to leave.

But there would be no escape today, Jennifer had decided. 'John, I called to your flat last night. I wanted to let you know that our submission had gone to Amsterdam. I saw you with her,' Jennifer said.

His face drained the same way it did the night Jennifer discovered he had not come home. 'It was a once-off. Just last night. It's no big deal,' he answered, the cogs in the lie machine taking up speed. 'I *am* single, by the way.'

'*Single?*' The word was an emetic to Jennifer, but she stayed calm. 'John, let me tell you what I think. I think that you have been having an affair with this girl for months. Let's face it, the night you didn't come home was a red flag, sloppy even by your standards of lying,' Jennifer said. 'What's worse, you have been giving me the impression that we might get our marriage back on track all the while sleeping with your student, who I believe you are also lying to. Your behaviour is the most despicable thing I have ever experienced in my life.' She was trying hard to suppress her emotions. She could see that John was going into self-preservation mode now. She had seen it so many times before.

'My relationship with her has nothing to do with us. My marriage was over long ago. She is just ...'

He can't even finish the sentence, Jennifer thought.

'... It's just a casual thing. It's not going anywhere,' he added.

'I wonder if she knows that?' Jennifer replied. 'I'm delighted for you that your marriage was over, John. Good for you. Haven't you got it all worked out? Well, you know what? My marriage was not over. I would have appreciated being told that it was before you started fucking the students.' She could feel herself getting rattled now. 'The least you could do is apologise for the lies and the game-playing, John. It's the least you could give me,' she continued. 'I could have gotten past the casual sex. We are all human, and sex is sex, but I cannot get past the never-ending stream of lies that flows from your mouth.'

John was floored by his wife's composed approach to the situation. 'Look, I'm sorry, okay? I'm sorry that you—'

'Found out about her? Yes, I bet you are,' Jennifer said. 'Well, John, I am glad that I did. At least I know what I'm dealing with now. I know that you cannot be trusted. I can see now that you are a man with no honour and no integrity. I did not realise that before now. But it's okay. This has been a valuable lesson for me. And as for the young one, she is about to learn a valuable lesson too. On Monday morning, I intend to write to the Dean of UCD and request a copy of their Code of Conduct and Fitness to Practise Policy for their physiotherapy placements. I doubt it allows for sexual relations with placement supervisors. She will be disciplined and likely removed from the programme. Ms. Sandy Gallagher is about to be taught a lesson she will not forget.' Jennifer spoke now with steel between her teeth.

John's eyes grew darker and narrowed. With fire in his face he stamped his fist on the table in front of Jennifer. 'Don't you fucking dare,' he thundered and stared at her as though to challenge a comeback. Jennifer stared back. 'Anyway, there is no evidence. What kind of a lawyer are you?' he asked, sniggering at her. He had never in his life been backed into a corner like this, and he was frantic.

'I took photos of the two of you kissing last night,' Jennifer said. She knew this was a lie, but they were playing by John Burke's rules now. 'We all have to live with the consequences of our actions, John: you, me and the innocent bystander. Let's face it, that's what she is. I mean, don't you think fucking the intern is a bit 1990s? Surely, even with your ego you can see that you are not exactly of Bill Clinton's calibre.' She threw a fake smile at him, mocking him now. 'Your little Monica is about to be fed to the wolves.' She had not intended such viciousness, but it flowed from her now.

John stood and shoved his body towards her in an act of sheer dominance. He glared at her and through gritted teeth said, 'Don't make me play the mental-illness card, Jennifer, because I will. You want to threaten me? I will make sure the whole country knows what you are.' He never moved his gaze from her, waiting for a reaction, but she was silent. The words slapped her in the face. They were the straw that broke her. Her steel melted, and she was shaken. The blow had come out of left field. The man she knew and loved no longer existed. It was as though she watched him die in front of her eyes. A stranger now stood in his place, towering over her, fist clenched, threatening to use the stigma associated with her mental illness to destroy her.

She picked up her purse and stood. She was shaking and vulnerable now. As she pulled away to leave, she turned to him and said, 'Please come to my house next weekend. We will tell the girls together that the marriage is over. I will be initiating the judicial separation proceedings within the week. Expect to hear from my solicitor.'

She turned and walked as steadily as she could to the door, realising that she would not make it to the car. She turned and rushed to the bathroom. There, she knelt on the floor of a cubicle and vomited until her stomach was empty. Trembling and bruised, she watched the life she had known flush away.

She barely remembered making her way home that evening. The girls were still out. They were helping to paint some benches in the town park as part of a tidy towns initiative and would be dropped home later by the mother of one of their friends. For a couple of hours at least, Jennifer could work on calming her mind and resting her exhausted body.

She reached for a bottle of wine on the shelf but stopped. A power outside of her instinctively intercepted. Her gut told her that she would need strength now, more than she had ever needed before, a reserve of coping mechanisms even beyond anything she had called on in her life. She would need to be alert and on top of her game for her very survival and for her daughters.

She boiled the kettle and made a cup of tea, watching the water turn golden and then dark brown. She examined the letters ARRABAWN on the side of the carton of milk. She listened to the tap dripping on the stainless-steel sink in her kitchen. She was practising mindfulness, instinctively, as she had been taught, and she was in the now. She was in the moment.

Her moment did not last long. The clatter of heels on her hall floor stirred her from her momentary peace. She could hear the thumping of women's shoes, more than one pair, and voices. *No way*, Jennifer thought, *I do not believe this*. This was the first time that the Burke sisters had come near her since the dinner at their father's house a couple of months ago. Jennifer naively believed that they would not have the neck to come back into her house after that showdown. *Unless it is to apologise to me?* she considered for a split second.

Liz and Geraldine made their way to the kitchen with great welcome for themselves. Jennifer did not have time to prepare herself. She was stunned. Stunned, but at an end point. She knew the minute she saw them that, for her, the years of keeping the peace were over. Tonight, all bets were off.

'Hi Jennifer,' Liz said, more sheepishly than in her usual tone. 'We won't keep you long. We are hoping that we can talk to you about whatever is going on with John.'

Jennifer's heart was racing at this stage, and her entire body was clenched. She didn't want to talk about John, not tonight, and not to this pair. She looked at Liz and then at Geraldine, who, incidentally, was not making eye contact with her. 'I'm sure that if you want to talk about anything then you can talk to your brother,' she said. She was not going to gift this to them.

'Jennifer, whatever is going on, we are sure that you will be able to work it out,' Liz said. Jennifer said nothing. Then Geraldine piped up. 'Living in a flat in the town? I mean, it's embarrassing.

Dad is mortified. Can you not sort it out and get him to move back home?'

Jennifer stared at the woman. She wasn't sure for a second if she was imagining all of this. Was Geraldine, the same woman who had screamed at her not so long ago, now standing in her home instructing her to 'sort out' her marriage? Jennifer just looked at her, expressionless, and said nothing.

'What we are trying to say is, Jennifer, for the girls' sake, you could put an end to whatever this carry-on is. Surely you can work it out. Whatever is going on with that young one won't last, sure anyone can see that,' Liz said.

Jennifer almost stopped breathing. *They know about her. Oh my God, everyone knows about her.* Jennifer thought that she would faint. She said nothing and prayed that the look on her face did not give her away.

'Well,' Geraldine said. 'Do you have anything to say?'

Jennifer's blood ran from cold to boiling in what seemed like seconds. Her head was melting. All the years of being subjected to aggression and bullying and shaming erupted from the vault. Then she spoke. 'Liz, Geraldine, I understand that you are John's sisters and that you have his best interests at heart. This is the situation. My marriage is none of your business. What I do need you to know is that this is my home, and I get to decide who comes into it and who does not. So here is the deal. I would like you both to stay out of my house. I have the right to privacy, and this house is off-limits to both of you from now on. Is there anything about that that you don't understand?'

Liz gaped open-mouthed at her and Geraldine bore the same vicious look on her face that she had the night at the birthday dinner.

'Now, if you don't mind, I'm very busy. Please leave,' Jennifer said.

'You are one stuck-up bitch. Do yourself a favour and get your husband to come home. You are the talk of the place,' Geraldine said, with venom this time.

'Goodnight ladies,' Jennifer said, and walked them to the door. She closed it and did not watch them drive away. *The final chapter*, she thought, *now complete*.

Part III

Chapter 22

The waves at Coumeenole were soft today as Jennifer strolled on the sand, breathing the West Kerry air deep into her chest. There was no air on earth like it. It was as though the calm rhythmic flow of the Atlantic was being absorbed into her lungs and injected into her veins. Here, on her home turf, she found sanctuary. The Great Blasket Island, uninhabited since 1953, rose from the sea in front of her. It was otherworldly.

Jennifer loved to imagine how life must have been for the islanders, how arduous it was for them compared to the comforts that she had today. Through hardship and adversity this intimate community had thrived. They had honoured their way of life and each other by leaving a legacy that the world could remember. Looking across at the rugged land mass now, Jennifer took solace and inspiration.

Before she knew it, she felt the dark November evening descend. She would have to get back to Castlebar soon. *Just a few more minutes*, she thought. It was the girls' weekend with their father. It galled Jennifer to watch her daughters forced to carve up their weeks and traipse from one home to the other, but for now it was out of her control. Watching her daughters go through the marriage break-up was by far the hardest part of it for her. She could have borne any heartache if it spared them.

She often thought of John's behaviour, his lying and general disrespect for others, and worried that he might treat his daughters the same way. She wondered if they would be scarred from the experience of their parents' separation and feared that she would not be able to protect them. But she resigned herself to the fact that they were intelligent young women, and she hoped that they were more astute in their judgements than their mother had been. In fact, she knew that they were. They were half Burke after all.

On her walk back to her car, Jennifer resolved to leave her haven on a positive note. She reminded herself that the separation had been as amicable as marital breakdowns went. They had mediated an agreement, and both parties were abiding by the contract. Jennifer had suffered through a few speed bumps initially when John refused to stay out of 'his' house, but once she declared her right to privacy and her intention to have it enforced in the courts if necessary, he backed down and handed back his key. As a result, Jennifer's life and her home with the girls had been more peaceful than ever. There was laughter and a general sense of calm in the house.

Jennifer kept minimal contact with John. It was early in the separation when she realised that keeping up their daily conversations was too heartbreaking for her. So, for now, she was investing all her energy in building a new little family of three. By making a few changes to their lifestyle she had turned their home into a place in which the girls enjoyed spending time and felt secure. Dinner was scheduled for 7 p.m. every weekday, and all three women took turns at cooking while the other two helped or hindered, depending on whether or not Alannah was the chef. Jennifer let go the cleaner and set up a rota of chores between the three of them. She was determined that from now on each would play an active part in the family, each would take responsibility for their duties, and, ultimately, all would reap the rewards. She knew in her heart that it was her daughters who saved her from the initial despair of the break-up. They were her biggest distraction and her greatest salvation, and she thanked God for them every day.

The drive from Dingle to Castlebar was a four-hour endurance test. While she stopped in Limerick or Galway for a break and some tea, it was always difficult going back on a Sunday night. She had discovered that the time she spent alone in the car with her own head was never productive. It invariably led to rumination, regret and often anger. What used to be her solace was the only place where she still struggled with her runaway thoughts. To that end, she had made a habit of ensuring that she had a distraction on these long journeys. The radio, a favourite playlist, an audiobook or a phone call. This evening she would give Sinead a well overdue call.

Sinead had taken John's affair badly. She didn't have Jennifer's more liberal attitude to sex, and also, more importantly, she had been lied to by John and was hurt. Sinead had recently gone back to work, and Jennifer hoped that she was finally getting her life back on track. But her recovery didn't last long. After a few months, she took another period of sick leave, and this time Jennifer felt that she had grown more introverted and generally sadder.

She visited and called her as much as she could. She even called on Sinead's parents in Ballina to discuss options for helping her. She could tell that they were heartbroken to see their bright beautiful daughter in this state and that they were worried. Jennifer cursed the affliction that was clinical depression. She had grown to understand it better in recent months as part of her research at BioWestPharma, but in truth the whole syndrome was a mystery to her. She could never understand why one person responded so well to a drug and another person did not. She hoped that the work that was being done by the brilliant scientists at her company would bring some relief to the people still suffering from depression, like her friend and hundreds of other friends around the world.

Sinead answered the phone and greeted Jennifer. 'Hey, Jen, are you on the road again? How are you getting on?' she said.

'Hi there. You sound great,' Jennifer answered, determined to keep the conversation upbeat and to encourage Sinead as much as possible.

'Ah, I'm grand,' Sinead said. 'Not much news really.'

'What have you been up to since I spoke to you? Have you been out? Met anyone?' Jennifer hoped that Sinead might have made an effort to get back into circulation; however, she knew from experience that if depression gets a good enough hold on a person they are just not able.

'I haven't really been up to it Jennifer, to be honest,' Sinead replied, her tone apologetic.

'Did you make it to the therapy session this week?' Jennifer asked.

Sinead didn't respond.

'Ah, Sinead, babe, you need more help than you are getting. Whatever doctor you are seeing and whatever medication you are on, they are not working for you. Depression is a treatable condition. I refuse to accept otherwise. And the therapy with a clinical psychologist is an integral part of it. But I do understand that without the right meds you will never be able for the therapy,' Jennifer conceded and changed her tone from reproach to support. 'Will you come with me to see my doctor and therapist in Castlebar?' she asked. 'They are fantastic. The treatment I got when I was diagnosed worked perfectly for me. I mean the condition went into remission in just one year and has never relapsed, not even now that I am going through the stress of the separation. Don't get me wrong, they said that I was particularly resilient' – here Jennifer enjoyed a smidgeon of self-pride – 'but, Sinead, they were so professional and caring. I would never have survived had it not been for them.' Jennifer suddenly realised the truth of the statement.

'Thanks, babe, I'm sure you are right,' Sinead replied. 'My parents called yesterday, and they already convinced me to change doctors. I have an appointment to see their GP next week. If I don't feel any better in a couple of weeks, I promise that I will ask for a referral to whatever Marvel Superhero team you used.'

Jennifer was happy to hear the humour. She wanted her friend back so badly. She recalled all the good times she had spent with Sinead and John over the years. She had lost one best friend already, and she would do everything in her power to rescue the other from the dark place in her head.

'Great, well done,' Jennifer said. 'Sinead, I promise you that this will end, and some day very soon it will just be a memory. You will emerge stronger and happier on the other side. I promise.'

'God, I hope so,' Sinead said. 'Because I can't see two steps in front of me right now.'

'You only need to take one at a time,' Jennifer immediately answered. 'And, in truth, babe, you don't even really need to see where it leads. You just need to take it.'

The friends bid their goodbyes, and Sinead promised to call after her GP visit next week.

It was almost nine when Jennifer pulled into the car park outside John's apartment. She never went in. She couldn't bring herself to look at his new life and how quickly he had become accustomed to it. She texted Alannah and waited for the girls in the car. Maybe someday, she negotiated with herself, someday she would no longer feel the thump in her breastbone. Someday she and John would be friends again. They would meet up for drinks and chat and laugh and share stories about their lives. Just not yet.

The girls were in great form but exhausted. Their father had taken them to Galway for the day. Pizza and new jeans were on the menu. Jennifer was aching to ask whether 'Monica' was in tow, but she didn't dare. She didn't want to upset the girls by thrusting them into the middle of a very uncomfortable situation, but equally she refused to let word get back to her husband that she cared.

Sinead had heard from her mother, who had heard on the grapevine, that the young one's plans to move to Mayo after her graduation mysteriously changed, but the women's detective skills ended there, leaving Jennifer bursting with curiosity about what had become of her.

Sunday nights in the Burke household meant hot chocolate and an early bed. Another addition to the new routine. Jennifer never pried into the girls' weekend activities. She still wasn't able to deal with how quickly they had normalised the situation, at least on the outside. She noticed that they instinctively knew not to talk about it too much in front of her. They were more mature than she realised, and the fact that they had each other to talk to always gave Jennifer comfort. More than that, Jennifer believed that her daughters were protecting her by practising discretion when it came to their relationship with their father. They were amazing young women, and she was very proud of them.

A quick shower before bed and then she would sleep through till morning. The ocean air always ensured that. She looked at herself in the mirror and wondered if she was really doing her best to look after herself, her body and her skin. How the priorities in her life had changed, she thought. She ran her fingers through her hair and felt sand. It made her smile.

'West Kerry sand is better than any serum or miracle hair treatment,' she said to herself. 'No, it bloody isn't!' She laughed out loud. 'Jennifer, it's time to get a grip. You have one life. Don't waste it. And for the love of God don't let John Burke be the reason you get old, girl.' She laughed again. But she meant it. It was time to get back on the horse.

She hadn't been outside the door in a social setting apart from her workplace in months. She knew that there would be plenty of difficult days ahead, but she vowed there and then, looking at her middle-aged ass in the mirror, that it was going to be best foot forward from now on.

Chapter 23

On her computer screen the following Friday morning, Jennifer stared at her email inbox. Caroline Montgomery was mailing her. Not all staff, just her. She sat a while wondering and worrying. Jennifer remembered this woman from her job interview. She recalled admiring her authority and her classy, controlled manner, even if it was a touch intimidating. But why would Head of Operations at the Castlebar site need to contact Jennifer today? Caroline never dealt with the help directly, Jennifer thought, with a smirk.

She clicked in, half looking, half shielding her gaze. 'Hi Jennifer, can you please call to see me in my office when you get a chance? Thanks very much, Caroline.'

What the hell was wrong? What was so wrong that Caroline Montgomery needed to speak to her about it? She knew that the current manufacturer's authorisation application was behind schedule, but that was Clinical Trials' fault, not hers, and so dismissed the theory. She guessed that it had to be serious if Caroline needed a face-to-face interaction.

Jennifer hesitantly considered this woman's reputation among the staff who had the benefit of a longer tenure than herself. BioWestPharma factory-floor legend had it that in the last plant Caroline managed she had caused the Head of Production to cry and leave her job, resulting in a hefty bullying case for the company in the courts. Here in Castlebar the employees were certainly afraid of her, but Jennifer had not heard of an actual incident to date. Whatever her reputation, Jennifer was now invited to a private showing.

She called Ruth. This situation required consultation.

'Shit, Jen. Sounds scary,' Ruth said in a particularly unhelpful manner. 'Just do it. Get it over with. Tell her you are free now and just do it.'

'Okay, I'm on it,' Jennifer replied. 'How bad can it be, right? Anyway, it's going to take more than one scary woman to upset me. I have a bloody PhD in crisis management at this stage.' The pair laughed.

Jennifer made her way to the third floor of the administration building and found Ms. Montgomery's office on the west-facing corner of the building. She took a deep breath and knocked, entering on command. The room was gorgeous: dark timber and blue carpet. So, this is what those massive windows encompass, Jennifer acknowledged silently. She walked to the desk and shook hands with the woman who stood up to greet her.

Caroline was an attractive lady. Mid-fifties with shoulder-length blonde hair and a well-tailored trouser suit. More importantly, she was smiling. Jennifer knew enough not to take that as a sign of things to come, but it put her at ease nonetheless.

'Thank you for getting back to me so quickly, Jennifer,' Caroline began. 'I know that you are very busy.'

Not particularly, thought Jennifer to herself, but she appreciated the vote of confidence.

'The reason I invited you in today,' Caroline continued, 'was to let you know that the board of management commended your work at their recent meeting and wanted me to make sure that you were satisfactorily rewarded.'

'Wow, thanks a million,' Jennifer said out loud. *What the fuck?!* was actually what she was saying in her head. She managed to stifle the urge to laugh. She had certainly not seen this coming.

'I realise that your annual performance review is not until the springtime, but in the interim management would like to document their appreciation for what you have contributed to the company, in particular the West of Ireland holding. Your efficiency and professionalism have not gone unnoticed. The standard of the document submission was commended by the EMA in their award of the recent authorisation. The templates that you created for the clinical-trials and production teams on the factory floor have enhanced the efficiency of the data collection. The board of management has the utmost confidence in you and hopefully your future with the company. We would like to award you a lump-sum bonus before the end of the year and review your salary at your annual performance meeting.' Caroline sat back in her chair, crossed her legs and waited comfortably for a reaction.

'I don't know what to say,' Jennifer began, genuinely taken aback. 'I am delighted that you appreciate my work. I had no choice but to put a lot of effort and research into the job initially as it was all so new to me. I guess starting from scratch pays off sometimes. It forces you to be thorough, not complacent. I am very grateful. Please pass on my appreciation to the board.'

'They will be writing it off against tax,' Caroline smiled and winked at Jennifer. 'Take it. You deserve it.'

Jennifer laughed and nodded in agreement. 'Okay then. I will,' she said, smiling back.

'This company needs as many strong intelligent women as it can get. I hope you decide that you have a future with us,' Caroline said, with sincerity in her voice.

'I'm very happy here,' Jennifer replied, not willing to commit. After all, God knows where she would ultimately end up now that her life had taken such a dramatic turn. But for now she needed her job more than ever and intended to keep it.

Making her way back to her office on the ground floor she texted Ruth, who must have been bursting with curiosity at this stage. 'Canteen. Now.'

'Fair play to you Jen,' Ruth said, beaming at the news of Jennifer's achievement. Ruth made no secret of the fact that she thought Jennifer was a spectacular lady in every respect and so was delighted that the board had recognised it. Jennifer likewise adored Ruth, who was so classy and confident in her eyes. She admired Ruth for her celebration of life and her 'live and let live' attitude.

Jennifer had always thought herself a confident and reasonable person, but, like the sea weathering the rocks on the coast, she felt that her confidence had been eroded over time, gradually and without notice. The weathering had accelerated in recent years following her bipolar diagnosis and her failed marriage. Now she looked at Ruth as a reminder of the person she wanted to be again. 'You know, Ruth, this is what I needed to help boost my confidence,' Jennifer explained to her friend. 'I'm losing my spark. I can feel it. I used to be so self-assured. Once I believed that I was able to take on the world with my kids on my back. Now I feel worn and old.'

'You are anything but worn and old!' Ruth replied in objection. 'Jesus, Jen, you are gorgeous! And look at what happened today. You are excellent at your job. In fact, you would be excellent at any job. That's how fabulous you are.'

'The problem is that I have to believe it, Ruth. I have to *feel* it,' Jennifer replied. 'Life has been chipping away at me since I moved to Mayo. I hate to admit it, but those two bitches in John's family succeeded in their attempts to knock me off my perch. I thought they hadn't, but now I can see that the gradual chiselling worked. And the stigma associated with bipolar disorder constantly hangs over my head and will always be there despite the fact that it is clinically over. That terrifies me. John's threat demonstrated that it is still very real. My husband left me for some young one in jeans. That was the last straw. My confidence is shot, Ruth.' Jennifer's words displayed a vulnerability that she would only ever disclose to Ruth.

 Ruth looked at her friend in disbelief at first but then compassion. She knew that what Jennifer was describing was not what others were seeing when they looked at her – but that was irrelevant. Jennifer needed to regain her confidence on her own terms. Ruth believed that this was inevitable given time, but Jennifer could not see through the fog right now.

 'Why did he do it, Ruth?' Jennifer asked, looking at her friend for answers. 'The rejection is unbearable. And look what I was replaced with.'

'You want my analysis of the situation, Jen? From an outsider looking in?' Ruth asked. Jennifer nodded. 'Men need to be adored, and they need to be needed, especially men like John whose older sisters put him on a pedestal his whole life. Clearly growing up he didn't have a mother figure capable of putting a smattering of manners on him, you know, the way mother dogs pull their pups into line when they get too cocky with her?' Ruth smiled then carried on. 'Of course, I may be entirely interpreting this, Jen, but I believe that John grew up believing that he should always get the last word and that lies are as good as the truth. He has no respect for women. He has no respect for his sisters. And he has no respect for you. He has an enormous ego that needs to be fed at all costs. As long as you were feeding that ego, Jennifer, you were useful to him. This man somehow managed to find a beautiful, intelligent, charming wife. I mean, how big must his dick be to have pulled a wife like you, right? That's what the lads must be saying, right?' Ruth smiled cheekily again and continued. 'When you challenged him, you challenged his ego. When you made him feel attractive or useful, then you were good for his ego. The key point is this – and, again, this is my interpretation of the situation – the minute you stopped needing him, the problems in the marriage really amplified. Think about it. You recovered famously from your mental-health breakdown. You showed strength. You didn't need him for that. In fact, you did it in the face of his denial of the condition. Then you got a great new job. You were successful. You were less stressed. You thrived. You made new friends. You were independent. You didn't need his support the way you did when you were previously struggling. And, let's face it, Jen, he waited until you had finished the final corrections on his master's thesis to fuck off. He literally had no further use for you. But more importantly than that: you didn't need him. The ego was running out of fuel.'

Jennifer looked horrified at her friend.

Ruth continued. 'And look at what he replaced you with: a twenty-five-year-old student. I'm sure she thinks John is ever so intelligent and handsome and grow-up and clever. I'm sure she appreciates him and needs him and feeds his ego to the brim.' Ruth took a breath. 'Do you see where I am going with this, Jennifer? Men like John need to be needed in order to feel strong – not threatened by a woman who is superior to them in every way. You said it yourself. He is insecure. And, Jen, I'm not for a second suggesting that he didn't love you. I'm sure he did. He probably still does. It's just that loving you was not compatible with his ego.'

Jennifer looked at Ruth for a moment but didn't speak. Her friend had puked up the truth as she saw it about her husband even though she must have known that there was a risk of objection, even insult. Ruth's way was always honesty first. Jennifer let the comments sit for a while. They made sense to an extent. She just didn't know if they made her feel any better.

'You have a point, I guess,' she accepted but didn't engage any further.

'What you need is to get out and about again, Jen,' Ruth continued, breaking the silence. 'You need to socialise more, meet new people. You can't spend the next couple of years in that house with two teenagers or walking on your own on a beach. It's time you got off your ass. Who knows who you might meet or where you might go?'

Jennifer was not enthused by this attempt at encouragement but knew for sure that her friend meant well. She knew that she wanted to embrace life again. She did not want to wither away. She wanted to thrive. She wanted to have a full future with people and happiness and love. She wanted to live again.

'I have an idea,' Ruth said. 'I am going to a black-tie event in Westport tonight. It's a media awards thing. I'm forced to go to all these events as part of my marketing role here. Anyway, I have two tickets. I usually go on my own, run in and run out once the photos are taken, but why don't you come? Get dressed up and come with me? You might enjoy it, and who knows what will happen?'

Jennifer's first instinct was to back away. The thought of a crowd and strangers, having to make conversation and a late night were a turn off. But she knew that Ruth was right. 'Tonight is a bit short notice isn't it? For black tie, I mean,' she said, attempting an argument.

'Jennifer Burke, are you sitting in front of me and telling me that you don't have a single ball gown in your wardrobe?' Ruth asked mockingly.

They both laughed.

'I am not,' Jennifer replied and dropped her head so that her friend wouldn't see her smile.

'I'll pick you up at eight. Be gorgeous.'

Chapter 24

'Holy shit, Mom. You look gorgeous,' Ava said as Jennifer picked her steps down the stairs and into the kitchen.

'Language!' replied Jennifer and Alannah together.

In her black backless halter-neck gown, Jennifer felt gorgeous. It dropped to her toes just above her ankles, exposing her Gucci sandals. No jewellery. Jennifer never decorated herself more than she needed to. And no wedding ring. She had removed it the night she witnessed John with his new lady friend and had not looked at it since.

In the mirror she saw a version of herself that reminded her of a time when she felt carefree and secure. Tonight, in this dress, she believed that she could find that place again.

The girls made her pose for photos for their Instagram stories. Jennifer secretly hoped that their father was a follower. She tried not to care about what he thought, but she couldn't help enjoying any potential opportunity to prove that she was blissfully happy without him. After a number of selfies and cryptic shots, they heard a car horn.

'That'll be my limo,' Jennifer said, grabbing her bag and coat. The girls stared with incredulous and very jealous faces. 'It's Ruth in a taxi!' she said, laughing. 'Don't wait up. And no pay-per-view this time!'

The conference centre in Westport had been transformed into a stunning award stage and banquet hall, perfect for the night's event. The atmosphere was bustling as Ruth and Jennifer made their way into the room. The tall elegant women were anything but invisible. Ruth modelled a red strappy thirties-style vintage gown with ease, and Jennifer's refined-chic look was striking. Heads turned, and onlookers whispered.

The friends joked that people were speculating as to whether Jennifer was Ruth's latest love interest. In truth, Jennifer was just a new face in the crowd and fresh meat for a flock whose job it was to find news.

Media gurus from outside of Dublin were primarily honoured at the ceremony. Television, newspapers and a host of online platforms were celebrated. Jennifer recognised many of the faces in the crowd and revelled in the 'behind-the-scenes' gossip that Ruth offered as a running commentary to the ceremony.

She was glad that she had decided to go. She felt relaxed as though she had given herself permission to have fun. Granted, she was on her second glass of wine, which she accepted may have played a part in her contentment. She had consciously stopped drinking the week she initiated the judicial separation proceedings. She realised that if she were to succeed as a single parent and carry the burden of a potential relapse in her mental-health condition, she would need to stay as healthy as possible. To that end she had decided that her home would be a wine-free zone from then on. As a result, she rarely drank anymore. Tonight, however, was an exception, and she was genuinely enjoying herself.

As the band performed and the party began in earnest, Jennifer's attention drifted to a man standing at the bar. He was engaged in what looked like the disclosure of national-security trade secrets, Jennifer laughed, such were the captivated faces of the other men in his company. He was handsome though, and in great shape from what the tuxedo would allow her to speculate. He had caught her eye. Worse than that, he was holding her attention.

She decided to consult the compendium of 'who's who in business' sitting beside her for some basic information. *Out of general interest*, she thought. 'Hey, Ruth? You see that man standing by the bar? The grey-haired, good-looking one with his jacket on? Who is he?' Jennifer asked, feigning indifference.

'Oh no, Jennifer, no way girl, stay away from him. He's a player,' Ruth answered, her impeccable intimate knowledge of everyone in the room still impressing Jennifer. 'His name is Gabriel Vaughan. He owns the Atlantic Press Newspaper group.' Jennifer immediately recognised the name of the media company. 'He is married, but I guess you could say they have an "arrangement". He still lives with his wife, in a mansion outside Westport, but rumour has it that in exchange for a nauseatingly comfortable lifestyle she looks the other way while he acts the bachelor.'

Jennifer was intrigued. She had no idea that people lived like that. She laughed as she realised exactly how naive she really was. She glanced over at him again. Yes, there it was, a thick shiny gold wedding ring. She could certainly see why women found him attractive, even at his age, which she estimated to be late fifties. She guessed that woman of all ages would undoubtedly be drawn to him, and his money. He was in fact very handsome. About six foot tall and slim. His hair was dark grey, and his tan, which Jennifer guessed was year-round from frequent sun holidays, gave him a vibrant and youthful look.

'Jennifer, I'm watching you,' Ruth said mockingly as she caught her withdrawing her gaze from Gabriel. 'The only place you are going with him is for a ride. But, of course,' she added, with a cheeky laugh, 'If it's a ride you are after—'

Jennifer opened her eyes wide and gasped at her friend, raising her hand to cover Ruth's mouth and cut off the rest of the sentence. 'He just caught my eye, okay?' she said, blatantly caught gawking.

'Well, it's too late now, babe,' Ruth responded. 'He's on his way over. Maybe I should leave you to it.'

Jennifer turned to face her friend. 'Don't you dare move!' she instructed, her cheeks starting to blush. She prayed it wasn't noticeable.

'Ruth, darling! How are you? You look absolutely magnificent,' Gabriel said, reaching past Jennifer and planting a kiss on Ruth's cheek. Then, turning to Jennifer, he asked, 'Who is your beautiful friend?' He held out his hand as a greeting.

'I'm Jennifer Burke,' she responded for herself and accepted his handshake. After all, what woman could have an objection to being called beautiful.

'Gabriel Vaughan. Lovely to meet you. Can I buy you ladies a drink?' Gabriel asked.

'We'd love one,' Ruth answered, clearly anxious to get Jennifer on her own for a final warning about the intentions of this man. Jennifer couldn't help but smile at her friend's motherly concern.

'I'm a big girl, Ruth,' she said, before he came back from the bar with the drinks. 'Don't worry. He's just a man.'

The trio chatted comfortably for the remainder of the evening. Gabriel was extremely charismatic. He was interesting but not boastful and very knowledgeable on current affairs. He listened absorbedly to Jennifer as she conveyed stories of her work and interests, keeping the details of her failed marriage to a minimum.

She saw him glance at her ring finger, but he did not enquire. Even Ruth found herself engrossed in his conversation and enjoying his attention. He really was excellent company.

Jennifer could not help noticing his spectacular green eyes and an old scar that ran deep underneath his left cheek at an angle towards his mouth. Perhaps a childhood accident or a sports injury. He was quite beautiful in an unconventional way, and she was a sucker for a beautiful face.

Bidding their goodnights, Jennifer was happy to discover that she had now been promoted to cheek-kissing status. It had been months since a man had put a hand on her. In fact, she realised that since her teenage years she had never gone this long without some sort of sexual contact with a man. This was a new chapter of her life, she thought, and she would take it as slowly as she wanted.

As Gabriel walked out the door, both friends watched how he greeted people and interacted with them, backslapping the men and kissing their wives. He was a salesman in his DNA, Jennifer thought. It seemed to her that everyone in the room knew him. Of course they did, she thought. He was a millionaire business owner, and he was a local. In any case, Ruth's intuition was correct: he was a player all right.

In the taxi home, Jennifer was more than tipsy. She thanked Ruth for encouraging her to go out and agreed to do it more often. 'You seemed to enjoy Gabriel's company tonight, Ruth,' she added, in an attempt to draw her out on some more information.

'Sure, what's not to like?' Ruth smiled in return. 'Once you know what you are dealing with.'

'Well, he wears his wedding ring, so he isn't trying to trick anyone,' Jennifer added. 'If he has an open marriage then more power to him – to both of them. I guess it's no one else's business.'

'This is Westport, Jennifer, not Dallas,' Ruth said, in hopeless desperation at her friend's naivety, and they both laughed. She had a point. The West of Ireland scandalmonger machine must lap him up for breakfast, Jennifer thought. But she had no doubt that a man like Gabriel Vaughan was able to turn it into good fortune one way or another.

A text alert on Ruth's phone jolted the pair of them from their thoughts. Ruth searched the bottom of her bag and eventually pulled it out. She read and smiled. Jennifer grew curious. Ruth glanced at her friend and giggled in amusement. Jennifer frowned in annoyance as she waited for Ruth to divulge the source of the alleged hilarity. When Ruth's drunken laughing eventually subsided, she handed over her phone.

The sender was Gabriel Vaughan. 'Hi Ruth. Fab to see you tonight. Let's not leave it as long again. Can I ask a favour? Will you please give my number to Jennifer? If she is interested I would very much like to buy her another drink sometime. Ask her to call me. Many thanks and hope to see you soon. G.'

Ruth stared at Jennifer so as not to miss a millisecond of her initial reaction. Raising her head and looking at Ruth, Jennifer covered her mouth with her hand in an attempt to mask her giddy delight.

'Oh my God, you really fancy him, don't you?' Ruth proclaimed.

'No. I mean, I don't know. Maybe,' Jennifer replied. 'There is something really sexy about him, but he is married, and the whole world seems to recognise his face. It's a stupid idea.'

'He's not asking you to marry him, Jen, and his marriage is his responsibility not yours,' Ruth said. 'Look, babe, you know what you are dealing with here. He is not a keeper, but if it's a bit of grown-up man action you are after, legend has it that he's more than qualified!'

Ruth had a way of always saying it straight out, Jennifer mused – *in plain talk, as they would say in these parts.*

'I'm sending you his number,' Ruth continued nonchalantly. 'You can do what you like with it. I'm leaving it with you.'

Jennifer smiled but didn't answer. She knew that Ruth would implode rather than accept not knowing every follow-up detail in the saga. 'I'll think about it,' she added casually as she climbed from the taxi outside her house. 'Thanks for a fantastic evening. See you Monday.'

Leaving her sandals inside the front door, Jennifer tiptoed to the kitchen. A pint of water with electrolytes was definitely on the agenda before bed. Another pint on her bedside locker and two paracetamol for the morning. She was getting too old for this carry-on, she thought.

While she removed her make-up in the bathroom mirror, she allowed herself to bask in the events of the night. Perhaps it was time to untangle herself from the tensions and fears that were engrained in her after the separation, and to try to have fun. She admitted how great it felt to be looked at and admired and wanted again. Yes, Gabriel Vaughan was a ladies' man and a player, but did it matter? She knew that she was not at risk because she knew that she would never fall for him. Her heart was stone. But the rest of her was very much alive.

Chapter 25

Christmas was in the air on the campus of BioWestPharma when Jennifer arrived at work. A magnificent tree stood inside the front door, and lights sparkled in every foyer. Kate had surprised her with her own decorated tree in her office, and Sean had installed a 'ho ho ho' bell that sounded every time the door opened. While she was sure that his gesture would grate on her after about ten minutes, she was thrilled with the surprise.

Christmas was her favourite time of year. Since she was a child she delighted in the magic and warmth of the season, especially Christmas Eve. Her lasting childhood memory of Christmas was of a roaring fire in the hearth, an asymmetrical, scantily decorated tree that her father had no doubt 'borrowed' from a local forestry, and *Willy Wonka & the Chocolate Factory* on the television. No matter how scarce money had been in the house, the happiness she got from Christmas prevailed.

This Christmas would be different. She resigned herself not to get upset about it. John had requested to have the girls on Christmas Day, and Jennifer didn't have the heart for a battle and so had agreed. Sinead's parents had invited Jennifer for Christmas dinner. She also had the option of going home. She would decide one of the days. Not today.

'Well?' a familiar voice said when Jennifer answered her office phone. 'Have you called him yet?' It had been three days since Jennifer got Gabriel's number from Ruth, and she had not yet acted on it. She hadn't decided. Her innate, decisive, even impulsive, self had evaded her of late. One part of her brain was telling her to go for it, but another was screaming at her to self-preserve. She couldn't decide whether her defensive instinct was based on this man's reputation or a newly acquired intuition to back away from all men.

'I'm still thinking about it,' she replied truthfully.

While Ruth would have done anything to protect her friend, she found it hard to suppress her thirst for a juicy story. 'Jennifer, maybe you need it,' she said. 'Let him wine and dine you, and whatever else' – Ruth's grin was audible on the line – 'and then walk away. It can be on your terms.'

Jennifer noted how Ruth had changed her tune about Gabriel considerably since Friday night, and was amused. Jennifer was well capable of handling the likes of Gabriel Vaughan, but she wondered about his wife at home. Had she really committed to an open marriage or was this a story that he was spinning to any woman who would entertain him? And, if so, was it Jennifer's problem? Her own overanalysis was irritating her at this stage. 'Okay, you have a point,' she concluded. 'I'll call you back later.'

At lunchtime, when the office was quiet, Jennifer stared at his number on her iPhone screen. 'I can't believe I'm doing this,' she thought, and dialled. She took a deep breath to keep the nerves at bay.

'Gabriel Vaughan,' the voice on the other end said, much quicker than Jennifer had anticipated.

'Gabriel, hi, it's Jennifer Burke. We met Fri—'

She was immediately interrupted by a charming and cheerful response. 'Jennifer, how great to hear from you. How are you?' Gabriel said, clearly expecting the call. She was delighted that he remembered her with ease. For all she knew there could have been a queue of women on standby to call him this week.

'I'm well, thanks, and you?' She would wait and see how he would handle himself now that she had taken the step to make contact.

'I'm all the better for hearing your voice again,' he answered. It made her smile. She didn't care how real it was. It was lovely to hear it. 'How would you feel about having dinner and a drink with me on Friday night?' he continued.

He wasn't wasting any time, she thought. 'Why not?' she replied, suddenly comfortable with him.

'Excellent,' he said. 'Can I text you the reservation details later today?'

She agreed and told him that she was looking forward to it. Hanging up the phone, she felt a tingle of excitement run through her body. Ruth was right. She needed this.

That Friday, her taxi dropped her outside the door of an intimate, modest restaurant in Westport. She had never heard of it. She hadn't realised how busy Friday nights were in this town. Did she really want to be seen in public with someone else's husband, she wondered. Was she naive enough to believe that no one would even recognise her? Standing in the doorway of this little cavern, she decided that it was time to shed her inhibitions and embrace a potentially enjoyable evening.

A gorgeous young Eastern European host greeted her. She wouldn't mind having a taste of him, she thought, suddenly realising that her bold intentions marked the re-emergence of the mischievous Jennifer she once knew and loved. Maybe that spark of hers had not vanished after all.

'Welcome, Ms Burke. Mr Vaughan is waiting for you on the first floor,' he said.

Jennifer was taken aback. How on earth did he know her? *Let it go, Jennifer*, she thought to herself. Tonight was going to be a night for going with the flow. She handed her heavy winter coat to the handsome boy and made her way up a narrow winding staircase. The place was tiny and exquisitely decorated, and the Christmas lights made it look like a scene from a children's fairy tale.

Stepping up onto the landing she saw Gabriel at a table. He was alone. Completely alone. Turning to her host, Jennifer said, 'Wow, it's really quiet in here. Is no one else booked in?'

The young man smiled and informed her that Gabriel had, in fact, booked the entire room out for the evening. *He must have some influence in this town*, she thought.

Gabriel smiled and stood to greet her, his eyes scanning her from head to toe. She looked incredible, and she knew it, but she hadn't gone to any effort for this man. Dark-blue skinny jeans and navy stilettos paired with a cream silk blouse. *Just like any other Friday night*, she smirked to herself. No halter-neck backless number tonight.

And as soon as her long thin legs disappeared under the table he would have to make do with the conversation – for a while at least, she thought. The difficulty rating associated with getting back out of said jeans had occurred to her, but she would cross that bridge when she was undressing on it.

No longer than a cheek-peck later, a bottle of Bordeaux arrived at the table, obviously ordered prior to her arrival. He had noted what she was drinking at the awards ceremony. *Very smooth,* she thought. She was looking forward to spending the evening with this man – the conversation, the compliments, the pampering – and he didn't disappoint. His tales of life in the media industry amused Jennifer no end, especially his stories about well-known public figures that had somehow managed to stay off the front pages. His memories from his early life growing up in Connemara brought her right back to her own childhood in West Kerry.

Jennifer could feel her attraction to him grow with every minute that passed, or perhaps with every sip of wine, she smiled to herself. Yes, his charisma and beautiful face were a perfect combination for her tonight. His eyes were magnetic. She couldn't recall ever seeing such stunning green eyes before. And the shallow lines in his face spoke of maturity and experience. This man oozed confident sexuality.

Stepping out into the cold two hours and two bottles later, he turned to face her. 'Would you like to come home with me for another drink, Jennifer?' he asked, moving noticeably closer to her.

'Why, Gabriel? Would your wife make me a cup of coffee?' she teased.

He smirked and dropped his head, reversing the step he had just taken. 'Please, let me explain,' he began.

'Please, don't,' she interrupted. 'It's none of my business.'

He explained anyway. 'My wife and I have an arrangement. We live our own lives. Don't get me wrong, I love her very much, but our physical relationship ended years ago.'

Jennifer did not respond, but she could understand the needs of a man in his situation.

'I have an apartment at the Mayland Hotel,' he continued.

Jennifer laughed out loud. 'I bet you do,' she said and laughed again. 'You really are the proverbial bachelor, aren't you?'

He couldn't help laughing too, and in the absence of an overt objection, he hailed a taxi. Inside the door of his top-floor apartment, Gabriel took Jennifer's coat. As he ushered her towards the kitchen, Jennifer grabbed his hand and stopped him in his tracks. Her face told him that he could dispense with the beverage and the foreplay. His body moved towards her and pressed her firmly against the wall. His mouth was gentle as it slid from her lips to her neck, his hands on her waist as though to anchor her to the spot.

This man was sensual and gorgeous, Jennifer thought. She put her fingers through his hair, encouraging him to continue, and gasped when he hit upon whatever erogenous zone had been lurking there all these months. It sent a wave of pleasure down through her body, and she delighted in the reminder that certain parts of her were still functional. Encouraged by her reaction, he untucked her blouse and ran his hands along the skin of her back. The feel of a man's touch on her body again was invigorating.

She unbuttoned his shirt and ran her fingers through his full chest of thick grey hair. It intrigued her. She had never slept with a man of his age before. It was incredibly sexy, she thought, as she restrained herself from pressing her face against it. Maybe later.

'Bedroom?' he whispered. She nodded. Little did he know, but she would have laid in a ditch for it at that very moment. She walked in ahead of him and stepped out of her shoes. She could tell that he was amused to see how short she really was. Now he towered over her. Quickly her blouse fell to the floor, but he stopped momentarily to consider the etiquette surrounding the removal of the jeans that she appeared to be vacuum-packed into.

Jennifer laughed and said, 'Allow me.' She peeled them off as gracefully as biology would allow and climbed onto the bed. Turning to face him, she was fascinated to see that he had shed all of his clothes, shoes, and socks, in what felt like two seconds. She laughed out loud and commended him on his expertise and skill. This man knew what he was doing. She was clearly in the hands of an expert now. He laughed and agreed.

With one arm around her waist, he positioned her underneath him. The strength that men had in their arms always took her by surprise and always turned her on. 'Tell me what you want,' he whispered.

'Show me what you've got,' she giggled.

He obliged. He must have kissed every inch of her body before he climbed on her. She wanted him now. Had he stopped at that moment she would have begged for it. As his body consumed hers, she barely suppressed the moans of pleasure. He was strong and masculine, and he knew exactly what he was doing. He was in control, and she loved it. With every move his body made she felt her blood volume shunt towards her inner thighs. She recognised the sensation. Gripping his face in her hands, she whispered, 'Harder.'

'Yes, I know what you want,' he replied. He grabbed her wrists and held her firmly down while he forced himself into her, hard and fast. Within seconds, she cried out, a euphoric release of pleasure shooting down her legs and up through her belly. The ecstasy engulfed her, and it drained her. She lay there for a minute, oblivious to even him.

Gradually her breathing and the throbbing in her body slowed. The sense of relaxation was intense. She always imagined that this must be what it felt like to get high. An aftershock flushed through her, up into her face this time, and she felt her ears start to redden. An unattractive side effect, she thought, but she didn't care.

Gabriel stretched out beside her in a comparable state of ecstasy. When they eventually looked at each other, they both burst out laughing. 'Wow' was all that Gabriel could manage. 'Ditto' was the best she could do.

Chapter 26

Monday morning brought December and sunshine. The air was crisp and icy, and the brightness of the day seemed to be lifting the winter spirits of the workers who were buzzing around the BioWestPharma campus. Jennifer was still basking in the afterglow of her intimate encounter on Friday night, and the stripes of sunshine shooting through the blinds in her office and landing across the desk in front of her enhanced her already cheerful mood.

She thought of Sinead. Jennifer wished that she could donate even a fraction of the hope and happiness that she was feeling today to her friend. If Sinead could find a treatment that allowed her to take just the first few steps out of her depression, then Jennifer believed she would have the strength to get back on her feet.

It was on days like today that Jennifer especially felt the pain of her friend's depression. It was a life-robbing, soul-destroying condition. She wondered if Sinead had seen the new GP yet. She dialled Sinead's number, but there was no answer. The less contact Sinead kept with the outside world the lower her mood, Jennifer had realised. She left a short message asking her to return the call.

Hanging up the phone, Jennifer recalled how Sinead had been there for her during her mental-health collapse. She had held her hand and helped pull her back to her feet at a time when she needed her the most, and now Jennifer was determined to pay it back.

Later, on the black couches, Ruth was practically drooling as she anticipated the details of Jennifer's dalliance. 'Tell me everything! Did he live up to his reputation?' Ruth asked, eager for entertainment.

'Well, let me explain it this way,' Jennifer began. Ruth moved closer. 'Do you remember the night we all went out to celebrate the EMA authorisation, and obnoxious Phil from Finance was drunk and attempted to sell us his sexual prowess by announcing that he didn't see the point of the female orgasm?'

'Oh yes,' answered Ruth. 'Misogyny leaking from every greasy pore.'

'And do you remember I piped up, "so she'll come back for more"? Well, it turns out I was spot on.' Jennifer smiled at her friend and waited for a reaction.

'Holy shit! That good?' Ruth responded, and the women giggled at their own childishness.

'Poor Phil really didn't get it,' Ruth said, still laughing.

'I doubt poor Phil ever gets it,' Jennifer added, and the giggling continued.

'I'm delighted for you, Jen. If anyone needed a good seeing-to it was you,' Ruth said in a tone of genuine concern.

'Thanks, Ruth,' Jennifer laughed. 'Always looking out for my welfare.'

'So, you'll see him again?' Ruth inquired, moving on to more pressing matters. 'A bit of pampering at the hands of a handsome wealthy man is the best prescription you will get right now.'

'True,' agreed Jennifer. 'But maybe I'll wait until the prescription needs refilling before I go back for more. In case I overdose, you know?'

The pair tried hard to suppress another bout of giggling, but the giddiness had already consumed them. Ruth was thrilled to see her friend laugh again. She believed that the time she spent with Gabriel Vaughan would work wonders for her waning confidence – to a point. Ultimately, Ruth knew that he would eventually move on to the next sparkly thing, and she was wary of Jennifer getting in too deep.

After lunch, Jennifer checked her phone, hoping to see a call or message from Sinead, but there was no word from her. There was, however, a voicemail from Jennifer's mother. It was a request for confirmation that she would be joining them in Kerry for Christmas dinner. Up to now, Jennifer had avoided thinking about Christmas Day, placing it at the back of the cognitive queue each time the thought surfaced. Normally, she would have loved nothing more than a Christmas in Kerry, but knowing that her daughters would be so many miles away from her on Christmas Day was more than she could bear. So, half-heartedly, she settled on spending the day with Sinead and her parents. She was ever so grateful for the invitation: at least she would be with friends, and she would get to see her babies opening their presents on Christmas morning.

For the most part, Jennifer was dealing well with the terms of the separation, but there wasn't a single day that she didn't think about John or remember the life she had planned for the four of them. She was dreading Christmas but knew that the first one would be the worst. The first of everything would be the worst. Then it would get easier.

She was suddenly distracted from her gloom by a text from Gabriel. 'I can still smell you' it read. She couldn't hold back the smile that consumed her face.

'You should have bottled it when you had the chance,' she replied cheekily.

She knew that what she was doing with him right now was superficial and temporary, but in this moment it was distracting her from sadness and the stress that still lingered from the separation. She was using him as much as he was using her.

Spending time with this man was a sort of therapy in itself. Some day she hoped that she would look back with fondness on her time with him and remember that he helped her at a juncture in her life when she was striving to heal.

'I'd love to see you again. How about this weekend?' said the next message.

'Sorry. You're good, just not good enough to compete with the love of my life ...' she replied.

'???' he returned immediately.

'West Kerry.'

Her daughters would be with their father this weekend, and Jennifer had plans to escape on Friday evening. Despite this, she was very inclined towards a rerun of last Friday night. She tried to convince herself that it was just the sex that she craved, but she knew at the back of it that Gabriel's company was also captivating her. He was clever and funny and very flattering.

The evening was already dark when Jennifer pulled in the long drive to her home. She was looking forward to getting into a pair of socks and helping Ava with the chicken curry she had decided to cook. *Perhaps a fire in the sitting room and an hour of the History Channel before bed*, she thought. She was getting used to spending the nights on her own now. Sometimes she even thought that she preferred it.

Pulling up to the door, she saw John's car in the drive. She was furious. What the hell did he want? She had made it clear when he moved out that unplanned visits were off the cards, and Jennifer was adamant that he would not gain access to her home without her permission.

She valued her privacy, and it was the principle of the thing that was at stake. It was probably something stupid that could have been settled over the phone or waited until he saw her at the weekend. Why was he pushing the boundaries now? She knew that if she gave in this time it would open the door for another push, and another.

Jennifer could just picture him inside with the girls helping with the dinner, knowing that she would be unlikely to cause a scene in front of them. *How bloody annoying*, she thought. As she approached the front door, she noticed that John was sitting in his car, not inside with the girls as she had assumed.

As soon as he saw her, he got out and walked towards her. Under the light of the front porch she saw his face. He didn't look well. It was drained and inert. He didn't react when he saw her. Not a smile or a greeting. He looked like he had just been in an accident or witnessed some tragedy.

'John, what's wrong? Are you okay?' Jennifer asked, anxiety rising in her now. 'Oh my God, the girls, where are they? John, where are they?' she cried, her anxiety suddenly promoted to full-blown panic.

'They are okay. The girls are fine,' he answered, putting his arm out to stop her from running into the house to look for them.

Jennifer took a breath. Whatever else was wrong, at least it was not the worst scenario, she thought. She looked at him, her breath barely strong enough to utter the words, 'Tell me.'

Reaching out to her and holding onto both of her arms, he forced out the words. 'It's Sinead. They found her today at her home. They think it was an overdose.'

Jennifer stared at her husband, as though still waiting for an answer to her question. Any second now, John would tell her what was wrong, right? Why was he saying Sinead's name? She pulled her arms from him as though annoyed and impatient.

'Did you hear me, Jen? Baby, Sinead is gone,' John said calmly, hoping that he would be able to stem the flood of grief when it hit her.

Seconds passed.

'What? No!' Jennifer said sternly, shaking her head. 'No way. She couldn't be. There is no way she would do that.'

John moved towards his wife, putting his arms around her to console her and protect her, but she was not ready to be consoled.

She didn't want to be touched. She stepped back from him, one foot and then another until she fell backwards onto the lawn. There, on the freezing ground, she screamed her friend's name. She begged her not to go. She pleaded with God to send her back. She pleaded with John to tell her it was all a mistake. She felt like someone had ripped a hole in her belly and pulled her internal organs out onto the grass.

John eventually succeeded in getting her to stand up. He wrapped his arms around her, and she clung to him, weeping into his chest and begging him to tell her why. John's tears flowed down his cheeks and into her hair. She was shivering now in the December frost. He moved to bring her inside. The unbearable task of telling his teenage daughters awaited him yet. He would do it alone, he thought. Jennifer would not be able.

Guiding her inside the door, John sat her on the couch in the sitting room and wrapped a blanket around her shaking shoulders. 'Will you be okay here on your own for a few minutes, babe?' he asked her. 'I'm going to go and talk to the girls.'

She nodded but didn't really register what he meant. John called the girls into the kitchen and closed the door. Jennifer sat in silence, thinking about her beautiful friend. Thinking about her alone and desperate and resigned. How could she have given up? How could she have believed that this was the only way? If Jennifer could have had just one more minute with Sinead, she would have changed her mind. She knew it.

Suddenly the kitchen door opened, and the two girls ran into the sitting room. They threw themselves on their mother and cried and cried. John followed, taking Ava and then Alannah in his arms and consoling them. Nothing was said. It was too shocking for commentary. After a few minutes, John asked the girls to go and make their mother a cup of tea while he sat with her.

'I need to go and see her,' Jennifer said, making to get up and leave. 'Where is she? I will go and see her now, I think.'

John held her hand and sat her back down. 'Baby, she's in the morgue at the hospital. You won't be able to see her for a while,' he said. 'Would you like to go to the house to see her parents?'

Jennifer nodded. She realised that what Sinead's mother and father were going through tonight was worse than what she was, and it sent a dagger through her. Her amazing friend was gone, and she did not know how she would survive another minute in this world.

Chapter 27

Sinead rested finally in a plot in Ballina beside her grandparents and a sister she never knew. They would meet each other at last, Jennifer took comfort in believing. She grabbed comfort from where she could right now. In the week that followed Sinead's death there had been no questions, no answers and only throbbing pain. For now, her friends and family could see nothing more than the tranquillity in her face and the beauty of the place where she would lie.

The week of the funeral came and went. Jennifer remembered some of it. Sympathisers flooded Sinead's childhood home to offer support and prayers. Sinead's parents and older brother were almost robotic, thanking their neighbours, friends and Sinead's work colleagues for their kindness, and feeding anyone who stepped inside the door.

Jennifer watched them go through the motions. Three lives destroyed. No one had begun to process the reality of it yet. Jennifer felt helpless but kept moving. She cleaned, made sandwiches, made tea, washed cups, made more tea. She spent the week at the house, doing little more than taking up space, if she were honest. It was a haze. But she could not imagine being anywhere else.

The short December days fused into night, and sleep came spasmodically. She watched people take turns sitting by the coffin while others slept. It irritated her. Sinead wasn't going to abscond. She was going nowhere, she wanted to tell them all. It was too late to be watching her now. But here in her mother's good room was no place for Jennifer's anger.

John collected her on the Sunday night. He had spent the week at home with the girls, helping them get to school and generally making sure that they were okay and the house was functional. Jennifer could not have managed without him. He had been strong and calm and compassionate, and he had provided the support for their daughters that Jennifer was unable to give this week.

When it was time to leave, Jennifer put her arms around Sinead's mother and held her tight, telling her that she would visit more and urging her to phone if ever she wanted to talk. Mrs

O'Malley agreed. As Jennifer turned to leave, she squeezed her hand saying, 'Why did she do it, Jennifer?'

Tears welled inside Jennifer's eyelids. Finally, Mrs O'Malley had uttered the words, Jennifer thought. She knew that the response she would give next would either console a desperate mother or cut an incision deeper into her heart. 'She didn't do it,' Jennifer replied. 'She was sick. She had a brutal disease that affected how she was thinking. It affects the way a person's brain works, even really strong, really clever people like Sinead.'

She thought she saw the slightest glimmer of comfort appear on the poor woman's face, at least for now. Jennifer herself did not feel a scrap of consolation from what she had just said. She wasn't buying the 'she's at peace now' bullshit that had been thrown around all week. With every day that passed since Sinead's death a doubt was burrowing a hole in Jennifer that more could have been done to save the life of her friend.

It was late on Sunday night when Jennifer got home. The girls were in bed, and she accepted John's offer of a nightcap. It was good to sit with him again. They chatted for hours about their daughters and how proud they both were of the stunning young ladies they had become. They had all been through so much in the past nine months with the separation and now losing Sinead.

Jennifer worried that the girls might struggle to cope. She feared that they would not deal with the stress of what they had been through. Her thoughts began to spiral. She wondered if they might fall into the same disgusting hole as Sinead had.

'Ava and Alannah are not Sinead,' John said comfortingly. 'They are perfectly healthy. We will offer them both a consultation with a therapist, and we will keep an eye on them. Don't worry, babe. They are tough, and they are safe.'

His words were calming and protective. Jennifer thanked God for him right now. He had been a rock of support this week and had made sure that she had no reason to worry about the girls for a second. This was John at his best. In recent months she had all but forgotten his kind, generous nature. The memories had been buried in a rubble of lies and cheating and threats. But the old John was still there underneath it all she felt.

As the small hours arrived, Jennifer pulled out some old photos of the three friends during their UCD days.

'We all looked so young,' John said. 'You looked stunning.'

'Looked?' Jennifer asked, mockingly. 'I have news for you, John Burke!'

John smiled as he admired her in her low-waisted jeans and grunge T-shirt. They both smiled at Sinead in her Doc Martens. 'She lived in them,' Jennifer joked. 'Oh my God, look at you with your Kurt Cobain hair cut! You really thought you were hot.'

They laughed.

'You obviously thought so too,' he said.

Jennifer smiled and nodded. 'Those were simpler times,' she said. 'Little did we know …'

She couldn't continue. The tears replaced the words, and she sobbed into John's shoulder. She couldn't comprehend the paths their lives had taken in the past year.

'Come on, Jen. I'll put you to bed,' John said to the exhausted woman in front of him. He guided her up the stairs and into her room. He hoped that her body would win the battle against her head and that she would sleep.

'Will you stay another night?' Jennifer asked as he turned to leave her room. He said that he would. 'Will you stay with me? Just tonight?' she asked. She desperately did not want to turn the light off and lie there on her own. She needed the comfort of the sound of his breathing and the warmth of his body beside her tonight.

He agreed without hesitation, and they climbed in beside each other, two weary bodies offering mutual comfort. She instinctively turned to him and wrapped an arm and leg around him, tucking her head under his arm and laying it on his chest like she had done hundreds of times before.

She had nested instinctively before she remembered that she had no right to do so. He wasn't hers anymore. She thought about pulling back but could tell he was not objecting. In that instant, her tense body relaxed, and her chest untightened. It felt so good to be in his arms tonight. She didn't care about tomorrow. If losing Sinead had taught her anything it was that there might not be a tomorrow. She vowed to never forget that.

His body was warm and inviting. He smelled of John. His chest was firm, and his arms felt strong around her. He tightened his grip on her and kissed her head. He too needed comfort. He had spent the past week taking care of everyone else. He felt her move closer, her legs wrapping tighter around his thigh, her nails gently scratching his chest. Jennifer's body was making decisions for her fatigued brain now. The familiar comfort of his body pressing against hers in their bed gave her solace.

'Are you sure about this, Jen?' he asked, conscious of her vulnerable state.

'I am,' was her reply. In that moment she wanted him. It felt right. He was gentle and tender when he made love to her, their closeness reassuring each other that the pain they both felt was bearable. She felt safe with him tonight. He was the only man she had ever loved. She could not imagine going through this nightmare with anyone else.

John was up and had brought the girls to the school bus by the time Jennifer stirred. The curtains were drawn back, and the room was dark and cold. She felt peaceful in the first split second of the morning, that period of transition from sleep to consciousness, before she remembered that her friend was in the ground. The pain returned much faster than it had left her the night before. She could not stem the flow of tears that soaked her pillow. It was unbearable.

She tried to focus her thoughts. It was time to face the world and get back to normality. She would stand up and keep going like she had done so many times before. One foot in front of the other, she reminded herself. That's what she had encouraged Sinead to do, wasn't it? In that minute Jennifer wondered if her 'one foot in front of the other' mantra was a farce, a lie designed to trick unsuspecting misfortunates into surviving when in fact what they were supposed to do was lie down and die. Why should she try so hard all the time? Maybe she should just take the fucking hint and give up. Maybe not everyone was supposed to survive.

Her mind was racing now, and her head was sore. She lay back into the bed and covered herself with the sheets. She wasn't going to face the world today. She was too tired. She was due back in the office, but she couldn't face it. She would work something out, but not today.

As the hours passed, she promised herself that she would get up soon. She would have dinner ready for the girls when they came home from school. She wouldn't waste the day, but she needed to rest now. She thought about John and what had happened last night. She knew it had been impulsive but consoled herself with the fact that they had needed each other. She realised that having him back in the house might confuse the girls, and the last thing they needed was to get their hopes up that he might be coming home. Yes, she would have to arrest any hopes of his return straight away. She would have to ask him to move back out immediately.

'Good morning,' John said as he answered her call. She smiled at the sound of his voice.

'Hi. Thanks for taking care of the girls this morning. And for last night,' Jennifer said with a pang of guilt in her voice. It was his pleasure, he claimed. 'Look, I was thinking,' she continued. 'Maybe it's not a good idea for you to stay here in the house now that I am home. Please don't get me wrong. I am grateful for what you did here last week. We would never have managed without you, but I think it might be very confusing and potentially upsetting for the kids if you were to stay any longer.' For all she knew he could have been planning to leave today anyway, but she wanted to be the first in with the decision.

Jennifer had been unsure at first and nervous about giving him access to the house, nervous about letting him get close to her. But her drained body and fried brain eventually accepted his offer. Now she felt bled of energy, as though she could sleep for days and not see another living soul.

Ruth phoned Jennifer later in the morning. She had expected her back at work that day and was concerned about her. Jennifer heard the call but ignored it. She didn't want to speak to anyone, not even Ruth. She could not even take a call from her mother. Not today, she thought. She didn't have the energy.

She would message later explaining that she planned to take another day or two off work. She was just not ready to deal with her colleagues at BioWestPharma. She couldn't even face speaking to the post lady. She would have more energy tomorrow and she would be better then. There was only one person she wanted to talk to, and she was in a grave in Leigue Cemetery. She would go and visit her later and talk to her, just like she had done every day since the burial.

Chapter 28

The earth was still dark brown on Sinead's grave, and the fresh flowers strewn across it had succumbed to the frost and dehydration. Jennifer removed the evidence of decay from on top of her friend and sat on the cold boundary stone of her family plot. It had been two weeks since they put her there. Jennifer had drifted since then, retreating from society and her duties. She had not yet returned to work but had taken shelter from the world in her house, only leaving it to make her daily pilgrimage to the graveyard.

Jennifer rarely remembered the half-hour drive to Ballina. Today was different. Her phone rang, and Caroline Montgomery's name flashed in front of her. Jennifer's body froze, and her reaction was to sit it out until it stopped ringing. She would surely leave a voicemail, right? Jennifer's heart was racing by now. *Fuck, fuck, fuck*, she thought. Then she remembered the five-second rule. *Just do it*, she told herself. Her entire body was telling her to run from all human contact, but her mind knew that she had to deal with this.

'Hello,' Jennifer said, and inhaled calmly.

'Jennifer, hello, how are you?' the friendly voice on the line said. 'It's Caroline, from BioWestPharma. I'm just checking in with you to see how you are.'

Jennifer was surprised – pleasantly, nonetheless. She had spoken to Caroline a handful of times, including that lovely encounter with her in her office earlier in the year, but they were by no means friends. 'Hi Caroline. I'm okay, thanks. I mean, it's tough, but I am getting on with it.' Jennifer literally did not know what to say. How much personal information are you supposed to share in this case? *My best friend just killed herself, and the last place in the world I want to be right now is at work*, she thought to herself.

'I noticed that you aren't in today,' Caroline continued. Jennifer's heart started thumping. She knew that she hadn't turned up for work today, or any day over the past two weeks, but she did not think that she would have to answer a call from Caroline Montgomery.

'Caroline, I'm really sorry. I had intended to phone this morning, but—'

Caroline interrupted her. 'The reason I'm calling, Jennifer, is to let you know that we are here for you.' Jennifer was silent. 'I wanted to call you to tell you that. If there is anything we can do to support you right now, then just let me know. We provide a counsellor as part of the support package for all our employees. It is entirely confidential. And, Jennifer, if you need some more time off right now then just let us know. We are here for you.'

Tears filled Jennifer's eyes, and she tried to speak, but the words came out as a whisper. She was overwhelmed with gratitude. In that moment, she felt supported. No, she felt loved. 'Thank you, Caroline. That means so much to me right now. I am really grateful,' she said.

'No problem,' Caroline said, 'take care of yourself. See you soon.'

The wind was cutting as Jennifer stepped out of her car. She was able to talk out loud here in this secluded place. She could speak to her friend without the worry of being overheard and judged. For the most part. However, she had not been able to say what she needed to say to Sinead. She talked about the girls and about John, how fantastic he had been to her and the kids since …

She wasn't able to say the word 'suicide' out loud. At least not in front of Sinead. She wasn't ready. Instead, she rambled on with stories from the news, as though Sinead were in isolation somewhere and had no access to newspapers.

Despite this daily dialogue, Jennifer received little comfort. One-sided conversation had a tendency to do that, Jennifer thought, recalling the number of times John had walked out of a room when she had initiated a dialogue that he didn't want to deal with. Or perhaps the lack of relief was due to Jennifer's dogged avoidance of the core issue. She had been sidestepping the one issue that was hanging over her, weighing her down and trapping her in ever-increasing isolation.

Her mood had been slipping more with each day that passed, and she knew it. She needed to act now if she were to drag herself away from the verge of depression. She knew the symptoms. She knew they were scratching on her bedroom door every morning as she woke. So far, she had kept them at bay, but she knew that it was only a matter of time before they took hold of her, like they had done to her friend. She knew that the faceless wrath of depression would crawl in and surround her in a heavy airtight shroud and consume her. She knew that she had to fight.

Jennifer's tears flowed freely these days amid bouts of anger and despair. She had asked herself the same questions repeatedly over the past couple of weeks, but she had not asked Sinead. There were things she needed to say to her friend. She wanted answers. Did she really believe this was her only option? Had she considered the grief-infused chaos in the lives of those she had left behind?

In that moment, an inner strength surfaced in Jennifer, or perhaps a final desperation. She looked at Sinead's name on the temporary wooden post that marked her spot and spoke sternly. 'How could you have done this?' she cried, tears rolling down her cheeks. 'How could you have done this and not told me what you were thinking?'

She waited for an answer, as if one were possible.

'I can't believe you gave up without asking for help,' she continued, her anger beginning to rise now. 'For fuck's sake, Sinead, what were you thinking? How could you have done this to us? We loved you so much. We would have done anything to help you. How the fuck did you think that this was the best option? Why didn't you just hang on?' She sobbed as she ran out of tears.

There were no answers. Jennifer knew Sinead well enough to know that she would never have asked for help. She never wanted to be a bother. Jennifer agonised in the knowledge that she should have done more. She should have forced Sinead to change doctors or go to therapy. She should have kept a closer eye on her. Why didn't she do more to keep her friend alive? she asked herself.

Her head dropped into her gloved hands, and she apologised. 'I'm sorry,' she cried. 'I knew what you were going through, and I didn't do enough. I should have been with you, not out on the town gratifying myself. I knew you were unwell. I knew you needed help, and I was not there. One more phone call or visit, and I might have changed the course of events. That's all it would have taken.' The tears flowed down her neck and into her scarf. 'I'm sorry,' she sobbed.

A bitter wind drove against Jennifer, and she wrapped her scarf around her face, breathing into it to warm herself. She knew that there was no such thing as turning back time. There had been plenty of times in her past when she had so desperately wished that she could have done so, but each time she had accepted the reality of the situation. *Accept what you cannot change and all that jazz*, she mocked now. Everything that life had thrown at her had been, for the most part, out of her control, and she was able to convince herself that minimal blame lay at her feet.

This time was different. This time she believed in her heart that she had not done her best. She had a duty of care to her friend in need, and she had failed. She should carry the burden of contributory negligence at least. She asked herself if she was in fact looking for forgiveness. Would Sinead ever forgive her for taking her eye off the ball? She tried to imagine what Sinead would say to her if she could speak to her right now. Would she scold her and tell her that she had been crying out for help but that Jennifer was too busy with her posh job and her new man to notice the state she was in? Would she be angry or just disappointed?

Jennifer imagined Sinead's beautiful kind face and gentle reassuring voice and realised that Sinead would be none of those things. What Sinead would almost certainly do would be to instruct Jennifer to get up off her self-pitying ass and get her shit together. She heard her friend's voice now in the swirling wind: 'Jennifer, babe, don't lie down. Get up. Keep going. You are strong. You are the strongest person I know. One foot in front of the other. I will always walk beside you.'

A sudden calm overtook Jennifer as she sat there in the dimming light. The Sinead who she had known for more than twenty years would have been horrified to see her thrown down, lying in bed, giving up almost. Jennifer could not bear the thought of disappointing her old friend. She would prove to Sinead that she had not been wrong all those times she had called her strong. She would not let her down. She would open her curtains in the morning, irrespective of how badly she felt, and she would put one foot in front of the other.

For Sinead.

Jennifer drove home that evening with less weight strapped to her. She would shed the guilt, she promised herself. Her selfless friend would want nothing less for Jennifer than for her to live and love and thrive.

John was cooking dinner when she arrived home. She had forgotten that he would be there. She didn't mind. He had been helping around the house, getting the groceries and chauffeuring the ladies. Up to now her head had not been able to process the sudden change in living arrangements. She would get to it, she thought. She greeted the three with a smile and sat down to join them for dinner.

'I think I'll go to work tomorrow,' she said, smiling across at John. He smiled back. For the first time in a fortnight Jennifer felt a glimmer of hope that things would be okay. Things would never again be the same. But they would be okay.

Later that evening, Jennifer picked up her phone and dialled Ruth. She had not spoken to her since the funeral and had only answered a few texts. She had not spoken to anyone. She didn't want to put them through the awkwardness and the gloom of having to deal with her in her current state of misery. Moreover, she didn't want to have to commit to going anywhere or doing anything.

Here goes, she thought. *One foot ...*

'Jesus, Jennifer, I was getting very worried about you. How are you?' Ruth asked, the relief in her voice clear.

'I've been better, thanks,' Jennifer answered. 'I've been slipping a bit the past week to be honest, but I have decided to get up in the morning and go to work. I don't know what I'm going to do when I get there, but I am determined to go.'

'Oh, thank God,' Ruth said. 'That's exactly what you should do. You will do better with people around you. And you will be distracted. You are fantastic. Well done you.'

Jennifer smiled at Ruth's overkill on the encouragement front but appreciated her sincerity and her concern. It was actively doing her good to hear Ruth's voice. It was like a painkiller.

'Kate and Sean are asking for you,' Ruth continued. Jennifer remembered seeing them briefly at the funeral. She had been delighted to see them. In fact, she recalled how half the workforce of BioWestPharma had come to pay their respects to Sinead's family, but especially to her. She had not really registered it until now. She was suddenly quite overwhelmed.

'They are so sweet,' she replied. 'I will see them tomorrow. Sean has probably moved into my office already, the brat,' she laughed.

Ruth agreed. 'And Gabriel phoned me,' Ruth continued. 'He hadn't heard from you and was worried. I explained where you were. He asked me to pass on his condolences and to tell you to call him anytime if there was anything at all he could do for you.'

Each friend knew that the other was smiling on the end of the line.

'Yes, I should contact him,' Jennifer said. 'Out of basic manners if nothing else.'

'Good idea,' Ruth said. 'You can't have too many friends, Jen.'

Jennifer smiled and said, 'Okay, see you tomorrow.'

The following morning arrived abruptly when Jennifer was woken by the sound of her 6.30 a.m. alarm. She froze initially as she looked around the dark room, the thought of getting up unbearable. She knew she had to. She had promised Ruth and John and the girls. And she had promised Sinead.

She thought of Mel Robbins. She knew she had just five seconds to get out of the bed and move her body before her brain talked her out of it. She thought about Sinead and she started to count. Five, four, three, two, one, move. She threw off the duvet and put her feet on the floor.

Stand up. Walk to the bathroom. Brush your teeth. Just do it. Don't think about it. Don't think about anything except brushing your teeth, she told herself. And that's what she did. Before she realised it, she had showered and dressed in a cosy grey woollen dress and pulled on a pair of black knee-high Kurt Geiger boots. She applied a light covering of pale concealer to camouflage her drained face, nude lipstick, mascara and a generous stroke of blush. When she looked in the mirror, she saw Jennifer. Sinead would have been proud of her.

Ava and Alannah were delighted when they finally came downstairs to find that their mother had prepared the breakfast table. They were young women now – independent to a point – but Jennifer knew that they still needed her. They needed to know that she was there, gently placed around them like a security blanket to help them get to sleep every night.

After a couple of minutes' chat at the table, Ava turned to her mother and asked, 'Hey, Mom, what's happening for Christmas?'

Oh my God, Christmas, Jennifer thought to herself, a wave of anxiety crashing. She had not even considered it. Christmas Day was in one week, and she had forgotten about it. It wasn't too late, she thought. It could be salvaged. 'It's all under control,' she replied. 'Will we put the tree up tonight?'

The girls smiled. 'Only if you are up to it,' Alannah said. Her mother nodded encouragingly.

Jennifer's thoughts turned to Christmas Day. How could they celebrate? How could they eat and drink and be merry? She thought of Sinead's parents and brother. How on earth would they get through it? It would be an endurance test for all. Then she had an idea. She would call Sinead's mother.

Chapter 29

Mrs O'Malley was silent on the phone to Jennifer, her brain still not processing the basic decision-making requirements of day-to-day life. She was functional, but barely. 'To be honest, Jennifer, we were going to ignore Christmas entirely, pretend it wasn't happening,' she said eventually. 'We are just not able to have a big slap-up dinner and celebration now.'

Jennifer explained her suggestion a bit better. 'How about instead of celebrating Christmas we celebrate Sinead, her life and our memories of her. Let's celebrate the gifts she brought to our lives over the years. We could invite her friends, cousins and work colleagues, and we could give her a proper send-off. Let's do what we were not able to do a couple of weeks ago. I was thinking that Sinead would have preferred that.'

Jennifer heard the sound of quiet sobs on the line. She prayed that she hadn't made things worse for the devastated woman.

'Yes, that's a great idea,' Mrs O'Malley answered. 'Sinead would have preferred that. She wasn't one for bawling and lamenting, was she? She would have wanted us to keep going.'

Jennifer exhaled in relief and felt genuine anticipation for a day that she hoped would help so many broken people to heal.

'Then we will have it here in her childhood home, where the memories began,' Sinead's mother continued. 'It will be turkey and ham sandwiches, cake and beer. How does that sound?'

'It sounds perfect,' Jennifer replied. 'I'll bring the soundtrack.'

After Mass on Christmas morning, the Burkes travelled to Ballina laden with food and wine. Jennifer had also packed a heap of photo albums and a playlist containing a few of Sinead's favourite records from over the years. Amy Winehouse's *Back to Black* and Adele's *21* were among her favourites. John insisted on adding 'What's the Frequency, Kenneth?' by REM as a nod to their college days. The pair of them smiled as they remembered dancing to that song in Fibber Magee's at the top of O'Connell Street on more than one occasion.

Jennifer was looking forward to being among friends today, and she was grateful to be with John and the girls after all. They all needed each other right now, she thought.

Sinead's brother, his wife and their three young children had already arrived by the time the Burkes pulled in. Among the guests were a selection of Sinead's aunts and uncles as well as a few of her first cousins and their families. A handful of her friends from Ballina and close colleagues from work had also decided to spend their day with the family.

Jennifer knew most of them and was thrilled to see them. She had worried that with the day that was in it people would prefer to celebrate at home with their families. But no, like Jennifer they were determined not to let a grieving family be alone on what was sure to be the loneliest day of the year for them. It filled her with a warm happiness and with hope to see so many gathered in this house, some of whom had only met for the first time a couple of weeks ago in tragic circumstances. Yet here they were, all with one thing in common. They loved Sinead and wanted to send her off properly, the Irish way, with food and drink and music and, of course, stories.

The fire was blazing in the front room, the same room where Sinead had rested not a fortnight previously. Today the atmosphere was transformed into one filled with lively chat and reminiscing. Everyone helped themselves at the kitchen table. There was enough to feed the town. A few of the neighbours called in the evening. They too wanted to make sure that the O'Malleys were not left without company that day.

Sinead's father was a well-known farmer in the community. He loved nothing more than to be in the middle of a crowd of people, be it at the mart or the local pub on a Friday night. He was a born storyteller, and, seated by the fire, he set the tone with tales of Sinead as a child growing up in her beloved Ballina. Her heart was always in the west, he said with pride. 'She loved her native Mayo,' he continued. 'She went off to Dublin for a few years, but we knew she would come back. She would never have settled anywhere else.'

'And her faith in the Mayo senior footballers to win the Sam Maguire was boundless,' her brother said with a laugh.

'If she was here until she was ninety, she'd still be waiting for that,' her father replied and laughed, as did Jennifer. 'You can well laugh over there Ms. Thirty-Seven All Irelands,' Mr O'Malley chuckled again. 'Tell me, does it ever get boring?'

'Never,' Jennifer answered, with a proud grin. 'We cherish every single medal and look forward to the ones yet to come.'

The laughter in the room was like medicine to the small crowd that gathered there. The immense pain in their hearts was eased temporarily by the power of their closeness and shared love of a magnificent lady.

Mrs O'Malley went on to tell of how Sinead always had it in her mind to study the law ever since she was a child. 'Do you remember?' she asked her husband. 'She was always glued to *Matlock*, and later it was the *Law & Order* obsession.'

'She was a great lawyer,' one of her close colleagues added. 'Her clients adored her, and they trusted her.' Jennifer agreed. Sinead was a far better lawyer than she was. She had an amazing memory for case law while Jennifer was more of a 'wing it and hope for the best in court' type of girl.

John recalled a story of how the pair of them, Jennifer and Sinead, had been thrown out of a lecture theatre in UCD for 'disrupting the lesson'. The very self-conscious professor had believed that they were laughing at him, and he had taken serious offence. 'Remember, Jen? You had to see the Dean and write a letter of apology,' John laughed.

Sinead's parents were less amused. Clearly this was a side of their daughter they had not seen before.

'In truth, I was the one talking and giggling,' Jennifer said. 'Sinead was trying to shut me up. She was always getting into trouble because of me. But she never complained, and she never tried to change me. She was a great friend. She had my back from the very first day we met. She was the one I turned to when life got on top of me. She talked me through more than one crisis. I will miss her every day.'

She dropped her head so as not to drag down the mood of the guests with the tears that threatened. Recognising her pain, John took her hand and squeezed it. He wanted to be there for her. He wanted Jennifer to know that he too could be a friend to her in the difficult days ahead.

That Christmas Day was one that none of them ever forgot. They drank and talked into the night. A few songs broke out as the small hours approached. Eventually the remaining guests found a corner to sleep in. Jennifer and the girls made their way up to Sinead's old bedroom while John fashioned a bed out of the small couch in the kitchen. And there they slept in the knowledge that they had sent her on her way with laughter and fond memories, in good faith that tomorrow would bring less pain and more hope.

Early in the morning, the Burkes piled into John's car, having thanked Sinead's family for a fabulous Christmas Day and promised to call very soon. Jennifer noticed Sinead's mother following her to the car with a small rigid gift bag in her hand. She thought perhaps it was some leftover cake and smiled. Well, she had consumed it very enthusiastically the previous day, she thought.

'Take this,' Mrs O'Malley said. 'We found it in Sinead's flat during the week. It was in her bedroom. I thought you might like it.' Jennifer put her hand into the bag and pulled out a framed photograph of Sinead, Jennifer and John from their college days. They were sitting on one of the fountains in St Stephen's Green on a beautiful sunny day.

Jennifer remembered the day – a Saturday. Sinead had taken her brand-new Polaroid camera into town and asked a passer-by, a complete stranger, to take the photo of them. Jennifer and John had joked that the scruffy-looking man was going to do a legger with the camera. But he didn't. She couldn't believe that Sinead had kept the photo all these years. The emotion of seeing it overwhelmed her, and she covered her mouth to shield her grief from an already stricken woman.

'You were very close, all three of you. I know that,' Mrs O'Malley said. Jennifer nodded, afraid to attempt words. 'She told me how much you were trying to help her in the end. She really appreciated it. I just wanted you to know that.'

With that, Jennifer's attempt to control her tears failed, and she sobbed. Both women reached for and held onto each other for a minute. Their hearts were broken, and their lives were changed – but not over. They promised each other that they would survive for their families and for Sinead.

Later that evening, Jennifer and John sat on the conservatory couch drinking tea and relaxing before John headed back to his flat. There was a calm hopefulness in the air and little conversation between them, just an acknowledgement that they were all in a slightly better place tonight.

Despite the trauma that she had suffered to her already delicate heart, Jennifer realised that her life was still full. Her daughters were growing up to be amazing young women. They were healthy and safe. She had a great job that could comfortably sustain them. She had friends and family. Her home in Kerry would always be there for her. And she was physically and mentally well. In fact, compared to a lot of women in the world right now, Jennifer knew that she was incredibly lucky.

'I've been meaning to ask you a question,' John said. She looked at him to encourage him to continue. 'Would you like to spend New Year's Eve with me?' he asked, unsure of the reception that he would get.

'Jeez, I hadn't thought that far ahead,' Jennifer replied. 'The girls are going out to a New Year's Eve disco, I'm told. Ruth has invited me to a party in Ballina, but I am in no mood for that. What did you have in mind?'

'I'll cook dinner,' he continued. 'Nothing special. Glass of wine and a film.'

She considered it for a minute. While she was grateful for his help and his company over the past couple of weeks, she was very reluctant to agree to spend an evening alone with him, just the two of them. In fact, it made her nervous. She had been so consumed with her loss that the pain of the separation had taken a back seat. In truth, she was reluctant to put herself in a position where she could get hurt again.

She knew that she had not recovered from the break-up. She knew that she was still in love with John. She had admitted that to herself the night she invited him into her bed. Did she really want to get close to him now only to be ravaged a second time when he left next time? Then again, if she refused his offer, would she spend New Year's Eve on her own, ringing in the new year alone on her couch, sobbing over her lost love and her old friend?

Maybe a friendly meal and a drink to welcome the new year would be no harm, she thought. 'Okay,' she answered. 'That sounds grand. Can we spend it here? It will be more comfortable.'

Chapter 30

The atmosphere in the Burke house on New Year's Eve was one of warmth and anticipation, in sharp contrast to the frost and freezing fog that were descending outdoors. The girls were in giddy preparation for an over-eighteens New Year's party in a nightclub in the town. They were in fact still several months shy of their eighteenth birthdays; however, Ava had acquired an ID card from an older girl at school, and both twins had formulated a strategy to use it simultaneously. One intended to gain access by presenting it to a bouncer, then a friend on the inside would casually exit and hand it to the other twin, who would show it to a different bouncer. Jennifer laughed at the enterprise of the whole thing and joked that the girls had a lot to learn about the razor-sharp skills of bouncers.

All in all, the outfits, hair and make-up took about two hours to perfect. Jennifer wondered at the procedure. She was certain that such priming did not exist back in her day. Fake tan, layers of contouring and outfits that were bought not borrowed seemed to be the norm today. Her little girls stood in front of her as adults now.

She wondered how she would be rated by them as a mother in the years to come. She believed that she had done her best, but whether she liked to admit it or not she knew that the years of parent-bashing suffered at the hands of her in-laws had scarred her. She hated herself when she realised that she had succumbed to self-doubt at their hands. She wanted to be strong and not care about what they had thrown at her over the years, but the damage was done. All she could do now was provide a balanced and supportive hand to guide her girls on their way and hope for the best.

The doorbell announced the arrival of their father. Bearing a bottle of Malbec and two fillet steaks, he wolf-whistled the girls as they posed for photos in the kitchen. His face too portrayed that of a man wondering how his babies had grown up without his noticing.

He was in great form, Jennifer thought, joking that he would be waiting at the door with a shotgun when the girls returned home. Jennifer wondered how the girls felt about having him back home these days. Tonight, however, they were far too preoccupied with their immediate seventeen-year-old concerns – which was how it was supposed to be, Jennifer thought.

Suddenly, in a flurry of heels and handbags, the pair disappeared out the door to a waiting parent in an SUV. The adults looked at each other and laughed. Despite their years of conflict, the girls always had the effect of bringing them together.

John had expert skills when it came to cooking steak, perfectly crisp and rare at the same time. Jennifer took responsibility for the potato gratin and the greens. John poured the wine as they cooked. He offered a glass to Jennifer, and they toasted new beginnings and, of course, Sinead.

When Jennifer thought of Sinead now, she realised that she had enjoyed a sort of relief since Christmas Day. Her heart was still broken, but she felt as though the soul-destroying burden of responsibility had lifted somewhat. She may never entirely forgive herself for not doing more to save her friend, but now she could at least accept the possibility that it had been, for the most part, beyond her control.

By the time the meal was served, John was opening a second bottle of wine. Jennifer was feeling a warm fuzziness from the alcohol, that whisper of silliness that always hit her with the first glass or two. This evening had been the first time there had been wine in the house in ages, she realised. As she clinked glasses with John, she reminded herself to revert to the 'no wine in the house' rule for the new year.

Resolution number one of this evening, she thought, and smiled as she sipped. The concept of a new year had really only occurred to her for the first time now. The year about to end had been the worst in her life, but a brand-new one was laying a path in front of her. *Keep moving*, she reminded herself.

'You are lost in your own world there, Jen,' John said, disturbing her from her musings.

Jennifer smiled and asked, 'Do you have any New Year's resolutions, John? Anything you want to accomplish or try this year?'

John smiled back and lowered his head slightly in the knowledge that they both knew he had tried plenty of new things that year. 'Hopefully, it will be better than the year just gone,' he answered. Then he looked at Jennifer and said, 'Jen, I've been wanting to talk to you about something for the past few weeks, but there has never been a good time. I thought tonight might be appropriate.'

Jennifer didn't interrupt. She knew better than to anticipate. This man had a history of shocking her with unexpected statements.

He continued. 'I think that I made a big mistake leaving you and the girls.'

Jennifer stopped chewing and picked up her glass. She sipped but did not look at him. She did not answer. She refused to help him by acknowledging his words or by giving him a scaffold on which to build his case. 'The past few weeks have thrown the worst at all of us,' he added. 'And it brought us all so close together again. It made me realise that we still make a great family.'

Jennifer looked at him now. She knew that what he was saying was right. He was the one she had turned to and relied on in the face of her crisis. He had come through for her when she needed him. More importantly, she knew that she had never stopped loving him. But he had devastated her once. He had lied, and he had threatened her. The sting of that remained carved into her heart.

In the absence of a response, John continued. 'Before you say anything, I know what you are thinking,' he said. 'What I did to you was unforgivable. I know. I swear, Jennifer, if I could change it I would. I don't know what the hell I was thinking. I was so stupid. I mean, our relationship had broken down. I didn't see a future for us. I was so confused. I still love you so much. I really think that we could make a go of it if you would have me back.' Then he drew a breath and rested. He had said his bit.

Jennifer put her glass on the table and looked at him. 'What did you do?' she asked him, not moving her gaze from his. He looked at her with confusion. She repeated herself more clearly this time. 'What exactly did you do that was unforgivable? You said that what you did was unforgivable, yet I'm assuming that you are in fact looking for some sort of forgiveness. So, I'm just wondering what for.'

John appeared confused, but he attempted an answer. 'Well, for Sandy, I guess,' was the best he could do.

Jennifer's eyes opened wide with disbelief, but his response was predictable given consideration. *Of course that's what he thinks he did wrong*, she thought to herself. 'You think a fling with some bit of skirt upset me, John?' she answered defiantly. John was floored. He did not understand her reaction. 'You walked out on me, the kids and our home and left us here to get on with it – which we did, by the way. You lied to my face and to Sinead when we asked you to tell us the truth about said bit of skirt. You swore a bullshit lie on the lives of your children. You knowingly led me into believing that I had a chance at getting you back when I did not. Instead, you played me. You played both women. Zero respect. And then, and I want you to write this one down so you don't forget it, you threatened that you would "play the mental-illness card" if I continued to challenge you. So, John, you have, as usual, completely misinterpreted the source of my grievance. The bit of skirt was insignificant. She was the forgivable bit. The rest is not.'

John was stunned. However, his immediate response was classic. He launched a defence, vehemently denying Jennifer's accusations and blaming her for the situation in which they found themselves. Jennifer sat back in her chair, casually took a sip of wine, and allowed him to continue. She had been here so many times before. In the past, she would have attempted to argue, to correct him, to try to make him see logic. This time she knew that she would not. This time, she did not care whether he accepted the truth or not. His ego was no longer her problem.

'I'm sorry, Jen. For all of it,' he said eventually, looking into her eyes and pleading with her. 'I'm sorry for all of those things. You are right. I really have no explanation for what I did. I knew that I was losing you, and I couldn't bear it. I will spend the rest of my life making it up to you if you will give me a chance.'

This time Jennifer was genuinely stunned into silence. She did not need to practise restraint. She had quite literally never heard those words come out of her husband's mouth before. An apology and an offer of future redress? Could he really have changed so much since their last head-to-head? Was it possible that someone could have been rehabilitated to this extent, change their personality this much?

John carried on. 'I know that I hurt you and the girls, Jen. I realise that. But I think that we still have so much potential as a family. Is it really too late? Could you see a way for us to start again? I still love you. If you love me then surely there is a way.'

Jennifer had no answer. All she wanted a few short months ago was to hear those words from her husband. In fact, years of anxiety and pain could have been prevented had he made an effort to modify his behaviour. But perhaps it took the reality of the separation for him to see that he had to change. Perhaps he had changed.

'John, this is all too much for me to take in right now,' Jennifer replied. 'I am really happy to hear you apologise and acknowledge the hurt that you caused to all of us, but there is no way that I can deal with it tonight. I've had a couple of glasses of wine for a start. Can we maybe meet again in a few days, when I have had time to think, and have a proper chat?'

'So you are not ruling it out?' John asked.

'I'm not ruling it out.' Jennifer smiled. 'Now, how about we park that subject and let's get on with the rest of this New Year's Eve. We have the best part of this bottle of wine to get through yet.'

The pair retired to the sitting-room couch and turned on the television. They would ring in the new year to the countdown of a clock at a mammoth party at Dublin Castle. There was no more talk of a potential reunion, only a comfortable enjoyment of the moment that was in it.

On the sound of the twelve bells, John turned to his wife and kissed her. His touch was gentle at first, and then more ardent, encouraging her body to respond to his as he knew it always had before. Jennifer accepted his advances. The physical attraction she had towards him had never wavered. She allowed her body to become engulfed by him, as her mind had earlier in the evening by his declarations of love and remorse. She had no idea how she felt or what she wanted. All she knew right now, at the dawn of a new year, was that she was in complete control.

Chapter 31

Jennifer returned from the first school run of the year to an empty house. It was the first Friday of January. Back to School Day had always marked the real beginning of the new year. She had decided to take annual leave until the following Monday when she vowed that she would tear into her own new beginning. Until then, the girls would be with their father and the weekend would be hers to own.

She had thought about nothing but John's proposition since New Year's Eve, but the more she ruminated the less resolution she found. Each time she asked herself whether a future with John was still what she desired, she found herself abandoned in the exact same state of indecision as before. She had not mentioned these developments to anyone, not even to Ruth. She knew that Ruth's reaction would be biased. Jennifer was an emotional mess, heartbroken and in need of comfort and counsel. She knew she was biased and could not be trusted to think clearly. What she needed was a balanced perspective. What she needed was Sinead. Always balanced and always kind, Sinead would have known what to say.

A note and a key on the hall table caught Jennifer's attention. The note was from Ava. 'Mom, will you please run to Dad's apartment and pick up my runners? I need them for evening practice. They are under the kitchen table. We are going to the gym with him straight after school, and he won't have time to go back and get them. You're the best, Ava xxx.'

Jennifer's stomach churned. Part of her methodology for surviving the separation was to stay out of the bachelor pad. What she didn't see couldn't hurt her. And it had worked. She was hoping that she could avoid the place indefinitely. However, on reflection of the new developments in their relationship, she thought, maybe there was no need for such a reaction. Surely if she and John were thinking about getting back together then the apartment and all of its former visitors would be insignificant. Perhaps it might even be a good idea to visit the place and get some closure. Jennifer didn't give herself time to think. She grabbed the key and jumped in the car.

Her heart was thumping as she turned the key in the lock. She was dreading being in the apartment but needed to at the same time. She would get the shoes and leave. *Stick to the plan, Jennifer*, she told herself. Stepping into the hallway she remarked how small the place was in comparison to the house John had left behind. *This must have taken some getting used to*, she thought. Had he really been so unhappy to have chosen this apartment over his own beautiful home? Or was the lure of the new woman simply too hard to resist?

At first Jennifer allowed her eyes to wander. Maybe a quick tour of the premises would be no harm to put her mind at ease. If what John had said on New Year's Eve was genuine, then she had every right to be here. As her eyes scanned the small hallway, she noticed a yellow raincoat hanging on a coat hanger behind the door. A woman's jacket. Her chest tightened.

Without thinking, she shoved her hands into the pockets and pulled out two small strips of card. Cinema tickets for the Eye Cinema in Galway. *Strange*, she thought. *The girls didn't mention going to the cinema.* She looked more closely at the items in her hand. They were dated two days ago. She examined the jacket once more. It had to belong to her. It definitely didn't belong to one of her daughters. Or did it? Jennifer felt sick. Her frustration grew as she feared the possibility that she was being fed more lies.

She reminded herself to not catastrophise, to stay calm and objective. Taking a deep breath to balance herself she headed towards the kitchen and retrieved the runners. The place was neat and clean. She scanned the room quickly, opened a few cupboard doors and poked her nose in the fridge. There was nothing of note. *Okay*, she thought. *You have the shoes; now leave.*

She was almost at the front door when she re-evaluated. She would not get this chance again, she realised. She turned and headed back down the narrow hallway. She wanted to see his bedroom. She needed concrete evidence that the other woman was still hanging around, if that were the case. She wanted to see for herself one way or another.

She was uncomfortable and nervous as stepped closer to his bedroom door, but she needed confirmation of what she had just seen. She knew that taking the word of this man would be a stupid mistake. She turned into the room and looked around, her heart pounding and her breath held. At first glance she only saw evidence of John. A few garments thrown around and the bed unmade. It looked like John. Just John. There didn't appear to be anything distinctively female in the room.

She walked to the wardrobe and opened it quickly and deliberately. John's clothes. Nothing that a woman would wear. She stepped back and breathed a sigh of relief. She felt a mild pang of guilt for not trusting John but immediately reminded herself of his history and form. *Right*, she thought. *You got what you came here for, now get out.*

With a sense of relief, she made her way towards the front door, sticking her head into the bathroom on her way out. It was a small bathroom but beautifully finished. She stepped in to have a closer look at the tiles – but she didn't see them. She saw four toothbrushes on the sink and a pink razor in the shower. Four toothbrushes were one too many, and Jennifer knew that she had recently purchased two white-handled Venus razors for the girls.

She scanned the room more carefully now. *Trust your instincts*, she told herself. Her head was pounding. Then, placed carefully on the windowsill, she noticed a pair of small black-framed reading glasses. Not John's and not her daughters'. Had she seen enough? Vomit climbed into her throat. She had lots of circumstantial evidence, but no real evidence. She knew from experience that John would turn it around in a matter of seconds, forcing her to doubt herself, leaving her worse off than she was at this moment.

Clinging to Ava's runners she turned and exited the apartment, locking the door behind her. She sat in the car, gathering her thoughts. Either John was still seeing that woman, or he was not. Either the evidence that Jennifer had just seen was definitive, or it was not. Of course it was not, but it was suggestive. It was corroboratory, but not conclusive. It was enough to plant a reasonable doubt, and that was what Jennifer had been afraid of. She could have handled the definitive, but not the niggling suspicion.

She drove straight from John's apartment towards the school, trying her best to think rationally about the situation. Ava would be wondering what had taken her so long with the runners. What exactly had she witnessed? A woman's jacket, a cinema ticket, a pair of glasses, a razor and toothbrush in an apartment where two seventeen-year-old girls spend every other weekend? *Seriously,*

Jennifer? She would have been laughed out of court, and she knew it.

So she considered her options. She could ask the girls if the items belonged to them. No, she could not, she scolded herself. In doing so, she would have to explain why she had been snooping around their dad's apartment. She would never have condoned snooping through a person's private possessions and had taught her kids the same. She did not want the girls to think that she was a hypocrite.

She could always confront John: ask him straight out whether the other woman was still paying visits to the apartment. She laughed at such a notion. She already knew how that would go for her. He would lie, followed by a deflection of some description. She knew better than to put herself in that position. She concluded that, until further notice, the not-knowing would be easier. For now, she would take one step at a time. She didn't have to do anything right now except find her daughter and hand over a pair of runners.

'Hey, Mom.' A voice came from behind her as Jennifer stepped out of the car at the school gate. 'Thanks, you're the best,'

Ava said and, turning on her heel, was gone as quickly as she had appeared.

'You're welcome,' Jennifer answered, talking to herself at this stage. 'See you later.'

The dilemma weighed heavy on her that day and into the next. Since their night together on New Year's Eve, the idea of putting her family back together had been growing inside Jennifer. She admitted to herself that she had been moved by John's change of heart. She had been given a glimpse of the John she had always wanted. She fantasised about the possibility of a fresh start based on the promise of his willingness to change. It was not that long ago that she had offered the same promise herself, she realised.

Maybe John had gotten his pathetic midlife crisis out of his system and was genuinely remorseful. Would Jennifer be crazy to give him the benefit of the doubt? She thought of all the good times, the happiness and the closeness. He was such a kind man and a great father. Was the fairy tale really possible, she wondered, or was this train of thought in fact the early symptom of a brain tumour? She laughed at herself.

With every attempt Jennifer made to clear her head and focus, the memory of the yellow raincoat and the cinema tickets reinfected her mind. It was gnawing at her. It smelled off. She began to ask herself if she really wanted to spend the rest of her life with a man whom she could not trust to tell the truth, looking over her shoulder and wondering if what he was saying to her was real. Could she live like that again now that she was finally emerging from the break-up and gaining some independence and peace of mind?

Her life and the lives of the girls had been so calm and peaceful in recent months. Did she want to risk even one more row in her happy home? Apart from the broken trust, she asked herself if she could ever forgive him for his threat to 'play the mental-illness card'. She was certain that she had not forgiven him for that yet, and she knew that the infliction of that deep wound would be a huge barrier to a reconciliation. She questioned whether he had the emotional intelligence to see that.

She realised that if she was willing to give her marriage another try with the man she still loved, she would have to take a massive leap of faith in the knowledge that her children would also pay the price if she failed. Then she asked herself if she could live with losing him again. Her mind was going into meltdown. She removed her shoes and lay on the couch, turning on one of her meditation recordings. This form of relaxation had rescued her time and again during her recovery from her breakdown and in her darkest moments after John left.

Mindfulness, spiritual focusing, active awareness – she didn't care what they called it, she relied on it. She closed her eyes and drew plenty of air into her body, allowing her muscles to relax systematically and completely. With that, her mind relaxed in perfect harmony. Perfect, that was, until the doorbell rang.

'Damn,' she said out loud. 'Can a girl have five minutes?'

Stepping back into her shoes, she walked to the door, hoping that it wasn't someone expecting a warm welcome and prolonged entertainment. She opened it to see Gabriel Vaughan standing on her doorstep clutching flowers.

'Gabriel. Hi. This is a pleasant surprise,' Jennifer eventually spluttered. Surprise was an understatement.

'Jennifer. How are you?' Gabriel replied. 'I hope you don't mind my arriving unannounced like this. Ruth told me that you would be alone this weekend. I wanted to pay my respects and offer my sincere sympathy for your loss. I was very saddened to hear about your friend. I just want you to know that I am here if you need anything.'

Jennifer suddenly realised that in her shock she had left him standing on the doorstep throughout his entire speech. 'Come in, please,' she said with embarrassment. 'Thank you very much. I really appreciate that. I am sorry that I have not kept in touch with you. It was my intention to get back to you.' She took the flowers and ushered him towards the kitchen where she clumsily searched for a vase.

'Actually,' Gabriel continued, 'I have an ulterior motive for coming today. Ruth called me. She thought that you might need to get out of the house for a while. She thought that you might not object to having a distraction. I think that's how she put it.' He smiled awkwardly.

Jennifer could just imagine Ruth calling Gabriel and telling him to go rescue her. She was mortified. She would kill Ruth on Monday. 'Yes, I bet she did,' she said, laughing now.

'So, I'm taking you away for the weekend,' Gabriel interjected. 'Pack your case. Your carriage awaits.'

'What?' replied Jennifer. 'Don't be ridiculous. I can't just go away for the weekend. Where are you going anyway?'

'Yes, you can. It's a surprise,' he replied. 'If you can give me one good reason why you can't drop what you are doing and come with me right now, I will accept it.'

Jennifer opened her mouth to answer, but her brain did not keep up. She tried hard to come up with a reason to say no, but in reality she had none. There was no reason. Was John a good enough reason? she asked herself. She had made no promises to him. She had the right to take her time with an answer to his proposition. She had a right to live her life.

'This is crazy,' she laughed. 'Do I even get a hint at where you are taking me?'

'Let's just say you will recognise the place,' he smiled. 'Now, go pack an overnight bag.'

Chapter 32

Before she had processed exactly what she was doing, Jennifer had climbed into the passenger seat of Gabriel Vaughan's 8 Series BMW. She shook her head in disbelief and laughed as he shot a satisfied smile across at her. She had always had an impulsive streak – at least the Jennifer of her younger days had.

This is crazy, she thought. This behaviour might have been perfectly acceptable at one stage in her life, but for now and into the foreseeable future her days would be focused on surviving more than thriving.

Gabriel must have been reading her mind. He glanced over and said, 'Sit back and enjoy it, Jennifer. You deserve it.'

She complied, sinking back into the seat and inhaling deeply. She would try to relax and enjoy it. Maybe she needed it. In the aftermath of Sinead's funeral, Jennifer's doctor had voiced his concerns regarding the risk of her becoming overwhelmed with stress – a known trigger for her condition. Her bipolar disorder had survived the trauma of her marriage breakdown, but, in her doctor's opinion, Superwoman herself would be tested with what Jennifer had endured in recent months.

Jennifer was acutely aware of the risks of relapsing into her disorder. The thought of it terrified her. While the symptoms themselves were a distant memory, the potential for her to be pushed over the edge again was something that she would always have to manage. With that in mind, she decided that this unexpected excursion with Gabriel was exactly what the doctor would have prescribed.

None of her attempts to coax their destination from her driver's lips held sway. He wasn't budging. The route was familiar to Jennifer. 'Galway?' she guessed. 'We're going to Galway?'

'Nope' was his only reply. She smiled at him, already easing into the day. It was easy. Gabriel made it easy. His laid-back nature and witty sense of humour made every minute of the journey a pleasure. The tension lodged in her body all morning was gradually disappearing. She couldn't remember the last time she had taken an excursion like this. She had avoided holidays and weekend breaks in recent years, and it had been a few years since she was last away on her own with John.

In realising that, Jennifer suddenly was aware that she had consciously sidestepped going away with John to avoid having to endure his aggression. *Were things really that bad?*, she asked herself. With John, holidays meant stress, not relaxation – stress that was invariably dumped on her. She had learned to avoid them as a necessary manoeuvre to keep the peace with a man who had never learned how to manage stressful situations.

The sharp contrast of the calm, enjoyable atmosphere with Gabriel today had taken her off guard. It was so comfortable. She reminded herself that she didn't really know him, of course, not like his wife did. She looked over at her companion and wondered how he might manage in what John deemed a minor crisis. Getting lost in a foreign country with no internet? Or perhaps something more serious. An intruder in the house at night? Those were the tests that the Catholic Church should include on their mandatory pre-marriage course, she laughed to herself.

Another hour passed in what seemed like minutes, and Jennifer tried again. 'Limerick?' she asked.

'Nope' was the response.

Jennifer commented to her travelling companion that she had barely noticed the time passing since they had left Castlebar.

'That must be due to the magnificent company you have on your journey, Ms Burke,' Gabriel said with a smile.

'Nah, it's probably the comfort of the flash car,' she replied.

'The car? If you give me any more of that cheek, I'll be forced to sort you out when I stop this flash car,' he teased.

'Now you're just encouraging me,' she taunted. He was spot on, she thought. She loved his company. She couldn't quite put her finger on it. He made her feel attractive. No, it was more than that. He made her feel young.

When Gabriel indicated for the N21, Jennifer beamed at him. 'We're going to Kerry?!' she said with delight. 'Where, where, where?'

Gabriel laughed. 'What is it with you Kerry people? There's no place like home, Toto!'

In what seemed to Jennifer like no time at all, the BMW was pulling into the prestigious five-star Europe Hotel on the picturesque lakes of Killarney. Life certainly didn't get any better than this, she smiled to herself. Killarney was a place that Jennifer knew well. The splendour of the accommodation that Gabriel had arranged for them, however, was a real treat. 'Gabriel, this is too much,' she began.

'It most certainly is not,' he interrupted. 'It's a small token. You have been through a lot lately. Here you can have twenty-four hours of relaxation and pampering. That's all. I just wanted to do what I could for you.'

Jennifer was overwhelmed with this act of kindness. She barely knew this man. Of course, she wasn't stupid – she knew that there would be something in it for him too. There was no doubt that their last encounter had left him longing for more of the same. In truth, however, he could have gone to far less trouble to get it. Yet he hadn't. He had gone to quite a lot of trouble and expense to be with her.

Gabriel continued. 'You are booked in for a massage in half an hour,' he said. 'Then I thought we might chance the heated outdoor pool under the stars before we dine in the main hall tonight. What say you, my lady?'

'Your lady is pretty speechless right now, sir,' she replied. She stretched across to the driver's seat and kissed him on the cheek.

'Thank you.' Jennifer was more than grateful. She was turned on by his confidence this morning, knowing that she would get into his car and go with him.

The entire night was one never-ending therapy session for a woman whose body and mind had been tested to their limits in recent months. Jennifer slept through the massage. Never in her life had she fallen asleep while another human being was touching her skin. She took it as a sign. Her soul needed the rest. Perhaps it was time to shut off the constant noise of her life and reboot her existence, to switch from survival mode to a new start filled with possibility. To flourish.

Was it possible to draw that proverbial line in the sand, she wondered? Would she and John be able to work on their relationship to the point where they could embrace a future as a new couple, not a re-enactment of the old? Is that what John was suggesting when he asked her for a second chance? Six months ago, she would have taken his hand off for the offer. Now she was not so sure.

The time she spent with Gabriel had given her a taste of another life, an entirely fresh start on her own, a life filled with the promises of the world laid at her feet. The very thought of it thrilled her and terrified her too.

Over dinner, they sipped wine and looked out on the floodlights oscillating on the lake. It was surely as beautiful as anywhere on earth, Jennifer thought. She felt as content in that moment as she could remember. How could it be possible to feel so comfortable and so happy with a man she had just met? She could have sat there the entire night with him, listening to his stories and sharing hers. It brought her back to when she met John for the first time, how they instantly fell in love and planned their lives together without a worry.

In this moment with Gabriel Jennifer didn't care that he was married or that she was supposed to be contemplating a return to her husband. In this moment they were two people infatuated with each other's company, and what the morning would bring was far from her thoughts.

Her night of therapy and rehabilitation ended wrapped around Gabriel in a state of physical bliss. His body was addictive, perfectly synchronised to the needs of hers. But in what should have been a perfect moment, her unease grew. A wave of fear descended upon her as she lay on his chest and smelled his skin. She failed to fight what was happening. She was falling for him. *Shit*, she thought. *No, this can't be happening.* There was no way she was willing to take one more hit. She was done with heartache.

Jennifer woke to bright January sunlight streaming through a huge window. Gabriel was standing at it, gazing out on the magnificent MacGillycuddy's Reeks. 'How about a walk before breakfast?' he asked. 'We might not get this weather again for a while.'

Jennifer willingly complied. She laughed to herself as she realised that she had never actually said no to this man. Not once. With every breath of cold air that she inhaled into her lungs, a sense of freshness and newness filled her mind. As they walked close to the lake shore and listened to the lapping of the water, Gabriel reached down and held Jennifer's hand.

The action startled her, and for a second she did not know how to deal with it. She never held hands with anyone. She was sure that she had held her daughters' hands when they were tiny little things, but that was it. She had never thought about doing it with John, and he hadn't with her. She was very tactile with him but usually in a sexual way. Despite her initial resistance, she went with it and moved in closer to Gabriel's side. It was nice, she thought, protective. She must remember to try it again.

'I've never met anyone quite like you, Jennifer,' Gabriel said, interrupting the silence.

Jennifer smiled up at him. 'I'll take that as a compliment,' she said.

'You should. I have met a lot of women over the years. Young women, mature women, beautiful women, wealthy women, educated women. No one like you,' Gabriel said. 'You have no shield, no barriers. You are open and straight.'

Jennifer wasn't sure how to respond. She wondered for a second if his compliment was in fact pointing out her weaknesses, her naivety and trusting nature, her willingness to take people at their word. These were not assets in her eyes. 'Thank you,' she responded. 'However, I'm not sure those traits have served me well over the years.'

'They are strong qualities in a person. Trust me,' he said. 'Jennifer, how would you react if I told you that I have decided to leave my wife? We have been talking about it for a while, and we came to the decision that it is time to move on.'

Jennifer was shocked. It was the last thing she expected to hear this morning. 'I guess you both know what's best for you,' she said non-committedly.

'I was the one who suggested the separation,' Gabriel added. 'For the first time in quite a long time I felt that there was a possibility of having a life with someone else.'

Jennifer froze. Had he just said what she thought he had? She stopped walking and looked up at him.

'Don't get scared! I'm not asking you for any sort of a commitment,' he continued. 'Of course not. I'm just telling you that I am applying for a separation with a view to divorce. Jennifer, I think that you are a spectacular person, and if you are interested in seeing me again then I would be delighted. I know that we have only just met and you don't know me at all. I am just laying my cards firmly on your table.'

For a woman who was rarely stuck for something to say, Jennifer wasn't formulating thoughts very clearly at that moment.

'You are allowed say something now,' Gabriel laughed nervously.

Jennifer smiled and said, 'Okay.' Still nothing came for a minute or so. 'I'll be honest, Gabriel, I really didn't see this coming,' she began. 'I love being with you. I have enjoyed every minute of it, and this weekend was possibly the best thing that has happened to me in months.'

'Is there a "but" coming?' Gabriel asked.

'John and I are thinking about getting back together,' she replied. She needed to get it out. 'I mean, he asked me. I am supposed to be in the process of thinking about it as we speak.'

'Yet you are here with me,' Gabriel interrupted.

Jennifer didn't answer. The speaking of the words out loud stuck in her. The pair continued in silence a few more minutes. 'Well, at least we both know the state of affairs now,' Gabriel said to break the stillness of the winter morning. He squeezed Jennifer's hand a little tighter as they walked back to the hotel. She could tell that he was doing his best to lighten the mood and ensure that they enjoyed the rest of the morning.

There, in beautiful Killarney, the lovers left the unanswered question of their future relationship hanging on the icy lake's edge. It would be Jennifer's to answer, but not today. She would not hint at her feelings for him. She would keep her secret love for him to herself for now for fear it would erupt and destroy her. She knew that the task of deciding the fate of her future with both men was looming closer, and she knew that she would have to make the decision alone.

Chapter 33

January advanced with a backdrop of grey sleet and rain. The lifelessness outside the window was offset by a vibrant and busy schedule in the Burke house. With two Leaving Certificates and an upcoming EMA authorisation on the agenda in the coming months, Jennifer's headspace was full – almost.

She thought about John as she stared at the streaks of water running down the glass, about the future she had planned, about how it had disappeared from her grasp. She thought about the second chance they had been given and wondered if it was God's way of telling her something. She thought about her weekend in Killarney, about her handsome man, her knight in shining armour. She wondered if it was God's way of telling her something. She wished he would spell it out.

Listening to the rain belting against her huge conservatory window, she realised that she wasn't able to recall the sunshine of the summer just past. It had come and gone while she survived in the haze of grief and desperation left in the wake of her separation. Looking back now, she did not know how she had survived it. By taking one day at a time, she assumed. She wondered if she would ever fully recover from John's decision to leave. She had not had enough time to advance through all of the seven prescribed stages of grief for her husband before the second wave of anguish had struck. She did not know how to grieve the loss of two loves at the same time.

She remembered how, months before, she had desperately pleaded with God to help her. In her despair she had asked him to do something, anything, to bring her some peace. Angrily now she chastised him. She had found no peace, only more pain. Was this his plan for her? Trauma after trauma until she succumbed? Or could it be that the grand plan was in fact to throw her marriage into so much turmoil that the repairing of it would be the gift? Would she and John be closer now given all that they had all lived through?

All Jennifer knew was that she could not spend another day recycling her thoughts, asking herself the same questions. She knew that no matter how she tried she would never be able to predict the future. Two men had come to her and given her new hope and opportunity for the future, while only a few months ago she was alone and terrified. John offered a mended heart and stability. Gabriel offered excitement and comfort.

The longer she ruminated, however, the further away her new beginning would be, and Jennifer knew that what she needed more than anything was a new beginning. She knew that there was only one port of call, one consultation to be had, before she settled on her decision.

The exposed graveyard was unforgiving in this weather. Jennifer sat at Sinead's feet and spoke to her friend, coat buttoned up and hat pulled well around her ears. She wondered how much of Sinead's passing had contributed to the dilemma she faced today. Had it not been for Sinead, she and John would not have had the opportunity to rekindle their love. Had it not been for Sinead, Gabriel would not have turned up at the weekend and made his declaration of intent.

'You have a lot to answer for, lady,' Jennifer laughed, as she waited in vain for Sinead to offer her inspiration like she had always done since the friends had first met. 'I wish you could just tell me what to do,' Jennifer said. 'What would you say to me now? Would you tell me to go back to my true love? That he made a mistake and is worth the risk? He was all I ever wanted, Sinead, but I wanted a better version of him. Less insecure, less angry, more considerate. Do you think it could be possible for him to see that and try harder? Or will I be walking back to the same stress? Maybe I was just as stressed without him. Maybe I was the problem all along. Maybe I am the one who needs to reconsider my failings.' She was no clearer. 'More importantly, could I ever trust him again?' she continued. 'He lies. A liar is a liar for life, right? Am I being too harsh?' Then her tone softened. 'I really do still love him. He is *my* husband – no one else's. I will never love another man the way I love him. I know that for certain.'

She stood and started to gather the dead flowers from Sinead's grave. There were fresh ones too, possibly from her mother, she thought. Sinead didn't even like flowers, Jennifer thought with a smile as she continued with the housekeeping.

'And you would love Gabriel,' she said. 'He's so charming and gorgeous. He makes me feel great when I am with him.' She recalled her recent trip to Killarney, how liberating it was. It had filled her with hope and possibility for the future. There was something about the unknown that excited Jennifer. It was the same excitement she felt when she arrived in Belfield for the first time, the same excitement she felt when she started her new job at BioWestPharma.

'Come to think of it, you would probably warn me to be more cautious of him, wouldn't you?' Jennifer continued. 'You could always see the dangers, and I always went running head first towards them.' She smiled as she remembered their friendship fondly. 'The thing is, Sinead, sometimes you were right, and sometimes I was.'

Almost an hour passed before Jennifer bid her friend goodbye. Her mind felt settled now, calm and resolute. As she rose to her feet and made her way back to her car, it occurred to her that she had known deep inside all along what her course of action was to be. It took her until today, at the graveside of her old friend, to say it out loud.

Jennifer left the cemetery lighter than she had arrived. There was a degree of anticipation in her now for the path she had resolved to take. She would speak to the men in her life today, and tomorrow she would wake to her new beginning.

Later that evening, she sat alone in a café across the road from the BioWestPharma campus. The winter darkness had already closed in. The Christmas decorations had conceded to the bleaker month ahead. Jennifer always regarded the month of January as a chance for a new start, the end of winter that paved the way for spring, but she understood that for many it was tough and depressing.

The door of the café opened, and Gabriel waved as he made his way towards her. 'This invitation is an unexpected surprise,' he said with a smile. He reached over and kissed her on the cheek, then signalled to the waiter for a coffee. 'You look gorgeous, as usual,' he said. She smiled up at him. The obligatory Irish conversation about the cold and rain followed until Jennifer brought his attention to the reason for the invite.

'Gabriel, I've been thinking a lot about what you said to me in Killarney, about us potentially having a relationship.' Gabriel focused his gaze on her. He wasn't really able to read her. He didn't know her well enough. There was a pause. 'I'm not going to be able to see you again,' she said, looking at his face for a response. Gabriel didn't respond. He was clearly disappointed. She continued. 'I adore you—'

'Then what's the problem?' Gabriel interrupted. 'Are you going back to him?' The words blurted from his mouth before he could control himself. He was annoyed that this woman whom he thought so highly of would put herself back in a situation he clearly believed she should not be in.

Jennifer did not answer but continued with her sentence. 'I adore you,' she said. 'You were there for me at a time in my life when I needed to feel wanted. You made me feel confident and beautiful when I had lost the ability to feel it. And I will always be grateful for that.'

Gabriel dropped his head momentarily. He had not been expecting this, but he understood the reality of the situation. 'You are a spectacular person, Jennifer. Please don't ever forget that,' he said as he rose from the table. 'You know where I am if you ever change your mind. Please take care of yourself.'

For a moment, Jennifer's chest tightened. If she ever had any doubt as to whether she had feelings for Gabriel, it had just been confirmed. She questioned herself and her decisions. He was fantastic in so many ways, but this was not the right path for her. He was a married man with an infamous reputation. She was as vulnerable as she had been in her life.

She sat there a short while with a pang of regret, but she knew it was momentary. As the minutes passed, she was confident that she had made the right decision. She had followed her gut. She remembered a time not so long ago when she had promised herself that she would always listen to her gut in future. There was no better guide.

Taking out her phone, she texted John. She needed to see him. 'On my way over to your apartment. You there?' The apartment that she had tried hard to avoid for so many months seemed as good a place as any to do this. She was no longer afraid.

'I'm here,' John replied. 'See you shortly.'

John opened the door with a beaming smile. It was met with Jennifer's. She was excited and a little nervous. As she walked into the kitchen and accepted a cup of tea, a sense of calm took over. Everything about this scene felt right. She looked at her husband, expecting to see the man she had known her entire adult life, but instead she saw someone new. Life had altered him. No, life had altered her.

She invited him to sit at the table and took his hand. 'John, I've loved you since the day I met you.' John smiled. 'I love you today, and I will always love you.' Jennifer knew that she meant every word of what she was saying. She continued: 'But I know now that I can't spend the rest of my life with you. The day you left me you changed my life. I thought at the time that I would die, that I would never survive without you, but I did. I have been given a chance to start a new life, a better life filled with opportunity and possibility. I know now that if I don't grab it I will regret it. We have both changed so much – too much. I want to spend the rest of my life with someone I know I can trust completely, and that person is me.'

John shook his head. He explained that they could go back to the way things were, just the four of them.

'Going back to the way things were is exactly what I don't want, John,' Jennifer replied. 'One night, shortly after you left, I was distraught, broken-hearted, crying and begging God to help me. I was a mess. I couldn't understand why you needed to leave, why you wouldn't try a little bit harder to make it work for all four of us. I prayed to God for help, but he didn't bother answering. He took Sinead, and he took you. I never thought of that night again until this morning when I realised that God wasn't ignoring me. He was helping me all along. He sent me Sandy Gallagher.'

    John did not respond. There was no denial, no defence and no attack. He realised that the woman in front of him was stronger without him than she ever had been with him.

    'So, I have no reason to hate you or her. I have no reason to be angry. I am grateful for everything that I have and everything that I am today,' Jennifer said. She stood and walked towards the door. He followed. Turning back to him, she could see that he was hurt. She moved towards him, and they hugged before she opened the door.

    There would be plenty more to say to each other in the future. They would of course have a joint role in the lives of their two beautiful daughters. But for now there was nothing more to say.

    Jennifer walked to her car a strong, single, independent woman. She knew that she already had everything she wanted from life, and she was beyond grateful. Her daughters were healthy and happy and had the potential to become anything they wanted.

Jennifer herself was healthy. She had survived an assault on her mental health. More than that: she had learned from it. She was more confident now than she had been in her entire life, and with her health intact she knew that her career would flourish. The possibilities were endless.

Sitting by Sinead earlier that morning, she had casually asked herself the question, 'Where do you see yourself in five years' time?' That had been the sealing moment in her decision-making process. The thought of knowing exactly where she would be and what she would be doing in five years' time terrified her. It was the glimpse of freedom that exhilarated her. What Jennifer needed from life was the not knowing. She had already taken the first steps into the unknown, and it had fuelled her. She could not turn back now.

Jennifer walked out into the freezing cold evening with the eagerness and excitement of a person setting foot in the place for the first time. The world felt fresh and new. The air filling her lungs was light and invigorating. For the first time in years she realised that she could walk around a corner and bump into someone who might change her life. It was the most exhilarating feeling she had ever experienced.

She wondered if Sinead would have approved of her decision. As she pulled out of the apartment block and turned her car for home, she pictured her friend smiling down on her and heard her reassuring voice.

'Babe, you've got this.'